The Lost Girl of Craven County

ALSO BY EMILY MATCHAR

In the Shadow of the Greenbrier

Homeward Bound

The LOST GIRL *of* CRAVEN COUNTY

A Novel

EMILY MATCHAR

G. P. PUTNAM'S SONS NEW YORK

PUTNAM
— EST. 1838 —

G. P. Putnam's Sons
Publishers Since 1838
An imprint of Penguin Random House LLC
1745 Broadway, New York, NY 10019
penguinrandomhouse.com

Book design by Fritz Metsch

Hardcover ISBN: 9798217048007
Ebook ISBN: 9798217048014

Printed in the United States of America
1st Printing

The authorized representative in the EU for product safety and compliance is Penguin Random House Ireland, Morrison Chambers, 32 Nassau Street, Dublin D02 YH68, Ireland, https://eu-contact.penguin.ie.

To my mother

The Lost Girl of Craven County

PART ONE

Chapter 1

New Bern, North Carolina
August 1939

I was three weeks past my twenty-fifth birthday when I discovered the woman lying in the gravel behind my family's pickle warehouse. Twenty-five: an old maid by the standards of Jewish New Bern, which was why I was the one sent to fetch a jar of pickles that afternoon.

If I hadn't gone—if my mother had remembered to ask Jesse to bring the pickles, or if she'd decided to make do without them—my whole life would have turned out differently. But that's the way things go, isn't it? Life can hinge on a thing as silly as a jar of pickles.

The other women in the family—my mother, aunt, sister-in-law, and three cousins—were gathered in our parlor, cooing over my cousin Violet's wedding dress hanging on the wire dress frame (ivory rayon with a smocked bodice and leg-of-mutton sleeves; Violet would look like an overgrown child in a nightdress).

What would Millie care about a wedding dress? the others must have thought. *She's never getting married! Send her off for the pickles.*

I was happy to go.

The pickle warehouse, an enormous rectangle of painted brick on the east side of Craven Street, overlooked the river. It was mid-August, mid-afternoon, white hot, with ragged clouds drooping in a pale sky. A fishy smell drifted up from the docks, mingling with the tang of vinegar, which grew stronger as I approached the warehouse.

Prickling with sweat, I picked my way across the expanse of crushed-oyster-shell gravel where the farm trucks parked each morning to unload their vegetables. To the side of the warehouse's massive metal doors stood the roof-high brine tank, where cucumbers were stored in salty water until they could be moved inside. Next to the tank was a double row of wooden pickle barrels awaiting pickup, bound for the rail yard. Any decent grocery in the Southeast stocked Felix's Famous Pickles. Sweet, sour, and dill, chowchow and relish.

Something—the barest hint of something—behind the pickle barrels caught my eye. I turned. A patch of pink. Then a movement. A soft sound. A moan?

It could have been a rabid dog, or a hobo blind with rotgut, but for some reason—perhaps because I'm as impetuous as everyone says—I didn't hesitate. I strode straight ahead and peered over the barrel.

There, lying on the crushed oyster shells, was a woman.

I gasped, my heart juddering, and took a step backwards.

She lay full-length in the shadow between the pickle barrels and the warehouse wall. Her face rolled towards me and her eyes fluttered open. The bridge of her nose was scraped, and her chin bruised purple.

"Hello? Are you all right?" I said.

The woman gave no answer. She was wet, utterly soaked through. Her pale hair was plastered to her forehead—it was so short I might have thought she was a boy, except her wet dress lay so heavily on her body I could see her little breasts and her hip bones poking out.

Only it wasn't actually a dress. It was a kind of garment I'd never seen before. On the top it appeared to be a toga, something like Julius Caesar might have worn—white, and tied in a knot at her shoulder. On the bottom it resembled nothing so much as the billowy pants of a harem girl in *The Arabian Nights*, its folds drenched and flattened against the gravel.

She moaned again. I looked around, to see if there was anyone who might help. But we were alone.

Could she be one of the warehouse workers? But the workers wore ordinary clothes and aprons. And anyhow, it was Sunday. A day off for the workers, though not for Jesse, who was likely inside doing inventory.

I leaned over slowly, so as not to startle her. "Can you stand up?" I asked.

She just stared at me blankly, her eyes the strange light gray of puddles on the sidewalk after a hard rain. Her face was as oval as a porcelain doll's, and just as white, though with spots of hectic color blooming on her cheeks. Her short hair was the color of wet sand. She could have been thirteen or thirty.

Perhaps she'd been hit by a car and knocked senseless? Maybe she'd fallen in the river and bumped her head? I knelt beside her, the oyster gravel prickling my bare knees. If I'd taken the nurse's training course my mother kept suggesting, I'd know what to do.

"Let me go get help," I said.

But as soon as I attempted to stand, she moaned and reached out for me with one thin wet arm, like a sick child reaching for her mother.

"I'll be right back," I said. "The doctor's clinic is just down on Pollock Street."

But again she reached for me and moaned so distressingly that I knelt back down. I could feel the North Carolina sun beginning to singe the back of my neck.

"Can you walk?"

She simply stared up at me again, her face as blank as a baby's. I wondered if she was deaf and quickly clapped my hands above her head to test the theory. She startled. Not deaf. I felt a small flash of triumph. Jesse would never have thought of that.

I picked up one of the girl-woman's hands and grasped it between my own. It was small and boneless feeling, and as cold as a fish. I tugged, attempting to get her into a sitting position.

In one quick motion she sat up, gasping, and began to cough. The effort caused a bead of blood to ooze from her swollen lower lip. Her cheeks grew even pinker.

I thought of Auggie, coughing so hard he turned purple. I had to shake my head quickly to remove the image from my mind.

After regaining her breath, the woman reached for my hand and pulled herself up. She stood for a moment, leaning against the hot bricks of the warehouse wall, gazing around herself in a curious way, as if she'd never seen her surroundings before. She *must* have hit her head. After another moment, she stepped out from behind the pickle barrels with the delicacy of a ballerina. She smiled at me despite her swollen lip, and dipped her head in what seemed like a nod of thanks.

"Let's take you to the doctor?" I asked.

No response. Of course not.

I tried to pantomime "doctor," feigning to take my own pulse. But the girl-woman simply looked at me wide-eyed.

"All right, then," I said. "You can come home with me."

I thought about pantomiming "home," but I couldn't think

of what to imitate. Perhaps my mother, shoving a brisket in the oven while using her free hand to wag her finger at me? Instead, I merely gave the stranger a smile and held out my hand. "Come," I said. "We'll figure it out."

If I'd known then what I know now, well . . . But that's the thing of it, I suppose: If we knew at the beginning what we know at the end, nothing very interesting would ever happen in the middle, would it?

THE SWISS PROTESTANTS who founded New Bern laid out the city in the shape of a cross, which you might think would have put us Jews off settling here. Yet here we've been for a hundred years, on this thumb of Craven County between the Trent and Neuse Rivers, a village within a village. People call Middle Street, the vertical part of the cross, "Little Jerusalem," on account of the number of Jewish-owned shops. We number no more than eighty, with fewer every year as more boys light out for Raleigh or Charleston or Baltimore for better work. Those remaining grow more and more desperate for gossip—I knew if any Jewish New Bernian spotted me with the stranger, the entire community would know in a matter of minutes, thanks to the party-line telephone and Mrs. Lefkowitz's extremely quick dialing finger.

Glancing around, I led the stranger down Middle Street, her cold hand in mine. She walked with a high, deliberate step, leaving a trail of little wet footprints. Being Sunday morning and hot as the devil, there were only a few people at Middle and Pollock Streets, normally the busiest corner in downtown New Bern. A lady with a parasol—Shirley Stucky's mother, I thought—turned to give me and the stranger a beady-eyed stare. I gave her a too-big smile, and she looked away quickly.

The mute girl didn't seem to notice. She was staring around in what seemed to be wonderment, her eyes going in all directions. You'd think she'd never seen a dogwood tree or a fire hydrant or an advertisement painted on a brick wall (DRINK NEW BERN'S OWN PEPSI-COLA: WORTH A DIME, COSTS A NICKEL!). We passed the Cohens' furniture store, my aunt and uncle's laundry, the narrow building where old Mr. Gelman repaired watches and jewelry, the fishmonger's run by my cousin's husband. As we passed the Marie Antoinette Boutique, I saw the shadow of Sophie Zucker—Sophie *Cohen*—in the window, tugging a dress off a mannequin.

The Marie Antoinette. Why would anyone name a clothing store after a queen who lost her head? But far be it from me to disagree with a graduate of Sweet Briar College.

I looked more closely at the stranger. She was almost certainly a young woman, not a girl, I decided. There was also something mature about the set of her jaw, despite her gawping expression. Her garment had nearly dried and now looked even more billowy and bizarre. Could she be a nun? Perhaps she'd lost her habit, and this was nun underwear? Maybe I should take her up the block to Saint Paul's and ask if they'd lost a sister?

By now I was nearly at my house. I pointed to it as we approached and patted my chest.

The woman looked up at our plain blue two-story house and smiled so big you'd think we were arriving at a castle. She nodded as if she understood.

We climbed the brick steps, and I swung open the front door. The woman, in her strange outfit, followed me silently.

The ladies sat in the parlor, holding glasses of sherbet, chattering like parrots. As soon as I stepped inside, the stranger clinging like a shadow behind me, they went silent. Fanny's eyes widened in concern. Violet wrinkled her nose. Lizzy, who'd been nursing one of the twins, nearly dropped him as her hands flew up to button her dress. Bea started to say something, but before she could, my mother heaved herself to her feet and swung her square body towards me. Her eyes narrowed.

"Millie," she said finally. "I sent you for pickles."

Chapter 2

All at once the parlor was a frenzy of activity. My mother, fearsomely efficient as always, swept the wedding dress into the back bedroom and brought down several old towels to lay on the rug in case the stranger's garment dripped. Violet and her sisters, Bea and Lizzy, and my sister-in-law, Fanny, made a circle around the stranger, examining her the way farmers might examine a cow at auction.

"You found her behind the pickle warehouse?" demanded Bea, my oldest cousin. Bea never asks—she demands. "Is she a thief?"

"Does she look like she could lift a barrel of pickles?" I scoffed.

The stranger stood in a dignified way, smiling tolerantly. Her hair, fully dried, was the color of cornsilk, the kind of hair you normally only see on small children. It stood out around her head like fluff on a dandelion. I noticed she wore a brooch pinned to the folds of her garment at her bosom. It was a gray metal flower with the petals folded in on themselves. In the center was a bloodred stone.

"Is she one of the Kirby girls?" asked my aunt, who'd just entered the room, squinting. She carried a coffee cake on one of my mother's blue-and-white china platters, which she set on the sideboard along with the Toll House cookies Fanny had baked. "There's always a Kirby girl getting into trouble, isn't there?"

My aunt Zora is my father's sister, though you'd think she and my mother were twins, with their matching square figures and jaws. She runs the business side of Adlon's Laundry—my uncle Abe does the actual washing—and she prides herself on her cleverness. "You can't get anything by me" is her favorite sentence.

"Couldn't be," said Bea. "The Kirby girls all have red hair."

My aunt's nostrils flared slightly, like a hound scenting game. "Is this some Masonic nonsense?"

"Why would a woman be wearing a Masonic outfit?" Lizzy pointed out. Lizzy is the middle daughter and the sensible one in the family, the one who clips cost-saving recipes from *Ladies' Home Journal* and talks Bea down when she's in a snit.

"You never know," said Aunt Zora darkly. She hates to be wrong.

The stranger was looking around the room with wide, fascinated eyes, as if our parlor were an opium den. My family's parlor was certainly nothing out of the ordinary: old-fashioned peach-striped wallpaper hung with portraits of my father and Auggie, a dark-green chesterfield, a faux Chinese-style sideboard, and an oriental rug my mother had brought with her as a young bride from South Carolina. I'd spent hours of my youth on the chesterfield, reading books about children in faraway places—*Kim*, *Anne of Green Gables*, *The Secret Garden*—a plate of shortbread or oatmeal cookies balanced on my stomach.

"Why is she here, anyway?" said Violet peevishly. She was sore to have the attention off her, after waiting so long in her older sisters' shadows to have her own turn in an ugly wedding dress. She'd wanted to have a "bridal shower," like she'd read about in film magazines, but my mother and Aunt Zora put the nix on that right away—"What, you want to invite the Evil Eye?"—so the dress-viewing party was the compromise. She'd begged for a Hollywood theme and was dressed for the occasion in a lurid green gown with lace cap sleeves, which I recognized as Aunt Zora's old bathroom curtains.

"What was I supposed to do, leave her lying behind the pickle barrels?" I said. "She's probably hit her head or something."

"She looks all right to me, except for her chin," Violet said with a sniff.

"Do you want me to fetch Dr. Dixon?" asked Fanny kindly, her soft German accent turning the *W* in "want" into a *V*. Unlike me, Lizzy, and Bea, Fanny had gamely dressed for the party in a pink dress with a bow at the collar, her hair arranged in old-fashioned finger waves.

"She seems all right physically," I said, thinking of Dr. Dixon's sour face and absurd little Vandyke beard.

I turned to see Lizzy had pulled a chair out for the stranger to sit and was plying her with a slice of Aunt Zora's coffee cake. Like most of the women in my family, my middle cousin is like a machine designed to feed people, whether people want to be fed or not. Lizzy has only gotten worse since she had her twins. You wouldn't think a woman could nurse a baby while simultaneously making pancakes, but Lizzy could. She could even nurse two babies at once, though then at least she had to sit down.

Twins seem like a foolish idea, though I suppose that's God's fault, not Lizzy's.

"Why doesn't she speak?" asked Violet in the same whiny tone. She's lucky she's pretty, Violet, since she's got the personality of a pickle. "Is she a deaf-mute?"

"She's not deaf," I said.

"She must not understand English," said Lizzy sensibly.

I bristled. Of course. Why hadn't I thought of that?

I eyed the stranger again. She sat very upright in the blue velvet chair now, her legs crossed at the ankles. Her face was pale with a sheen of sweat on her upper lip; it was still hot indoors, despite the steady thwack of the ceiling fan and the window shutters closed against the sun. What language might she speak? She must be from Europe—where else do people have such light hair and eyes?

"*Parlez-vous français?*" I tried, dredging up my best high school French.

She just stared at me as blankly as before.

"*Sprechen Sie Deutsch?*" asked Fanny gently.

Another blank look.

"Are the hobos at the train yard ever girls?" asked Lizzy.

"I don't think so, they—" I started, but was interrupted by Aunt Zora.

"*Redstu Yidish?*" she asked in a suspicious tone.

"Mother, of course she doesn't," said Violet. "No one younger than forty speaks Yiddish, and we know every Jewish family from Atlanta to Baltimore anyway, don't we?"

This was an exaggeration, but it certainly felt true. The world of Southeastern Jews sometimes felt like a child's game of cat's cradle, where everyone is connected by a dizzying zigzag of thread, the ties understood only by yentas like my mother and Zora.

"You never know," said Zora again. "She could be a spy."

"A spy!" exclaimed Bea, Lizzy, and Violet all together.

"Mother, that's absurd," said Bea, who, due to having three sons already and being pregnant again, considered herself senior even to her own mother.

"There are people who would pay top dollar for that pickle recipe," Zora said. "Everyone says Felix's pickles are better even than what you get in Baltimore or New York!"

Felix of Felix's Famous Pickles was my father. He died when I was three.

"Recipe? Cucumbers, vinegar, salt, dill," said Bea, one hand folded proprietarily atop her belly. "There! If the girl's a thief, she can have it for free." She shot a smirky smile at her mother.

Aunt Zora narrowed her eyes. "So smart, you think you are. I remember when you were a little *pisher* who thought eating apple seeds would grow trees in your stomach."

Bea scowled.

"What language does Guster, or whatever his name is, speak?" I asked Bea, thinking of her husband Benji's sulky young assistant at the fishmonger's.

Bea thought. "He's from Switzerland—no, Sweden. I told Benji to fire him—he's been skimming from the till! Benji caught him red-handed. But the Swede told Benji some tale about needing medicine for a sick mother, and you know how Benji is."

Benji is kind to the point of being soft brained. Who else could stand to be married to Bea?

The stranger sat upright with a neutral expression and an air of patient expectancy, like someone used to waiting for others. She gave a slight yawn, covering her mouth delicately with a small white hand. There was no way she was an ordinary thief or a farm girl like the Kirbys. There was something special about her. I could tell.

"She's tired. I think I should take her upstairs for a rest," I said.

My mother, who had been standing in the doorway with her arms folded the whole time, suddenly stepped forward, and all the chattering stopped. I froze, certain she was about to say "Certainly not" and demand I take the stranger to the police or the train station so everyone could get back to sherbet and dresses. *Must you spoil the party, Millie? Must you always make life more difficult, Millie?* But instead she simply said, "Go make the bed in Auggie's room."

I CARRIED THE fresh sheets from the linen closet upstairs and pushed open the door. Inside, Auggie's room was the same as always: somehow brighter than any other room in the house, the dust motes suspended in light as thick and golden as syrup.

Aunt Zora had more than once offered to redecorate, to make it into a sewing room or a library. But then she would look at my face and stop talking.

It had been three years.

The air in there was utterly still, as if the very molecules of the room were holding their breath, waiting for Auggie to come back. On the shelf above the bed, Auggie's old teddy bear, Cornelius, sat expectantly, his glossy black eyes staring into the middle distance. Next to him was Auggie's camera, his miniature globe on its wooden pedestal, and his favorite books—a set of Jules Verne bound in blue leather, a volume on polar exploration, a dictionary, and a slightly mildewed copy of *Practical Photography* by O. E. Wheeler. On the wall was a periodic table of elements chart, rescued from the garbage bin behind the school.

I heard a loud thump, then an outbreak of giggles. I turned to see a big brown eye peeping through the crack in the doorway. One of Bea's boys.

"I'm going to eat you!" I yelled.

There was a fresh round of laughter and a stampede of footsteps as the children ran back down the hall.

Children seemed to prefer me best when I pretended to be a monster.

I made the bed with fresh sheets and left one of my old nightdresses folded on the pillow. Then I went downstairs to fetch the stranger.

"Come on," I said to the stranger, pointing up the stairs. "Rest." I folded my hands and leaned my head against them, miming sleep. The stranger smiled and immediately got up to follow me. *She trusts me*, I thought, and, for just a moment, I thought I might start to cry.

Chapter 3

When I returned downstairs, the cousins and Aunt Zora had left and Fanny was having her nap in her and Jesse's room in the back. Dr. Dixon has warned her that if she's ever to become a mother, she needs rest and tranquility. Fanny listens dutifully and takes a daily nap, though I hardly know how Dr. Dixon expects her to be tranquil, given what's happening back in Germany with Mr. Hitler. Fanny worries about her cousins and aunts and uncles so much she's tugged herself a bald spot at the back of her skull, poor thing.

Having caught me alone, my mother started in immediately.

"Millie," she began in that particular tone she uses with me, like she's talking to a grouchy five-year-old, wiping her hands on her apron.

"What?" I snapped, knowing exactly what she was going to say.

"Have you thought about Richmond?"

"What about it?" I said, though I knew perfectly well what she meant. I picked up the last Toll House cookie from the platter and took a bite, without using a saucer or napkin. There's nothing that bothers my mother more than crumbs on the floor.

"Can I tell the Teppers we'll come in October?"

I shrugged and watched my mother struggle not to say anything. She needed my cooperation.

"They'll need to get the guest room ready."

"It's August. October is two months away."

"There are other . . . preparations."

Preparations. It made it sound like I was a goat to be sold at auction. Which was essentially what my mother was hoping to do, if you thought about it. Richmond would be the sixth time she'd dragged me to a distant acquaintance's house to sit in their parlor and meet eligible young Jewish men. We'd already done Raleigh and Durham and Winston-Salem and Charleston and Norfolk, nearly the full Southern Jewish marriage circuit. I'd already failed to match with a widower, a door-to-door sewing machine salesman, and an engineer with pimples so bad they looked like the illustration of smallpox in my *Encyclopedia Britannica*. My mother was getting desperate now. The next stop after Richmond would be Baltimore, and if I didn't make a match in Baltimore, I would be considered hopeless. My reputation—strange, difficult, *loony*—would have preceded me all the way to the Mason-Dixon line.

"I'll think about it," I said.

"Good," my mother said, stooping down to pick up a cookie crumb. You could tell it was as satisfying to her as releasing a sneeze.

Sometimes I wonder what my father would have made of me. Would he think I was crazy? Would he think I was useless? Or—perhaps—would he be the one to understand me? My mother and Jesse are two of a kind—practical, unflappable, no time for nonsense. My mother kept the pickle business running nearly on her own after my father died, stalking the warehouse floor like a short, stout general from dawn to dusk, haggling with buyers, not a cucumber or an onion escaping her notice.

Now Jesse does the same, though with much more hot air. Auggie and I were the opposite of that—heads in books, full of dreams, forgetting even to eat lunch. I bet my father would have been on our team—he must have liked to read, at least; Auggie's Jules Verne books once belonged to him. I'd know more if my mother ever talked about him. But she's not one for dwelling in the past, she says.

I was jolted from my thoughts by the clatter of shoes on the front porch. Ugh, Jesse was home.

"Shhhh," I hissed, as Jesse and my uncle Abe came through the front door. "There's a girl sleeping upstairs."

"Sleeping? Who's sleeping?" said my uncle, pulling a handkerchief out of his pocket and wiping the sweat off his forehead.

"What's for dinner?" asked Jesse, completely ignoring me.

"Tongue, your favorite," said my mother. She couldn't wait to get me married off, but she would have been thrilled to have her firstborn baby boy live at home for the rest of his life. Jesse and Fanny had been married for nearly five years, but still lived in the back two rooms of our house. Jesse said he'd look for their own house when they had children to fill it. Every time he said that, poor Fanny's eyes glistened.

"Enough for me?" asked Abe. "Zora's at her Sisterhood do, and there's nothing in the icebox but cold grits." He and Aunt Zora lived next door.

"When have I ever not made enough?" my mother said scornfully.

"I found a woman behind the pickle warehouse," I said, feeling like a child interrupting the adults for attention but unable to stop myself. "She's sleeping in Auggie's room."

My uncle gave my mother a look.

"She can't speak," I said. "She doesn't know English. Or she might have hit her head. We don't know."

"What are you talking about?" said Jesse, snatching a piece of bread off the table, folding it in half, and shoving it into his mouth. He was wearing his dumb shiny suit with the narrow lapels, the one he thinks makes him look sharp. It just makes him look like a gangster in a film, and not the brains of the operation either.

Just then, the stairs creaked, and everyone looked up. There stood the stranger, at the bottom of the steps. She was wearing my white nightgown, and her fluff of pale yellow hair made a halo around her head. Framed by the blackness of the stairwell, she looked like an angel in a painting. She smiled at us all, looking perfectly at ease, her gray-and-red brooch pinned at the neck of the nightgown.

Jesse swallowed.

"Millie?" said my uncle, turning to me, eyebrows raised.

"I told you," I said. "I found her behind the pickle warehouse this afternoon. She was wet. I think she fell in the river."

A look of concern crossed my uncle's face. He stepped closer to the stranger. "Hello, dear," he said.

"She doesn't speak," I said again.

My uncle reached out his hand and the stranger took it, stepping off the bottom stair like a duchess out of a carriage.

Everyone gazed at her.

"She's wearing a nightgown," said Jesse, who never found anything too obvious to say aloud.

"She was wearing a strange dress when I found her," I said. For some reason it felt important to repeat it: *I found her*. Me. "It was white and knotted, like a toga, but with some kind of trousers underneath."

"Toga?" said Jesse. "Like in China?"

"Ancient Rome," I said. Jesse was always careful not to learn a single thing at school. It would have interfered with his football playing.

"She's a Roman?"

"No, Jesse, she's not a *Roman*, I'm just explaining what her dress looked like."

My mother wedged herself between us. "We're all hungry. The girl must be hungry too. Let's eat."

We all moved to the dining room and sat down: my uncle at one end, my mother at the other, and Jesse and me in our childhood spots, backs to the window. The stranger sat opposite on the right, next to Fanny. Auggie's old spot.

My mother began to serve the food, beginning with our guest. The instant she laid a slice of tongue on the stranger's plate, the woman fell upon it like a wolf. My mother narrowed her eyes, not sure whether to be bothered by poor table manners or pleased that someone was so enthusiastic about her cooking. She put another slice on the plate, and the stranger fell upon that as well.

My mother smiled. "It's nice to see a girl eating properly," she said, giving me a significant look. She's always complained I don't have enough meat on my bones. The stranger devoured several more slices of tongue and cornbread, heaped with spoonfuls of chowchow from the crystal pickle dish. She held her fork crudely, using it as a shovel rather than a spear. She bent so far over her plate that all you could see as she ate was the top of her fuzzy blond head bobbing up and down.

Jesse gave a low whistle.

"That little scrap of a thing must have a hollow leg," my uncle said.

"I hadn't made a dessert, but there's some lemon pudding in the icebox," my mother said. "Do you think she'd eat that?"

"I think she'd eat the icebox itself," my uncle said.

When the pudding had been served and the bowl scraped clean, the stranger gave a little sigh and her eyes fluttered, like a child about to fall asleep. As my entire family stared, awed, she once again held out her arms with her hands clasped, brought them to her chest, then extended them outwards, dipping them towards each of us—my mother, my uncle, Jesse, me. *Thank you*, the hands said. *Thank you*.

I knew at that moment, with as much certainty as I've ever known anything, that I was going to help her. This time would be different.

Chapter 4

When I came downstairs in the morning, the stranger was sitting at the dining table with Fanny, devouring a slab of challah fried in egg. The kitchen smelled like cinnamon; there must be a fresh coffee cake in the oven.

"You'd think she'd never had food before," said my mother from the kitchen doorway, sounding delighted.

"Has she spoken?" I asked.

"Not a word," Fanny said.

"I'm going to the station to talk to Zeke. He might be able to help."

My mother shook her head. "Feh. That boy. All those brains, but can't pin a tail on a cat!"

My mother had been angry at Zeke ever since he left college without a degree. You'd have thought he didn't have an angry mother of his own. Continuing to shake her head, she cast an eye at my dress—an old navy cotton shift with a drooping hem—and cleared her throat. "I meant to ask—have you picked out a dress for the wedding?"

Ugh. Violet's wedding. "I'm wearing the yellow one I wore to Lizzy's."

"Don't be silly. You can't wear the same dress to two of your cousins' weddings. People would think the factory was failing, that we're on our way to being hobos, God forbid."

"God forbid," I repeated sarcastically.

"Go to the Marie Antoinette," she said. "Let Sophie help you pick something. She always had such nice taste."

Perfect Sophie and her "nice taste." I could feel my jaw clench involuntarily.

"I will not!"

My mother put her hands on her hips. "I don't understand why you're being this way. I've hardly seen you and Sophie even look at each other since she came back from New York. You used to be such good friends. Peas in a pod!"

"A lot's happened since then."

"Fine. Wear an old *schmatta* like a—" She closed her mouth. The unsaid words hung in the air between us.

I blew air out through my lips. "You know, Mother, it's too bad Jews don't have convents, or you could send me there and stop having to worry about what I do and what I wear. Shall I go join the Catholics? It's not too late."

"She thinks she's funny," my mother said to no one in particular. "Ha ha ha, I say."

IT WAS BARELY after eight, but outside the air was already swampy. I felt the armpits of my dress dampen as I walked along Broad Street, through the Negro downtown at Five Points. It was already bustling with shoppers, though fewer than when I was a girl, before the Negro neighborhood to the north burned in the Great Fire, and the city wouldn't allow the residents to rebuild. A *shonda*, my mother called it.

The train station was, like the pickle warehouse, in Riverside, at the south end of Pasteur. Before I entered, I stopped to stare across the expanse of oyster-shell gravel towards the pickle warehouse's back doors. I don't know what I was expecting to see—a clue of some sort? A search party dressed in odd white garments? But all I could see was a farmer unloading bushels of cucumbers from the back of a rickety truck. He wore a pair of much-mended overalls and homemade leather brogues; the Depression had lifted for many of us here in town, but the farmers were still struggling.

Could the stranger be a runaway farm girl? A worker from one of the textile mills upriver? A fisherman's wife?

Whoever she was, she wasn't from New Bern. We're big enough to count as a city—we've got two cinemas, a white high school and a Negro one, a cannery, a boatyard, a Coca-Cola bottling plant, and a fancy new post office with a bell tower so tall it gives me the shivers. More than anything, we have churches, which is how everyone seems to organize themselves—the Catholics, the Presbyterians, the Methodists, the Salvation Army, the Baptists who don't dance and the Baptists who play gospel music and the Baptists who wade in the river off Front Street and holler hallelujah so loud it wakes you on a Sunday morning. Then there's Chester B'nai Sholem Synagogue, which has splendid Corinthian columns but no permanent rabbi. It was founded by my grandfather and a handful of others at the end of the last century, back when people thought New Bern would be the next Charleston or Baltimore. Instead, the town remained stubbornly small enough that you can still recognize most everyone by face.

So where did she come from? How did she get here?

I may not have finished college, but while I was there I did work on the staff of the *Carolinian*, our student newspaper. One thing we learned from our adviser, Miss Leda Snett, was that when you have a question to solve, you approach it methodically, one possibility at a time, following every lead like a thread. The most obvious possibility was that the stranger arrived in New Bern on the train. Zeke could answer that question.

Zeke's office was on the upper floor of the station, with a window overlooking the tracks. You had to climb a rather rickety open metal staircase to get there, which never failed to make me sweat, but I managed it well enough by clinging to the rail and taking deep breaths until I stepped inside. The office's brick walls were completely papered in maps and timetables. The crooked ceiling fan made a thumping sound with every rotation, the air lifting the edges of the papers that covered the desk.

Zeke himself was sitting on the top of a filing cabinet, his feet on the arm of his desk chair. He was wearing no shoes, and there was a hole in the toe of one sock. On his lap was an enormous railroad atlas. He had a pen in his left hand and was making notes directly in the book.

I knocked on the open door, but he didn't look up. I knocked again. "Zeke!"

Zeke startled, and the atlas slipped off his lap and clattered to the floor. "Oh, hi, Millie," he said, bending down to pick it up. "I think I've figured out a way to reduce the delays on the Seaboard Line. We've just got to get them to put the hopper cars ahead of the flats, then reorder them again after the dairy stop—"

Ezekiel Abramowitz and I have known each other since we were babies in prams. In school, he was my only rival for spelling bee champion. He and Auggie were great friends, always getting into one scrape or another. Now he was the only person in Jewish New Bern who was as much of a disappointment to his family as I was. He was the assistant timekeeper for the railroad and spent most of his off hours tinkering with inventions in the workshop behind his parents' house on Rhem Avenue, where he, like me, still lived in his childhood bedroom.

Zeke has always reminded me of one of the great egrets that stand in the mudflats at low tide, all gangly legs and sharp angles. His nose is beaky like a bird's too, set below a pair of startlingly blue eyes and a scramble of curly black hair. He's always in motion—jiggling a leg, tapping a toe, drumming his fingers.

"Zeke, what was the schedule yesterday afternoon?" I asked.

Zeke didn't blink. "Excursion train from Wilson at twelve oh one, freighter from Goldsboro at one thirty-seven, and Atlantic Coast Line at three thirty-two."

Zeke has a perfect memory for this kind of detail—and a highly imperfect one for things you might think were more important, like where he put his shoes.

"Who was on the excursion train?"

"A bunch of people from a Negro church, going to see the ball game."

"How about the freighter—anyone get off it?"

Zeke shook his head. "They just unloaded some tin."

I moved a pile of atlases off a chair and sat down across the desk from Zeke. "I found a woman behind the pickle warehouse, not fifty feet from the tracks. She can't seem to speak, at least not English. I'm trying to figure out where she came from. If she came by train, maybe she got off by accident or is lost."

Zeke looked up, curious, and pushed a rogue curl away from his eyes. "Weird," he said.

Zeke had always been fascinated by trains and everything else that moves. He was studying engineering at NC State but left without graduating to take the job at the train station.

The two spelling bee champions of New Bern Elementary, now unmarried college dropouts living with our parents. Pathetic.

"Could she have got off the Atlantic Coast Line?" I asked.

"Nah, it was just Butch O'Brian, the engineer, and the other two."

"What other two?"

Zeke gave me a strange look. "You didn't know?"

"Know what?"

"It was . . . you know. Harry Morgenthaler and . . . the girl."

"What girl, Zeke?"

Zeke looked like someone was sticking tacks in his backside. "Harry's new wife. The one from Charleston. The wedding was last Sunday. Harry's parents have fixed them up with a house here. The yellow one, kitty-corner from mine."

"Oh."

"Sorry, I thought you knew."

I felt a deep flush of anger and humiliation begin to rise from my stomach. "Don't be that way, Zeke."

"What way?"

"Don't act like I'm some cracked china doll that needs to be handled carefully or it'll break into a million pieces. I don't need to be *handled*."

"I know you don't. Sorry."

"It's not like Harry and I were ever steady. I would never have been serious with someone like Harry. Ridiculous."

Poor Zeke. He was wriggling like a worm on a hook. I knew I shouldn't light into him. He was one of the few people who didn't normally treat me like I was crazy.

"It's all right." I sighed. "So she didn't come in on the train. I'll have to start looking at other leads."

I NEVER EXPECTED to marry Harry Morgenthaler; I figured he'd be the first in a long line of affairs I'd have, each more interesting than the last. He and I "dated"—if you can even call it that—back when I was in college, and miserable in the stupid way you can only be before anything truly bad has happened to you. I knew I should have been grateful to be at college at all—of my high school class, the only girls to go on with their education at all were me, Sophie Zucker, and Effie Piggott, whose father was the foreman at the Coca-Cola bottling plant.

But, even with Harry to neck with after the movies on a Saturday night, oh, how desperately I hated being at the North Carolina College for Women! All those dishwater-dull girls with their cardigans and their church groups, only in college to get schoolteacher certifications so they'd have something to do until they got married. I thought myself so superior, with my Nellie Bly books and my fantasies of being a famous reporter.

Things were different at Sweet Briar College, according to Sophie's letters. They had a Poetry Club and a Greek Club and they put on elaborate theatricals, with girls blackening their upper lips with cork to play the male parts. On weekends they piled into cars and drove over the mountains to play pranks on the boys at Hampden-Sydney. There was a summer term in Paris.

It's an awful feeling, jealousy. Doubly bad because you feel both the pain of the jealousy and the shame of being jealous all at once.

Anyhow, mazel tov to Harry and the girl from Charleston. I couldn't be less jealous of her if I tried.

Zeke had stood up and looked at the road map on the wall. "She could have come in a car, right?" he asked.

"Sure," I said. "That won't be much help, though—there must be hundreds of cars coming through town every day."

"Thousands now, with the Ocean Highway, though most of them don't stop except for gas. Oh, speaking of cars." Zeke bent down and rummaged through one of the stacks of paper on the desk. It looked a mess, but Zeke knew where everything was. "Aha," he said, pulling out a sheet. He held it out towards me. "I found this the other week. Auggie's calculations for his derby car. I thought you might want to have it."

I gazed down at the sheet of paper. It was a large pencil sketch of a car with a pointy nose like a canoe and a sharp tail-fin. The page was covered in Auggie's familiar chicken scrawl handwriting. Auggie and Zeke used to make things like this in Zeke's workshop. They could spend hours there together, barely speaking, just calculating and measuring and cutting and mixing. When Auggie was thirteen and Zeke and I were sixteen, the two of them built a hot air balloon that actually flew a few hundred feet before crashing in Union Point Park. Auggie got a bloody nose, and Zeke got a caution from the sheriff.

"That one would have been really fast," Zeke said, gazing at the drawing. "Maybe the fastest yet."

I imagined Auggie in his driving goggles, flying down the wooden ramp he and Zeke made, his mouth open in a yawp of joy. Wherever he is now, I hope every moment is like that.

"Thanks," I said.

Normally thinking about Auggie made me wander off into the past and get stuck, like a fly in syrup, but today I had a question important enough to tack my mind to the present. What was my next lead? If the stranger came by car, that was no help. But if I couldn't figure out *how* she came to New Bern, I could perhaps find out where she was from.

"Zeke," I said, "who in town knows about languages?"

We looked at each other, and at the same moment we both said, "Captain Kennedy."

"Of course!" I said. "Captain Kennedy. I'll go there now."

Zeke made a face. "Better go tomorrow first thing, if you want to talk to him sober. And watch out—you know what they say about the dead wives in the attic!" He gave a mock shiver.

I stuck out my tongue at him and flew down the steps, barely noticing the height.

Chapter 5

I returned home to find my cousins and aunt in the parlor, yelling at one another. The stranger sat in the center of the chesterfield, calmly holding one of Lizzy's twins (Adam? Aaron?). Bing Crosby was on the radio, and there was an empty platter with a few cake crumbs on the side table.

"What's wrong with Mary?" Bea was saying, eyes narrowed, nostrils flaring.

"'Mary' is a goyisch name," said Aunt Zora.

"Why does that matter?" said Bea, reddening around the nostrils.

"It should be 'Ann,'" said Lizzy in the same firm, motherly voice she uses on her twins. "That's a good, plain name."

"Plain as in boring!" whined Violet.

I cleared my throat. "Uh, shouldn't Bea name her own baby? And how do you know it'll be a girl? Going by history, I'd think you'd need boys' names."

"Don't be silly. You know we'd never name a baby before it's born—you think we need bad luck?" said my mother, whisking the empty cake platter into the kitchen. "They're trying to name the girl," she called over her shoulder.

Oh. I felt a surge of heat in my chest, the way I used to when

I was a child and Jesse or one of the cousins snatched a toy from me. I looked at the stranger. She was completely absorbed in the baby, who was gripping the tip of her finger and trying to pull it towards his mouth. She looked up and caught my eye, and I felt certain there was a flash of understanding between us. I wondered if she came from a family full of noisy women too.

"How about Myrna? Or Ginger?" said Violet, who saw every film that appeared at the Masonic Theatre or the Show Shop at least twice, no matter how stupid it was.

"Mary!"

"Myrna!"

"Mary!"

"All right, if we can't agree, maybe we should draw lots," Lizzy said. "Auntie Rose keeps paper in the little cupboard there."

Something about Lizzy's sensible voice and the bossy way the cousins were talking about the stranger, like they were adults and she was a child, made the heat in my chest grow fiercer. "She already has a name!" I said, far more loudly than I'd intended.

Violet and Bea and Lizzy and Aunt Zora and Mother and Fanny all went silent and turned to stare at me.

"Please do tell us, Millie," Aunt Zora said, arching her eyebrows and tilting her head.

"Well, I don't know it," I said. "But she has one. And she'll tell us when she's ready."

Violet was smirking faintly. *Madwoman Millie,* she was thinking, I was certain. That's the thing about everyone thinking you're cracked: Even perfectly normal things are taken as evidence of your craziness. You can't fight it.

I silently whispered a prayer that Violet's husband-to-be had a limp pecker.

The stranger was wearing one of Lizzy's old housedresses—taffy pink, with a print of tiny strawberries. It was huge on her, but somehow looked dignified anyway. Maybe it was the way she sat on the couch—straight-backed, her small hands circling the baby's waist like a bride holds a bouquet. The extra fabric puddled around her like a queen's robes.

"Did Zeke have anything useful to say?" Zora asked.

"It doesn't seem she was a train passenger," I said.

"If you can't find the girl's family, will you go to the police for help?" Lizzy looked away when she asked this.

"Absolutely not." I felt my face go hot. "The most important thing will be to figure out what language she speaks, and find a translator. I'll go see Captain Kennedy tomorrow."

"Good idea," said Lizzy, nodding her head so hard her bangs came unpinned, as if she was trying to make up for mentioning the police.

I stood up. "I'm going to go drop off the food. I'll be back in a little while." I picked up the satchel I'd prepared the night before, which was sitting on the chair by the kitchen door.

"Why don't you take the girl with you?" said Fanny, who was sitting in the corner of the chesterfield with her needlepoint. "She could probably do with a walk, and maybe some quiet." She looked meaningfully around the room.

I shrugged. "Why not?" I looked at the stranger. "Would you like to come with me?" I said, gesturing at the door.

The stranger smiled and stood, handing the baby to Lizzy. Everyone looked up as she swept out the door, as rapt as fans watching a film star swan down the red carpet.

ON MONDAYS I left food for the dirty-faced young men who hopped off freight trains in New Bern, looking for work in the cannery or the bottling plants or on the docks. Auggie used to do it, so now it was my job.

As we walked in the midday heat, I began chatting to the stranger. It felt strange at first—speaking to someone who couldn't understand—but only for a moment.

"We're leaving food for the hobos who ride the rails," I told her. "There are less of them these days, now that there's more work, but still plenty. People can be so cruel to them—the police burned down the tent camp they used to keep by the rail yard—but most of them are just boys whose families can't afford to feed them."

The stranger gave no sign of recognition, but her face looked calm and peaceful, so I figured she was happy to just let my words wash over her.

"People don't realize that bad things can happen to anyone," I said, feeling the familiar anger in my throat. "They think they'd never be so unlucky as those boys. But really, what's the difference between them and us? A few hundred dollars? A bad season at work? After the banks failed, my mother only kept the pickle factory running by the skin of her teeth, she says. Almost gave herself a stroke of apoplexy, working day and night. Now Jesse's in charge, and he thinks it's doing so well because he's clever. But most of it is luck, surely."

The thick air smelled briny: the scent of the muddy Trent and Neuse Rivers meeting the seaweedy Atlantic. I could feel my thin, straight hair, deflated even further by the heat, slipping out of the ribbon I'd haphazardly tied around my head to keep my bangs out of my eyes.

The stranger was sweating, but looked unbothered. I wondered if she was from somewhere hot too.

"Anyway, when the Depression started, we began to notice

these terribly odd symbols written in chalk all around town—on fence posts, on mailboxes, on the pylons under the bridge. Like Egyptian hieroglyphics or something. Auggie and Zeke puzzled them out. They were messages from one hobo to the next, see. To let others know where to go and where to avoid. Two *W*'s stuck together meant 'careful: mean dogs.' A *U* meant 'you can camp here.' A circle with an *X* inside meant 'good place for a handout.'"

"So Auggie, he got a piece of chalk and drew one of the circles with an *X* on our mailbox. Pretty soon, hobos were showing up at our door every day. Our mother was so angry! But Auggie found a bunch of Talmud passages—'Charity is more important than all the Lord God's other commandments put together,' that sort of thing—and quoted them at my mother until she screamed, fine, he could leave food if he'd hush up and stop noodging her. It was funny because Auggie never really believed in God at all, but he figured if he could do some good in his name, he would."

As we crossed Middle Street, old Mrs. Lefkowitz, Jewish New Bern's biggest gossip, waved at me from her perch in front of the jewelry store. I could tell she was desperate for me to stop and introduce the stranger, but I just waved back and quickened my step. Mr. Gelman was sitting outside his little watch repair shop, a newspaper folded on his lap, his eyes shut, his small wrinkled face tilted towards the sky like a sunflower. His right hand, which lay atop the newspaper, was missing half the index finger. The story is that when Mr. Gelman was a young man in Russia, he hacked the finger off himself to avoid being drafted into the tsar's army. As children, Sophie and I used to peer into the shop window to catch a look at the famous missing finger. If Mr. Gelman caught us, he'd holler.

"Auggie was my younger brother." I felt compelled to explain, though it hardly mattered to the stranger. "Three years younger than me."

The stranger was silent, but it was a companionable silence. It felt different from the silences I felt alone in my room, on those nights I couldn't sleep or even lie still. It felt nice.

"There were three of us," I told her. "Jesse is first. Then me, then Auggie. His real name was August, but no one ever called him that. He was born early and was tiny as a gnat. August seemed like too much name for somebody so small. So it was Auggie from the start."

The stranger looked at me, and I could tell she was listening, even if she didn't understand.

"Jesse is the big dumb one, if you couldn't tell," I said. "He was the star of the football team—*and* the basketball team *and* the baseball team—in high school. The thing about him is he doesn't know how dumb he is, so he just kind of shoves ahead and gets what he wants. He took the pickle business over from our mother when he finished high school, and now he loves playing the big-shot businessman. He bought a bunch of business books from a door-to-door salesman last year—*The Magic Ladder to Success* and that sort of rubbish—and now he's always saying the most absurd things you can imagine."

The stranger's expression didn't change, but her head inclined towards me sympathetically.

"He's lucky to have found a girl as nice as Fanny to marry him," I said. "She came to Baltimore from Germany when she was eighteen—both her parents had died, and she wasn't keen on staying after Mr. Hitler came to power. A cousin was supposed to meet her at the port and look after her, but he never showed up. She only spoke about ten words of English, but she managed to find a job in a soap factory. Jesse was up in Baltimore for a wedding and spotted her in a coffee shop. It's funny, she thinks she's the one who got lucky. I guess she sees herself as having been rescued."

Why do women love to be rescued?

"All she really wants now is to help her cousins get out of Germany and to have a baby," I went on. "It hasn't happened, the baby, even though she's tried all the old wives' tales—eggs and jellied calf's foot and all that. She even told me she tried standing on her head after, well, after *you know*."

At Craven Street, I spotted Helly Riggsby, who was in my year at school. She was carrying a brown package and dragging a yowling toddler in short pants. She pretended not to see me, and I pretended not to see her. It was truly like living inside a jar, New Bern.

"I was supposed to be the literary one," I continued, wiping sweat from my brow with the back of my hand. "I was going to be a traveling journalist, like Nellie Bly—fly on planes, have adventures, and write all about it. But it didn't work out that way."

Her silence was calming. Maybe this was what it was like for Fanny, after I got out of the hospital, taking me on those walks by the river, not minding that I wouldn't talk.

We turned down Johnson Street, where pavement gave way to the Neuse River Bridge. Stretching nearly a mile over the flat brown water, it was built of thick wooden slats that clattered unnervingly when you crossed in a car. On the side of the bridge was the storybook-small bridgetender's cottage; Auggie and I used to come down to watch Mr. Everington raise the swing span when tall boats came through. Two little boys sat on the edge of the bridge with cane fishing poles, their dangling feet nearly touching the reeds below.

By the first pylon was a small wooden barrel. I placed a brown paper bag full of sandwiches and apples inside. Above the barrel, written in white chalk on the wood, was the symbol of the circle with the cross inside. Using a small piece of chalk I'd tucked in my dress pocket, I refreshed the circle.

If Auggie drew the symbol three years ago and I've refreshed it a hundred times since, is it still Auggie's writing? I wondered. Do any of his original chalk fragments remain? Or is it just mine now?

"Auggie was the smart one," I said. "He was some kind of genius. He could talk before he was nine months old. Our father died when he was tiny, and my mother was busy running the pickle factory, so he and I were together all the time. We used to read every book in the library. He was good at everything. Math, Latin, piano, building derby cars. He saved all his money to buy a camera and took portraits of everyone in town. He was going to go to Duke University. He had the grades to do it."

The stranger was facing the river, but her head was inclined towards me, her hair blowing like dandelion fuzz in the breeze coming off the water. She seemed far too delicate for the setting, the hot mud and sunbaked wooden planks and fishy smell. I imagined her somewhere cool, somewhere with clean white snow.

Depositing the last of the sandwiches in the barrel, we walked north up Front Street, where the old captains' houses with their storm shutters and their widow's walks decayed genteelly beneath the ancient oaks. A few blocks later, the trees and homes gave way to the warehouses and factories and crushed-oyster-shell lots of Riverside. A cluster of women stood outside the pants factory, eating hasty lunches and laughing. Across the way, a group of young hobos crouched in the shade of the dogwoods along the rail yard fence.

"Spare a nickel, miss?" said one, peering up at me from under the brim of a dirty cap.

I rummaged around the bottom of my pocketbook and found five pennies. I bent over and threaded my arm through the chain link, pouring the coins into the boy's outstretched hand.

"God bless you, miss," he said.

I used to imagine God looking like the picture of my father on the parlor wall, only drawn in stars against the sky, like a constellation. I'd talk to him as I fell asleep, the way I'd talk to a father—telling him about my spelling tests, about what Sophie and I had eaten for a snack. Now I wonder why, if he exists at all, does he not help the ones who need him the most—the ones like this boy?

"Auggie used to do photos of the hobo boys, and give them the prints to keep," I told the stranger. "He said it was the only time they got to get their pictures outside of a police station. They all loved him. Everybody loved him."

I didn't notice I was crying until the stranger touched the side of my face. Her pale eyes were soft with concern. She made a gesture, reaching one hand to her left shoulder and patting her chest above her heart. The meaning was clear: *I understand. I understand your pain.*

But then her expression shifted. Her mouth went flat, and her nostrils flared with a sudden inhalation of breath. Her whole body seemed to shrink backwards, as if being pulled towards the wall. Her eyes darted back and forth.

It was a look of fear. Of terror.

Whipping around, I followed her gaze, prickling with fear. But there was nothing out of the ordinary—no mad dog, no swerving automobile. Then I saw. It was a man. He was just turning the corner, and the summer sunlight cast him briefly in silhouette. He raised his arm.

The stranger's lips were moving, but she wasn't speaking.

She was trembling ever so slightly, like a leaf in the faintest wind.

"What's the matter?" I said, raising my arm to wave at the man. "It's just Mr. Zucker, my friend—*former* friend—Sophie's father."

As I spoke, Mr. Zucker drew nearer. He was wearing, as usual, his long white coat and carrying his leather pharmacist's case. Even if he hadn't been in work clothes, I'd have recognized him from half a mile. He's stout and rather tall and walks with a slight stoop from bending over the pharmacy counter all day. He was, I presume, walking home for lunch—the Zuckers' house was two streets away. He looked lost in thought, his mouth set in its usual thin, sour line. His beard was much longer than the last time I saw him.

He looked up and saw me. "Hello, Millicent," he said, nodding.

"Hi, Mr. Zucker," I said, then turned in puzzlement towards the stranger.

As Mr. Zucker passed, the stranger's whole body seemed to melt in relief. She shook her head back and forth, a faint smile on her lips.

We looked at each other.

"You thought he was someone else, didn't you?" I said. "Someone who scares you?"

The stranger, of course, didn't answer.

Chapter 6

I looked up at Captain Kennedy's house and shuddered. The Kennedy house squatted at the very top of Middle Street, its five turrets looming over downtown like something from a Gothic novel. Back when the lumber mills were booming, the owners competed to build the biggest, most ridiculous mansion, and Captain Kennedy plainly won. It had dozens of windows and three chimneys, its series of exceedingly steep roofs covered in shiny gray fish-scale shingles. The whole thing was surrounded by a columned porch like a hoop skirt on a Civil War belle, all topped with an evil-looking iron weather vane.

I swallowed. I just hoped the captain would be sober at this time of day.

"Captain Kennedy used to own a lumber mill, but now he just sits inside his house, reading," I explained, though of course the stranger wouldn't understand. Mostly I just wanted to make sure my voice was steady. "People say he speaks a half dozen languages. Maybe one of them is yours?"

The stranger looked at me agreeably. She was wearing the same strawberry-print dress as the day before, her odd metal brooch pinned to the neck.

As I pushed open the wrought-iron gate, I noticed small

signs of neglect not visible at a casual glance. The paint on the ornate porch railings was peeling, and the plants in the enormous Grecian cement planters to either side of the porch steps had long since withered into corpses. A blue-tailed skink darted across the path and disappeared under an overgrown bush.

Nobody had seen Captain Kennedy much since his wife died and Kennedy Lumber went bust, along with most of the mills on the river. The mill buildings have stood there, rotting, ever since, becoming crusted with seagull droppings.

The stranger looked uneasy. Or maybe I just felt uneasy.

"It's all right," I told her. "The worst that can happen is he won't help us."

I didn't believe the stories about the dead wives in the attic, of course. Still . . .

The porch creaked as we neared the large red-lacquered double doors. Swallowing, I picked up a lion's-head knocker and let it fall.

For a minute, nothing. Then, faint footsteps. The footsteps grew louder, then, just as I expected the door to open, there was silence. The captain must have been standing on the other side of the door, waiting.

"Captain Kennedy?" I called out, my voice sounding high and childish. "It's Millicent Green, Rose Green's daughter from Felix's Pickles. I have a question I was hoping you could help me with a—a . . . a language question."

The door opened. In the blackness of the entryway stood the captain, looking older and smaller than I'd remembered. He blinked at the sun, dust motes falling softly in the columns of light let in by the open door. He was wearing a dressing gown in some rich Chinese fabric, tied at the waist with a braided rope. On his feet were slippers in wine velvet, with the monogram *AKJ* on the toes.

"It's rather early for language questions, ladies," he said. His voice sounded creaky, like an old chest opening. In his hand was a small silver flask.

"I'm not sure, sir," I said, stammering slightly. "I think it's at least half past eight. Should we come back?"

The captain made a dismissive noise and beckoned us in. "Come on, come on."

I looked at the stranger. She looked back at me. Her pale face looked unsure. I smiled and nodded.

We stepped across the threshold and into the entryway. It was dark, unbelievably dark for a bright August morning, and I had to blink several times before I could see anything. Once I could, I took quick stock of our surroundings, hoping the captain wouldn't notice me gawping. We were standing in a double-height entryway, a vast curving staircase before us. The floor was an ornate tile mosaic, depicting—I think—Plato's Academy in Athens (unlike Jesse, I paid attention in history class). The staircase was covered in an oriental carpet the same wine color as the captain's slippers. The windows, double height like the ceiling, were hung with dark velvet drapes, which admitted not a crack of light. On a marble-and-gilt side table sat a Roman-style bust. Above that hung a portrait of a woman in a blue gown, a faint and mysterious smile on her lips. The captain's late wife?

We followed the captain into a room to the right of the stairs, which turned out to be an office of sorts, dimly lit with only a bronze floor lamp. And—this was the amazing thing—three of the walls were *bookcases*. Floor to ceiling, nothing but bookcases, absolutely stuffed with leather-bound volumes of all sizes. I spotted the complete works of Shakespeare, Audubon's *Birds of America*, volumes of Ruskin. Then there were books in languages I didn't speak, and even in letters I didn't recognize. A mahogany ladder on wheels reached the upper shelves, where it was attached at the top to a bronze rail. Everything was coated in a fine layer of dust. The air smelled darkly of mildew, with a whiff of spoiled food.

The captain had fired his house staff after his wife died. Geneva, the cousin of Sophie's maid Pearlie, had been his cook. She'd said the captain didn't know which way to butter toast and that he'd surely starve without her. It looked like he didn't know much about dusting either.

I looked at the stranger. In the murky light, her skin was as pale as the Roman bust on the table beside her. Her mouth was hanging half-open as she gawked at the bookcases.

The captain seated himself behind an enormous leather-topped desk, his knees creaking as he bent down. He gestured to us, palm up. "Sit."

We sat.

"A language problem," he said slowly. "A language problem."

"Yes, sir," I began. "You see, this lady here, she, well, she doesn't seem to speak English. Or any language that my family knows. Not German or Yiddish, not French. It's a bit of a mystery. We thought that you, sir, with your . . . your intellectual reputation, might be able to help."

"Never be afraid to use flattery," Leda Snett once told our journalism class.

The captain stared at us from across the desk. He had a large, craggy head, with the thick neck and underbite of a bulldog. His silver hair, unbrushed, clung to his head like milkweed fluff caught on a boulder.

I waited, a polite smile frozen on my face.

"Where did she come from, this . . . young lady?" the captain finally asked.

"Well, that's part of the mystery, sir," I told him. Maybe I shouldn't say "sir"? It made me sound like a schoolgirl rather than a journalist. "We have no idea. I found her lying behind the pickle barrels outside my family's warehouse, quite distressed."

The captain frowned and stroked his chin, its silver stubble glittering in the lamplight. After a moment, he leaned forward. "When she does speak, how does the language sound? Of a Romance nature? Or more Germanic, perhaps? She certainly has an Aryan physiognomy, though her jaw is small."

"That's the thing—she doesn't speak," I said.

"Then she's a deaf-mute, surely," the captain said, shaking his head as if I were stupid. I wondered if stories of my past had reached him.

"She can hear," I said. "She startles at loud noises."

The captain tilted his head. He seemed for several moments lost in thought. Finally, he said, "*Vy russkiy?*"

The stranger looked at him, her gray eyes keen, but gave no sign of recognition.

"Hmm, not Russian," the captain said. "*Spreek je Nederlands?*"

Nothing.

"Not Dutch. Alas, I don't speak any of the Nordic languages—Swedish, Norwegian, and the like. She does have a Scandinavian aspect about her. Let's see . . . *Kya aap Hindi bolte hon?*"

Again, no response beyond a polite, slightly embarrassed smile.

"That was Hindi," the captain said. "Unlikely, obviously."

The captain proceeded to try a startling variety of languages—Spanish, Italian, Arabic, Serbian, even Chinese ("for amusement—why not?"). Nothing generated even a glimmer of recognition from the stranger, who sat as still as ever in the high-backed mahogany chair, her posture perfect, her hands folded neatly in her lap.

Eventually the captain leaned back, frustrated. Sensing we were losing his interest, I resorted again to flattery: "How many languages do you speak, Captain? It's so impressive."

The captain puffed back up. "Fifteen fluently, and another twenty at a more basic level. I'm currently engaged in learning Sanskrit. Do you know it?"

I had to admit I didn't.

"It was a language of the late Bronze Age, from the Indian subcontinent," the captain said, growing in enthusiasm. His whole body seemed to gain energy as he spoke, his blue eyes flashing. "Its speakers were the elites, the cream of ancient society. I've been studying from *A Practical Grammar of the Sanskrit Language* by Theodor Benfey—do you know of him?"

"Is he from North Carolina?" I asked.

The captain chortled, which made him cough. "Benfey was from Germany, though he died years ago. He was one of your people."

"My people?"

"The Hebrew race, girl."

I kept my face neutral. Inside, I felt a growing annoyance.

"You know, the Germans are quite correct about the importance of racial hygiene," the captain went on. "Only they're wrong about the Jews in specific. Any man with half a grasp of history can see that the Hebrew race has made superior contributions to science, medicine, and linguistics. Not to mention finance. But there's a certain coldness there, a certain lack of fellow feeling for those outside their group. No offense to present company."

I felt my jaw tighten. Naturally I was familiar with the fact that some New Bernians felt there was something clannish about us, and something slightly distasteful in the way Middle Street was so thick with Jewish-run businesses. But most people accepted us without much issue. We were Masons and Rotarians and members of the Women's Club and the Park Beautification Committee.

This wasn't Germany, after all. Although, as Fanny often said, Germany wasn't Germany either, until it was. She sometimes shared letters from cousins back home, talking about how Jews are now not allowed to sit on public benches or are forbidden from owning certain shops. Her cousin Shmuel had been engaged to a gentile girl—she was going to convert—but then a law was passed that made it illegal for Jews and non-Jews to marry. Because of this, Fanny was especially sensitive about the race separation rules in North Carolina. She would get so angry her eyes would tear up when she saw Negroes turned away from whites-only shops or made to use the outhouse when there was a perfectly good bathroom nearby. I always disliked it as well, but in the way you dislike something that seems to be the unchangeable way of the world, like hurricanes in September. You'd shake your head and wish it otherwise, but what could you do? *Something!* says Fanny fiercely, and she's right, of course. But what?

I cleared my throat. "I suppose my 'race' is as varied as any other, but I'm certainly not the expert you are. As to her origins, which are so much more interesting, being a mystery—do you have any suggestions on how to investigate?"

"I don't suppose the police were of much use?" the captain said. "Feebleminded, the lot of them. Scots-Irish, of course."

The captain, I remembered, had been taken to the drunk tank the year before after disrupting a town council meeting.

"No, the police haven't helped," I said. Which technically was not a lie.

The captain grunted and shook his huge head in disgust. Then he pushed back his chair and stood up, his knees creaking again. He went to one of the bookshelves and stood before it at length, muttering to himself. "Aha!" he said at last. He turned to me. "The volume I'm looking for is on the top shelf, and I'm afraid my legs are no longer up to the task. You look spryer."

"You want me to climb the ladder?"

"Indeed. It's the green Morocco-bound volume on the far left."

My heart began to hammer like a metronome in the cage of my chest. Why would the captain ask me to do this? Why?

Of course, the captain didn't know, I reminded myself. How could he? He wasn't trying to be cruel. Even if he knew what had happened to me, he'd have no idea I'd rather eat a bag of spiders one by one than climb a ladder. That my horror of heights was so profound I didn't even go too close to second-floor windows anymore. Climb a ladder. Oh God.

I looked at the stranger. Her face was so tranquil and innocent looking. She was counting on me.

I stood and smoothed my skirt, trying to remember whether or not I'd put on a slip that day. I often didn't bother when the weather was this hot, which horrified my mother. I wished I'd worn my sailor pants instead. I wished I'd never come. I wished I'd never been born.

Don't be stupid, I told myself. This is your chance to redeem yourself. Don't turn it into another opportunity for humiliation, another chance to show everyone how Millie is cracked. The stranger thought I was normal. Perhaps . . . perhaps she even found me a bit impressive. I couldn't risk losing that.

Carefully, I stepped onto the mahogany ladder, which felt solid though slippery under my foot. I gripped the brass railing so hard I could see my knuckles go white. What if my hands sweated? Oh God, they were sweating already. Taking a deep breath, I took a step. Then another. My heart was going so fast. What if I fainted? I tried to inhale and exhale the way Dr. Hoffstedder had taught me. Of all the doctors at the hospital, he was the only one I didn't hate. *In and out*, I could hear him saying in his soft Austrian accent. I took another step.

Then I made a mistake. I looked down. "Aah," I croaked, seeing the floor swaying six feet below me.

"Are you quite all right, girl?" asked the captain, staring up at me.

"I—I pinched my finger," I managed.

In and out. In and out. I took another step. My legs felt made of aspic. I was halfway at most. I reached for the next rung of the ladder and felt my sweaty hand slide on the varnished wood. I saw stars. *In and out. In and out.*

A memory of Auggie at six or so: I was nine, tasked with minding him on a summer afternoon. I was reading on the chesterfield, thinking he was playing with his tin soldiers upstairs. Then came a frantic knocking on the front door. It was Mrs. Callahan from across the street. I flew outside and followed Mrs. Callahan's pointing finger skyward. There was Auggie, standing on the very top of the chimney. Between his thighs was his wooden hobbyhorse, Billy.

"Auggie!" I screamed.

"I'm not Auggie," he shouted back, calm as can be. "I'm Bellerophon, and this is my flying horse, Pegasus."

I should have known better than to read to him from *Bulfinch's Mythology*.

"Bellerophon, come down this very moment!"

"Not until we kill the Chimera!"

It took minutes—though it felt like hours—to convince him that the Chimera was actually hiding behind the rosebush in the backyard. Once he agreed, he lowered himself from the chimney and skittered down the shingles as casually as if he were walking on the lawn. It was only when he popped back through the attic window that I allowed myself to take a breath. And I wasn't even afraid of heights back then.

In and out. In and out. Somehow, I'd reached the top shelf. Gathering every bit of strength, I reached for the green book. But it was heavy, too heavy to lift with one hand. I'd have to let go of the ladder completely. *In and out. In and out.* I felt my mind leave my body. It seemed to float above me as I reached both hands to the left of the ladder and slid the weighty volume towards me. As I did, my center of gravity shifted and my upper body pulled away from the ladder. I swayed. I let go of the book and gripped hold of the ladder, steadying myself.

No, I said to myself. No. No. No. I can't. I can't. I descended the ladder, legs quaking.

At the bottom, the captain stood, looking at me inquiringly. "What's the matter?"

"I—ah, I . . ." I began to explain, but before I could finish, the stranger stood and, quick as a flash, scurried up the ladder in her ridiculous oversized strawberry-print dress and grabbed the green book with both hands. She then backed down the ladder holding the book, without so much as a stumble. The next thing I knew, she was standing between me and the captain, smiling. The volume in her hands was titled *Atlas of European Languages* by Professor Milton van der Voost.

"You may borrow this," the captain said. "Let her browse the pages—perhaps she'll find a language that matches her own, assuming she's literate."

"Thank you," I said, my tongue like a dead fish in my mouth.

The stranger and I saw ourselves out. As we walked back down the path towards Middle Street, I felt overwhelmed with a hot white anger. *You can't even climb a ladder*, I said to myself. *You can't even get a book off a bookshelf. What good are you? Why do you even exist?*

"I'm sorry," I said to the stranger. "I'm afraid of heights. It's a long story."

The stranger looked at me in her pleasant blank way.

"It's not something I really talk about," I went on. "But I guess I could tell it to you. Would you like to hear it?"

She smiled.

"All right," I said. "It all starts with me standing on top of the Lucky Strike water tower in Durham. But maybe I should begin at the actual beginning. With Auggie."

Chapter 7

1936

It was Fanny who first mentioned Auggie's knee, buried in the third paragraph of one of her long letters.

> *Auggie fell in Union Point Park and hurt his knee. He is walking like an old man now! But the doctor says it is not broken, thank G-d. Zeke is back, working in the rail yard now. He and Auggie are "thick as thieves," your mother says. Can you explain what this means?*

Sitting in the dormitory parlor, with its stale air and sagging couches, I read the letter and immediately forgot the bit about the knee. Auggie was always hurting himself. This was the boy who took the brakes off his bicycle to see if it would go faster.

A few weeks later, I came home for Lizzy's wedding. I noticed Auggie sat during the hora, when the rest of the men and bigger boys raised Lizzy and Pete up in chairs and paraded them around the reception hall, laughing and singing.

The next night I was up late rereading *Around the World in Seventy-Two Days* by Nellie Bly. She'd taken the Jules Verne novel—my favorite as a little girl—and turned it into reality, besting Mr. Phileas Fogg by more than a week. She traveled by steamship and train, by rickshaw and sampan, even once by donkey! At the end, her publisher had arranged a special train to speed her from California back to Chicago.

Imagine, a woman having such adventures! And more than forty years ago, when Mama was still a little girl.

My head was swirling with images—pet monkeys in India, junks with red sails in Hong Kong harbor—when I went downstairs for a snack, sometime well after midnight. As I passed Auggie's room, I heard a low whimpering. I knocked and the sound stopped. Auggie must have been having a strange dream. But the next night, the same thing happened. This time I knocked and Auggie opened the door. He was pale as linen and sweating, taking deep gulps of air as he leaned against the doorframe.

"What on earth, Auggie?" A cold fear began to spread through my chest and throat, like I'd swallowed ice water too quickly.

"It's just my knee," he gasped. "Banged it. Just a bruise. Hurts worse at night."

"Auggie! That's not right. It must be broken."

"Nah, doc sent me for an X-ray."

"Still, something must be damaged. You look terrible."

"Thanks, Sis." Auggie managed a pained grin. "But, look, I made something to help." He hobbled over to his bed, sat down, and rolled up his pajama pants leg.

I had to laugh. His leg was wrapped in some kind of contraption, with tubes going every which way. Of course. That was Auggie.

"The rubber hosing is full of water, and I've covered it with a layer of the cellophane we use to line the pickle barrels—that bit was Zeke's idea," he explained. "Then—see—there's a bag of ice wrapped in flannel, then another layer of cellophane."

He went on for a while, describing the system—cooling tubes, freezing points. For a moment he seemed his regular self, and the fear in my chest began to ebb. But then his face spasmed and he stopped speaking mid-sentence. He tilted slowly, so slowly I didn't realize what was happening. Then he was toppling to the floor, hitting the rug with a sickening thwack.

DR. DIXON CAME in the morning to give Auggie an injection that allowed him to sleep on the train all the way to Durham. My mother and I rode with him, each of us holding one of his hands. She was praying silently, while I sat with every muscle in my body tensed, like my attention was needed to hold the train on the tracks, to hold Auggie in his bed, to keep the world from coming apart. The Silverbergs, family friends from my father's youth, met us at the station, and Laurence, their son, carried Auggie to their automobile for the ride to the new hospital at Duke University.

Everyone said Duke had the best hospital in North Carolina, maybe in all the South. It certainly looked like the kind of place that would be the best, an enormous gray stone building with arches like a cathedral. Inside everyone walked fast and purposefully, like they knew exactly where they were going and what they were doing. As soon as they put Auggie on a crisp white bed in the ward, I felt my body relax. Whatever was wrong, surely they'd solve it here. Maybe we'd even get on the morning train back to New Bern tomorrow. I'd return to college, Auggie would continue his senior year and be back at Duke in the fall to start his own degree.

They wheeled Auggie away for some tests, and my mother

and I waited on a bench in the shiny white hall. I got us a cup of coffee and some cookies from the hospital canteen, and we sat there, eating and drinking, confident that Auggie's problem was being solved at that very moment.

I still had a bit of cookie in my mouth when the doctor appeared. I'll never forget his face. Long and thin as a weasel's, with a weaselly mustache and beady black eyes. He had a French name—Du Clerc or Du Pont or something—and wore a Phi Beta Kappa key on his lapel. I hated him on sight. I hated him even before he spoke that hateful word. That word that plunged our family into an entirely new universe.

Cancer.

"We'll amputate, of course," Weasel Face said. "But these cancers typically spread to the lungs or the liver. Sometimes both!" He chuckled.

He actually chuckled.

I wanted to punch him so much my fists itched. I've never wanted to hurt someone so badly in my life.

But I kept my hands balled in my lap, twitching. My mother sat, looking down at the floor, her lips moving in silent prayer.

When they let us into the ward to see Auggie, he was sitting upright. They'd given him a better medicine for the pain. "So the doctor says it's just a sprain, then?" he said sleepily.

My mother nodded. "It will all be fine, *shefele*," she said, using a Yiddish baby name she hadn't spoken in years.

Auggie locked eyes with me. He shook his head slightly. I shook mine back. He knew our mother wouldn't call him *shefele* unless something was terribly wrong. I couldn't hide the truth from him. We had always been honest with each other, Auggie and I.

Later, when our mother went to the ladies' room, I told Auggie exactly what Weasel Face had said. He nodded slowly, taking it all in. Then he smiled.

"We'll do our own investigation," he said. "It's 1936, there's got to be new science that can help. We'll just have to find the right scientists, the right information—you've learned all about research and stuff at college, right? If anyone can figure it out, it's us."

"Yes," I said, feeling a thin ray of hope glowing in my chest. "You're right. If anyone can figure it out, it's us."

Chapter 8

As we turned on to our street, I saw Louise Nathan and her mother, Yetta Lieb, on our front walkway, and I stopped talking abruptly.

Gawkers. I could have guessed. They'd heard about the stranger and had decided to stop by for a nosy visit. Louise had on her nice dress, the green one with flowers she wears to synagogue. Louise's mother, Yetta, was holding a yellow enamel cake carrier. Knowing her, the carrier almost certainly contained the awful honey cake she made for every wedding, bris, Rosh Hashanah lunch, and break-the-fast dinner.

"Get ready to meet Little Jerusalem's second-biggest gossip," I whispered.

The stranger just smiled, clutching the captain's book to her chest with one hand.

Normally I'd be annoyed to have unexpected guests, but at the moment I felt oddly light, almost cheerful. I'd never spoken so freely about Auggie to anyone.

"Hi, Mrs. Lieb. Hi, Louise," I said as we turned on to the front path, which was lined with the jaunty pink and yellow flowers Fanny had planted. Louise and her mother turned around. Louise blinked in surprise, and Mrs. Lieb's lipsticked mouth rounded into a little O shape before jerking into a smile. They were probably more surprised to see me address them cheerfully than they were to see the stranger standing there in the flesh.

"Millicent, hello, so good to see you! You look well," said Mrs. Lieb, leaning down to kiss me on the cheek. She was Zeke's aunt, and shared his tall, lanky egret proportions, if not his good nature. Louise, Zeke's cousin, resembled her father's side of the family, plump and sweet faced.

"Good to see you too," I said, trying not to bristle. It was hard to hear *you look well* and not also hear the unspoken part: *for a lunatic!*

Louise smiled at me in her shy way. She'd had polio when we were small, and one of her arms was withered. The yentas had thought she might have to go as far as Charleston or Baltimore to find a husband, but Joe Nathan surprised everyone by proposing right after high school graduation. Louise and Fanny were good friends; I think they shared the feeling of having been rescued from a fate of aloneness by a man. Unlike Jesse, Joe Nathan was at least a decent person, if not much of a looker.

"Hello, dear. I'm Yetta Lieb," Mrs. Lieb said, holding out her hand for the stranger to shake.

The stranger took her hand and shook it with an odd little bob of her head and shoulders, almost like a small curtsy.

"She doesn't speak," I said for the dozenth time.

My mother opened the door to see all four of us standing on the porch. "Yetta, Louise, what a nice surprise!" she said, not looking at all surprised. "You just missed Mrs. Lefkowitz—she stopped by with some mandelbrod. Come in."

A few minutes later we were all sitting in the parlor with cold sweating glasses of sweet tea. God, I hoped Louise and her mother would leave quickly, so we could open the book Captain

Kennedy gave us. But I obligingly performed the motions of a normal Little Jerusalem daughter, slicing the honey cake and passing out my mother's blue-and-white china plates.

"So, where is your friend from? She's foreign, I take it?" Mrs. Lieb asked with a wide, false smile. Obviously, she'd already heard the story.

"I found her lying behind the pickle warehouse," I said, repeating what Mrs. Lieb surely already knew. "We're not sure where she's from or what language she speaks. We're trying to figure it out."

"What a kind heart you have, Millicent," she said. "Your mother must be proud."

I gave a wan smile. *Witch.* She knew perfectly well no Jewish Bern mother with an unmarried twenty-five-year-old daughter was *proud*.

"Millie's acting quite the little detective," my mother said, laughing lightly. "You'd think she was in one of those radio play mysteries. They went to question Captain Kennedy this morning."

Oh, how I wanted to throw my glass of iced tea across the room. *Quite the little detective?* As if I were an eight-year-old playacting in the backyard. Mrs. Lieb raised her eyebrows. "Kennedy? Is it true he keeps a stuffed tiger in the parlor? My girl Nanette's sister cleaned for him before the war, and she had stories about the decor, let me tell you. Paintings of women"—she lowered her voice—"in a state of nature."

"I didn't go in the parlor." I got a small satisfaction from the disappointment on Mrs. Lieb's face.

"Did he have anything useful to say?" My mother looked at me skeptically over the rim of her glass.

"He gave us a book. We'll look at it as soon as we have a free moment."

Mrs. Lieb scrutinized the stranger. "She reminds me of the wife of my second cousin, the one with the jewelry store in Virginia Beach. Hungarian girl. She had the same pale eyes. She made the most interesting soup—something to do with cherries. I'd telephone her to see if she'd talk to your friend in Hungarian, but she passed in June. Infection of the kidney, poor thing."

"May her memory be a blessing," my mother said.

There was silence for a moment. I could see the stranger looking longingly at the honey cake, having wolfed hers down in three bites. God willing she should eat it all before my mother could place another slice on my plate.

"Zora must be excited for Violet's wedding," Mrs. Lieb said, changing the subject. "Three girls, all married—what good fortune."

Louise cringed down at her teacup. For Mrs. Lieb, conversation was a blood sport.

"Such good fortune," my mother said, then quickly added, "*kein ayin hara,*" and pretended to spit, to keep away the evil eye.

"*Kein ayin hara,*" Mrs. Lieb repeated. She took a sip of tea and looked up, a sly little expression on her pointy face. "How about you, Rose. Do you not think of remarrying? Mrs. Lefkowitz was just telling me that her widowed daughter in Wilmington is marrying a man from up north. She must be fifty if a day, and not half as clever as you. Though I suppose being clever doesn't always help when it comes to finding a husband." Here, she looked at me, her eyebrows raised.

My mother's expression didn't so much as flicker. "Oh no, certainly not. When you have such a wonderful husband as God gave me, anyone who came after would be bound to feel in his shadow, and that wouldn't be fair."

"May his memory be a blessing," Mrs. Lieb said, her smile tight.

I knew some of the women in town gossiped about my mother when she was younger—running a business like a man, not accepting visits from the matchmaker. Yet she remained bound and determined to marry me off posthaste.

"Anyhow," said Mrs. Lieb, "what will you wear to the wedding?"

"Me?" My mother looked down at herself. "Green crepe. What else would be suitable for a stout old lady like me?"

"You'll look very handsome, I'm sure," Mrs. Lieb said. "And you, Millie?"

My mother laughed; only I could hear the angry catch underneath. "I wish she could tell you. She still hasn't gotten a new dress, she's been *so* busy trying to help the poor girl here. I keep telling her to go to the Marie Antoinette, buy anything she likes. I know most families still can't afford new clothes, but we're so *lucky* with the pickle factory—Jesse's been running it so marvelously. He just ordered a whole case of these fancy cigarette lighters with the logo on the side, for advertisement, see—" She picked up one of the lighters that was sitting on the side table and held it up for everyone to admire. It was silver, with an engraving of a pickle and the words FELIX'S FAMOUS PICKLES on the side.

Mrs. Lieb smiled insincerely. Her husband had more heart than business sense. He owned an import business but spent much of his time down in Wilmington, helping to establish some sort of farm colony for Jews leaving Europe. I supposed Mrs. Lieb would be wearing the same dress to Violet's wedding that she wore to Fanny's or Lizzy's. "Millicent is so slim, just like the girls in the magazines," she said. "I imagine she'd look beautiful in anything. It's funny how little daughters can resemble their mothers. I've always been slim too, and just look at Louise."

Louise's plump red cheeks went even redder.

My mother cleared her throat. But before she could speak, I had a thought. "I'll go to the Marie Antoinette tomorrow," I said. "I'll get a dress for myself and one for her."

"The girl?" My mother looked briefly aghast, then quickly rearranged her face.

"Why not? She's our guest. She should come to the wedding." With me as her chaperone, I could avoid the receiving line, the hora, and—dread of dreads—the tossing of the bouquet, which surely Violet would turn into a Hollywood production.

"Well, yes, of course. But don't you think she'll have found her people before Sunday?"

"Maybe. Maybe not."

"Do you think she'd . . . enjoy a wedding?"

"I don't see why not. But if you don't think we ought to spend the money, well . . ."

"No, no," my mother said. "Get her a dress, of course. Something with a little lace, perhaps?"

"I'll let Sophie pick," I said, smiling poisonously. "She's got *such* nice taste."

AS SOON AS Mrs. Lieb and Louise left, the stranger and I sat down on the chesterfield with the *Atlas of European Languages*. On the first page was a photograph of Professor Milton van der Voost glowering from behind a desk, as if angry anyone should dare read his book. Each language had its own page, in alphabetical order, with a brief description and a handful of phrases and their translations. I started at the beginning. Albanian. Oh dear. So many little dots above the letters.

Not knowing whether the stranger could read, I tried a phrase aloud: "*Përshëndetje*." (Hello.)

The stranger looked at me, a hint of a smile on her lips but no recognition.

I flipped to the next language and kept going, stumbling over unfamiliar letter arrangements and arcane accent marks. Aragonese. Aromanian. Asturian. Some of the languages were utterly indecipherable, with alphabets that looked like knotted rope or the hobos' chalk symbols. If the girl was a speaker of Avar or Azeri Turkic, we'd have no luck.

I kept stealing glances at her face, hoping for some change that would give me an idea of her thoughts. Did she know what we were looking at? Could she read? Her brow was furrowed in concentration, but of what kind?

By the time I got to "Corsican," I looked up to see the stranger's eyes closed, her head lolling against the back of the chesterfield. I closed the book and sat, watching for a few moments as she slept, her eyes flickered under bluish-white, nearly translucent eyelids. What was she dreaming about?

"Who are you?" I whispered, staring down at her.

Who would *I* be, I wondered, if I came ashore one day in a strange land, knowing no one? Who would I be, free from the narrow boundaries of the Trent and Neuse Rivers? Free from being Millicent Green, daughter of Rose, sister of Jesse. How would it feel to have no one know my family, my story, or even my name? Would it be liberating? Or would I fall apart? In college I'd imagined myself as the next Nellie Bly, setting off for Mexico or Hong Kong with nothing but a suitcase. But maybe that had always been a delusion. Maybe I'd always been destined to stay here, the old maid with the sad past, never quite strong enough, never quite brave enough. I'd been foolish to think I could have a big life one day, that I was bound for something special, something different.

I walked upstairs, the feeling of shame like a coat over my shoulders, heavy but familiar. Tomorrow I'd have to see the person who'd known my hopes and dreams better than anyone, who knew exactly how deeply I'd failed.

Sophie Zucker.

Chapter 9

It was another hot morning in Little Jerusalem, and everyone we passed seemed irritable. The Sussners were arguing outside their tailor shop, Old Mr. Gelman glowered as we passed his watch repair stall, Sy Lipinor dropped a box he was carrying into the furniture store and let loose a string of cusses. The smell of fish billowed up from the canal, where crates of oysters and gar sat in the sun, waiting to be picked up. By the time we got to the Marie Antoinette, I was sweating and edgy, my jaw working back and forth in a way that would give me a headache later.

Most of the shops on Middle Street were red brick, but Sophie had had the Marie Antoinette's exterior painted pristine white and topped with a blue-and-gold awning. On the door was a silhouette of a woman with a feather atop a mountain of hair, her nose pointed in the air.

I reluctantly pushed open the door, the stranger following closely. The bells jingled, and in the back of the shop I saw a blond head pop up from behind the counter.

Her married name of course was Sophie Cohen, but I'd never think of her that way. She was Sophie Zucker—teacher's favorite, the town's first-ever Jewish May Queen, graduation speaker at Sweet Briar College, now chatelaine of the Marie

Antoinette Ladies Boutique on Middle Street. Did I mention that Sophie has blond ringlets? I prayed for hair just like hers when I was little. I guess God didn't hear me, since my hair's as straight and brown as ever.

"I'll be right with you!" Sophie sang out. She hadn't noticed it was me yet.

The stranger stood in the middle of the shop, eyes wide. She looked the way Bea's older boys looked when I'd take them to Jacobi's Sweets on an occasional Friday afternoon and tell them they could pick anything they wanted.

The racks in the front of the shop held the new fall inventory. Wool dresses in greens and oranges, swing coats, felt fedoras and berets, even a rack of sickly-looking marten stoles, the martens' dead beady eyes gleaming in the artificial light. Who in New Bern wore fur, honestly? The air was laced with the heady fragrance of rose and jasmine. Jean Patou's Joy. For a moment I was eighteen again, at Sophie's birthday party, watching Sophie unwrap her present and squeal at the gleaming cut-glass perfume bottle. *Every woman should have a signature scent*, she'd said, turning to me. She'd always known things like that. What perfume to wear, how to talk to a boy, how to pick a dress color that flattered your complexion.

"Millie."

I looked up. Sophie was standing in front of me. She wore a pink dress with puff sleeves and a pearl necklace draped in a stylishly casual way, looking, as usual, twice as elegant as any other woman in New Bern. I'd never seen the necklace before. I wondered if Sam bought it for her.

"Hello," I said, mustering as much dignity as I could. "How are you, Sophie?"

"I'm fine, Millie, I'm fine. It's good to see you." Her eyes looked sincere, but I still felt the twist of shame in my gut.

I decided to get down to business immediately. "This is my . . . friend," I said, gesturing towards the stranger, who was staring at the marten furs with an air of bafflement. "She needs a dress for Violet's wedding. And some shoes, I suppose." The stranger, I noticed now, was wearing a pair of Lizzy's scuffed school Mary Janes, so loose her heel rose out of them with every step.

"Of course," said Sophie. She stepped towards the stranger. "Hello, I'm Sophie Cohen, I'm pleased to help you."

The stranger smiled and gave a polite little dip of her head.

"She doesn't speak," I told Sophie.

"Oh," said Sophie. I could tell she was desperately curious but knew it would be gauche to pry, of course. Funny—I would have thought she'd have been one of the first stops on the Little Jerusalem gossip circuit.

I certainly wasn't going to give her the satisfaction of an explanation.

"You would look nice in blue," Sophie said to the stranger. "It would bring out the color in your eyes."

"Blue's fine," I said. "How about these?" I pointed to a rack of cotton dresses farther towards the interior of the store; the remainders of the summer stock.

"Of course. But maybe she could try something a bit more formal as well?"

"It's just a Jewish New Bern wedding," I said. "We're not going to any Broadway shows or fancy New York dinners." The words came out more harshly than I intended. I tried to give a little laugh, but it sounded raspy and metallic.

"I see," said Sophie. She turned and, after considering for a moment, plucked two dresses off the rack. She held them up for my approval. One was a navy rayon with buttons and a swing skirt. The other was powder blue crepe, high necked and puff sleeved, like something my mother would have made me wear to synagogue as a little girl.

"I guess she should try them on," I said.

"Of course."

I motioned to the stranger, and we followed Sophie past the racks of nightgowns and bras to the fitting room, which was a closet that had been fitted with a lilac curtain where the door used to be.

"Go on," I said to the stranger, taking the dresses from Sophie and handing them to her.

She still looked confused, her pale features frozen in her oval face.

How strange. Where on earth could she have come from that people didn't have fitting rooms? My aunt once told me about an enormous bargain store up north called Filene's where the ladies simply stripped down to their underwear in the aisles to try on dresses. *Can you imagine a New Bern lady showing her girdle in public?* she'd said, laughing.

I pointed and made a motion of pulling clothes on over my head. Finally the stranger nodded slowly and stepped into the fitting room. Sophie pulled the curtain shut and trilled, "Just let me know if you need any help!"

"She doesn't speak," I said again.

"Of course," said Sophie. "How silly of me."

We stood on the other side of the lilac curtain, both of us looking in slightly different directions. *Please don't say anything, Sophie,* I thought. An uncomfortable silence would be better than small talk with Sophie Zucker.

GROWING UP, I spent as much time at Sophie's house as my own. My house was always noisy, with three children plus cousins running in and out, and my mother—when she was home—bustling around muttering to herself about factory invoices and the price of pickling salts. Sophie is an only child, and the only sound at her house was her housekeeper, Pearlie, humming to herself as she did the laundry. Sophie had a shelf of porcelain dolls and a Steiff horse on wheels we used to take turns riding on as little girls. Her bedroom had blue rose wallpaper and the most darling canopy bed. We used to lie there together after school, eating Pearlie's cookies and talking about the future that shimmered in front of us, so close we could almost touch it.

Sophie and I were going to go to Sweet Briar College, just like her glamorous older cousin Lili from Richmond. Sophie was going to study art and be a dress designer like Coco Chanel. I was going to do English, and be a foreign correspondent—*I'll make you a dress for the ceremony when you win a Pulitzer Prize!* she'd said, and we'd screamed with laughter at the idea, but we'd also, deep in our hearts, believed it could happen.

Well, Sophie did go to Sweet Briar, of course. I was accepted too, but Jesse said we couldn't spare the money, not when there was a perfectly good public women's college in Greensboro for fifty dollars a year. I begged my mother to intercede, but she just said that Jesse was the man of the house now that he ran the pickle factory. I was so angry I didn't speak to Jesse all summer.

Later, I would wonder if crying like I did over Sweet Briar made God angry, and that's why everything happened. I knew it seemed silly, but was it? The God in the Torah was awfully vengeful sometimes.

"I SAW FANNY the other day." Sophie broke the silence. "She's looking well."

"I'll tell her you said so." I wondered if Sophie was also having trouble having a baby. She and Sam had been married more than two years, after all. Imagine, Sophie not getting something she wanted. It would be the first time.

Another long silence. I stared at the rack of Bakelite bracelets next to the cash register.

"And Jesse? How is he?"

Fortunately, before I had to respond, we were interrupted by the rustling of the lilac curtain. The stranger pushed it aside and stepped out. She was wearing the navy rayon, though the belt had been done up wrong and the dress's lapels were turned inside out.

Sophie rushed forward and straightened them. The stranger flinched slightly at her touch. I could see that Sophie noticed; a questioning look crossed her face, only to disappear under a bright smile as she stood back to look at her handiwork.

"Beautiful!" she said. "What do you think, Millie?"

"Fine," I said. "We'll take it."

"But don't you want to try the other?" Sophie said.

I could have argued, but it seemed simpler just to agree. So I gave the stranger a reassuring look and sent her back to the dressing room. I turned to stare at the Bakelite bracelets again, but when I looked back I saw the stranger had not closed the lilac curtain all the way. She pulled the dress over her head, and as she did, I saw the skin of her stomach.

Her stomach.

Oh my God.

Her pale flesh was riven by a gleaming pink slash. It stretched from hip bone to hip bone, curving like a terrible smile. I thought absurdly of a magic show I'd seen as a child, where the magician cut a woman in half. What on earth could make such an awful scar?

Before I could take a second look, she was dressed again. I tried to smile as she came out of the fitting room in the puff-sleeved dress, but my mouth was suddenly so dry my lips stuck to my front teeth. I began to paw through the dresses on the nearest rack, just to have something to do with my hands.

Sophie looked at the new dress and gasped. "Don't you look just as cute as a bug's ear!" She guided the stranger towards the mirror.

She looked ridiculous. All poofs and ribbons, the fake flower as large as a cabbage flopping around on her shoulder. It reminded me of one of those faux wedding cakes brides used to save on butter and sugar, laid thick with swags and rosettes, because why not go all the way when it's just plaster anyhow.

I started to shake my head, but then I noticed the way the stranger was looking at herself in the mirror. Her eyes were large and soft and shining. Her lips trembled. Her hands flitted up and down, stroking the ribbons and the flower, as if she wasn't sure they were real. It was as if she was seeing herself for the first time.

"I think she likes it," Sophie said softly.

"We'll take it," I said. "And this too"—I grabbed a yellow dress off the rack, which appeared to be vaguely my size.

Sophie wrapped my dress, as well as a set of socks and underthings and a pair of white pumps, in tissue paper the same pale blue as the Marie Antoinette's awning. She let the stranger go home wearing the new dress.

"I hope I'll see you again soon, Millie," she said as we stepped out into the thick August air.

"Yes," I said.

Never, I thought. *Not even if I have to learn to sew my own dresses.*

I hurried out of the store, the stranger on my heels in her new dress.

"I'm sorry," I said, turning to her. "I know I was acting strangely. You see, Sophie and I used to be best friends. You think you can count on a person who's been your best friend since you were five. But you can't."

Chapter 10

1936

By that September, Auggie was back at Duke, but not for college. He lay in his bed in the ward with his eyes half-closed, his yellow skin standing out against the white pillow. His eyelids were puffy, showing a sliver of darker yellow underneath. Most alarmingly, his stomach had swollen up like he'd swallowed a whole watermelon.

"Don't worry, Auggie," I said, holding his hand, which felt thin and papery in mine. "I'm still doing research. There are so many science books in the Duke library; you'll be amazed when you finally see it. Next semester, I'm sure of it." He smiled, but it was more of a grimace, like the act of smiling was painful.

Every morning I'd go to the library at opening time and check out heavy stacks of blue and green textbooks with Laurence Silverberg's library card. When visiting hours started, I'd sit in the uncomfortable chair next to Auggie's bed and read the most interesting passages out loud. Auggie didn't always seem to be awake, but sometimes his eyelids would open a crack and he'd whisper "Wow" or "Read me that part again." Evenings, back at the Silverbergs', I'd make a thermos of coffee and sit cross-legged on top of the flowered quilt in the spare bedroom until three or four in the morning, reading about the effects of aniline dyes on tumors and the benefits of "radiotherapy." I held a medical dictionary on my lap and flipped through it frequently, like I was translating a foreign language. I'd get up at seven and do it all again. Despite the schedule, I felt full of restless energy, like my body understood there were more important things than sleep right now.

One night, reading a book called *The Cancer Problem* in the dim amber light of the bedside lamp, I made the discovery:

> *It is undeniable that a certain number of sarcomata disappear under, or are profoundly influenced by, Coley's toxins.*

Wait. He was saying that something called Coley's toxins could kill the sarcomata—the cancer—that was invading Auggie's body?

I read more, growing more and more excited and angry and agitated: Coley's toxins were a sort of vaccine made of bacteria. It made patients ill for a brief time. But it could kill any tumors.

Why had Weasel Face not mentioned this?

I didn't sleep at all that night. In the morning, I slammed into Weasel Face's office, my mother at my heels. "How did you not tell us about Coley's toxins?" I said, my voice trembling with fury. "Auggie needs them now, right away!"

Weasel Face raised his eyebrows. "Coley's toxins?" he said in a tone of distaste. "Sounds like nonsense."

"Nonsense!" I cried. "There was a girl with a tumor on her neck who was cured by Coley's toxins, cured completely. In hours! I read about it!"

"Miss Green," he said, his black rodent eyes gleaming like he was laughing at me in his head. "I'm a graduate of Yale University and the Johns Hopkins School of Medicine. I've been treating cancer victims for a decade. I assure you, if there were a cure that worked within hours, I would be using it. Everyone would be using it."

"If you know what to do, then why aren't you doing anything?"

"Millie!" my mother said, aghast.

Weasel Face was quiet for a moment. He looked at my mother, who sank into a chair against the wall.

"I suppose I might as well tell you, since it won't be long," he finally said, as casually as if he was telling me the weather. "As I expected, the cancer has traveled to the liver. Unfortunately, there's nothing more to be done."

"But what about the radiotherapy?" I suddenly felt very, very cold, and like I needed to sit down. "We've been reading about so many new advances."

"All we can do now is give him morphine," Weasel Face said. "To keep him comfortable, you understand."

My mother dropped her head to her chest and began to pray.

Mi shebeirakh avoteinu
Avraham, Yitz'chak v'Ya'akov
Mosheh, Aharon, David uSh'lomoh
hu y'vareikh virapei et hacholeh

The one who blessed our ancestors
Abraham, Isaac, and Jacob,
Moses, Aaron, David and Solomon,
may He bless and heal the sick one.

I wanted to tell her to stop. I wanted to tell her prayers weren't what Auggie needed; he needed better medicine, better doctors. He didn't even believe in God! But I found I couldn't move my mouth to speak. I was so cold. My arms and legs felt very far away, like they weren't part of my body. The hallway began to shimmer and dissolve in front of my eyes.

The next thing I knew, I was lying on a gurney in the hallway with a pack of ice on my head and a nurse tsking in my face. My mother sat on the bench next to me, her eyes far away, lips still moving. Still saying her useless prayers.

Chapter 11

The stranger and I entered the house to the smell of vinegar and spiced beef and sticky burnt sugar. Sweet-and-sour stuffed cabbage. "You're in luck," I whispered to the stranger. "Fanny has made her very best dish."

My mother and Fanny took turns in the kitchen; I was as useless at cooking as I was at everything else. Fanny was the better cook of the two, though the rest of the family teased her about her old-fashioned attitude towards kosher laws—burying meat forks in a flowerpot of dirt if they accidentally touched milk and so on. Most of us in Jewish New Bern just avoid shrimp and pork and consider it good enough; I once even caught my uncle Abe eating a pork barbecue sandwich. ("It's not tref if it's chopped small enough," he claimed.) My mother wobbled through the door moments later, carrying a sack from the laundry. She heaved the sack onto the bottom stair, and looked at the stranger in her new dress.

"Such a *shaina maidel*!" she exclaimed. Then she turned to me: "I hope yours is half as pretty."

I didn't answer. The stranger stood by the kitchen door, eyeing the cabbage rolls. Her posture was as perfect as ever, but she was sniffing like a hungry hound.

"Help set the table, at least, Millie," my mother said, getting a pitcher out of the sideboard and filling it with water. As irritated as she sounded, she was still using the nice pitcher. She still wanted the stranger to feel welcome.

I set the table with my mother's blue-and-white wedding china and we all sat down. The cabbage rolls lay under a glistening blanket of orange sauce, studded with raisins. A tureen of hot rice steamed. There were fresh rolls and oleo, and the crystal pickle dish was full of sweet mixed pickles.

The stranger sat next to me, straining almost imperceptibly towards the food, like a sprinter awaiting the gun at a track meet. *Oh, that's rather good*, I thought. *Like a sprinter awaiting the gun*. I should write that down.

We were about to serve ourselves when the door flew open and hit the plaster wall with a muffled bang. Jesse. He always entered a room like a defensive lineman about to tackle the other team's quarterback. The stranger jolted back in her chair, startled.

"Smells good," Jesse said loudly, with an exaggerated lip licking.

"Who's minding the factory?" my mother said, frowning. "It's a packing day, no?"

"I put Baxter in charge. I wasn't gonna sit there and eat a cold tongue sandwich like a schmo, not when Fanny's cooking up her famous cabbage rolls."

"Are you sure? I can go over there to help, I'll eat later."

"Ma, sit down. Relax. It's fine. Your days of working yourself to death are over, all right? And don't worry—old Bax knows I've got eyes everywhere, he won't try any nonsense."

My mother sighed, but didn't say anything. Jesse has never been scolded in his life.

Jesse sat down at the head of the table and began serving

himself. It wasn't until his plate was heaped that he looked up and noticed the stranger. "She's still here?"

"Yes, Jesse, she's still here," I said tartly.

"What are you gonna do with her?"

"We're working on it," I said.

"They went to see Captain Kennedy," my mother said, giving me another skeptical glance. "He gave them a book."

"That old souse?" scoffed Jesse, shoveling a forkful of rice and cabbage roll into his mouth. "What the heck is a book gonna do to get her out of my house?"

"*Your* house?" I said, my voice rising.

Here, Fanny interjected. Dear, sweet Fanny. "Jesse, I forgot to tell you—I have finished with your new suit. Let us have a fitting after lunch, and you can wear it for the wedding."

Jesse smiled in his infuriating cat-that-ate-the-canary way. "Sure, sweetheart. You might have to take it out in the middle, after this lunch." He patted his stomach, then pulled out one of his stupid Felix's Famous Pickles lighters and lit a cigarette. He turned back to me. "I had a thought."

"Oh? That must be a new experience for you."

Jesse narrowed his eyes. "Har, har. Yeah, my thought was that maybe she's faking it."

"Excuse me?"

"You heard me. Maybe she's a phony. Pretending she can't talk, so she can eat our food and sleep under our roof. Pretty nice racket."

"Jesse," Fanny began, laying a hand on his arm.

He shook it off. "I'm surprised you didn't think of that yourself, Millie—you're supposed to be the smart one now."

I felt a slow swirl of fury rise in the pit of my stomach. "Oh? So you think she just came from nowhere and lay down behind the pickle warehouse, hoping someone would find her and let her live in their house forever, so long as she couldn't speak?"

"I don't think she came from nowhere," Jesse said, picking up his fork again.

"Please, do tell us where she came from then, Jesse, since you know so much."

Jesse chewed like a cow, his plump cheeks bulging as he worked the cabbage roll like a cud. He finally swallowed. "She's probably a . . . how should I say it, so I don't offend the ladies present? A *lady of the night.* Maybe from the cathouse out in Five Points."

"Jesse!" my mother said, which is as close as she'll get to an admonishment.

Jesse shrugged. "Makes sense. A pretty young girl with an honest reputation would have a family looking for her. And it would account for her weird clothes, huh?"

"We don't know if she has a family or not, Jesse," I said, almost hissing. "We don't know anything. That's what we're trying to find out. And *ladies of the night* are not known for wearing togas, but I guess you know much more about them than I do."

He grinned. "Don't get all hot under the collar. I'm just helping."

"You know you're not. You've never helped a minute in your life."

"Never helped?" Jesse's voice had gone low. "I'm the one who's running the goddamn pickle factory! I'm the one who stepped up to keep this family afloat! Who are you to talk, the girl who's living in my house, eating food I pay for with money I get up at the crack of dawn to earn?"

"It's. Not. Your. House!" I growled.

Fanny seemed to shrink in her chair.

"Like hell it's not," Jesse said. "You want your own house? Go get married!"

Bang!

The table jumped, rattling all the plates and glasses. Everyone froze.

My mother had slammed her hand down like a judge's gavel.

Even the stranger, who'd been nearly horizontal over her plate, looked up.

"Stop this at once," my mother said. "I will not have this kind of talk in *my* house."

Jesse shot me an evil look but stopped talking. He bent over his plate in silence for several minutes, shoveling food in like a farmer baling hay. Then he stood and left the room.

Fanny hurried to clear his plate. Poor Fanny. Was this really so much better than a boardinghouse in Baltimore?

I thought Jesse had left through the back door to return to work, but suddenly he was there again, looming in the doorway of the dining room. He was holding something behind his back, like a parent about to give a present to a child.

"This ought to do the trick," he said, turning to the stranger. "Hey, sweetheart, look at me."

"Jesse, you know perfectly well she doesn't understand," I said.

"Right." Jesse smirked. He tapped the stranger on the back. When she turned, he pulled out the object he was concealing behind his back.

It was Auggie's camera.

"What are you doing with that?" I shrieked.

"What do you think, Millie?" he said. "I'm gonna take a picture of her and we'll make a missing persons ad for the papers. Have you really never thought of that?" He crouched down by the stranger and aimed the camera in her face.

It happened so quickly. The camera shutter clicked. The stranger reared back. One arm flew up to cover her face. The other arm shot out and smacked the camera out of Jesse's hands. For a moment the room held in utter silence. Then came two crashes. The first was the stranger's water glass, upset by her elbow, shattering on the floor. The second was the camera. It spun across the room and hit the edge of the coffee table with the violence of a skull cracking.

I gasped and froze, my hand clapped over my mouth. The camera kept moving. The lens flew off and went spinning across the parlor like a top. It seemed to go on spinning for years.

When it finally came to a stop, my ears were ringing. "No, no, no," I cried, though I wasn't sure if I was actually speaking or the word was simply echoing in my head. "No."

I RAN DOWN Pasteur Street, the camera wrapped in a pillowcase. When I got to the station, I took the stairs two at a time, not minding the height.

Zeke was standing by the back wall of his office, marking something on a map. Hearing me enter, he whirled around, his blue eyes blinking in surprise. "Millie? What's wrong?"

"Can you fix a camera?" I managed.

"Sure—I mean, probably. Depends on what's wrong with it. What kind of camera?"

"Auggie's Leica," I whispered. I pulled the camera and lens out of the pillowcase and placed them on Zeke's overflowing desk.

Zeke just looked at me and didn't say anything. He came around my side of the desk and picked up the camera. "What happened?"

"Jesse," I said bitterly. "He took the mute woman's picture, and she got scared and swatted it away."

"Scared?" he said. "But why?"

"I don't know. Maybe she'd never seen a camera before?"

"That would be odd," he said, rubbing the lens on his shirt and holding it up to the window. "It's not like they're rare these days. Even the hobos knew what they were, and some of those boys were really from the back of beyond."

"I suppose you're right."

"I'll try my best with this," Zeke said, still squinting at the camera. "If I can't do it, there's a guy in Chapel Hill who knows Leicas inside out; I'll write to him."

"Thank you," I said, feeling relieved about the camera, at least. But now I had a new thing to feel uneasy about. Zeke *was* right. It would be quite odd if the stranger had never seen a camera before. More likely that she knew exactly what it was, but didn't want her picture taken.

Why not?

Chapter 12

That night, the day's strange events and Jesse's words rolled around in my head. *Maybe she's faking it. Maybe she's a phony.*

She wasn't faking her scars. She wasn't faking her hunger. She wasn't faking her fear.

Still. Jesse's smug voice itched at my mind. I couldn't sleep. The freshly laundered sheets were starched and scratchy. The air was soupy. Every cricket chirp or distant train whistle was as irritating as a nail dragged across a blackboard. I thrashed, trying to get comfortable. I knew my hair would be a bird's nest of tangles in the morning, just like when I was a little girl.

Eventually I got up. I meant to go to the bathroom, but somehow I found myself outside Auggie's room, silvery moonlight falling slantwise across the hall. The house was utterly silent except for the crickets outside. I strained my ears towards the door. Faintly, ever so faintly, I could hear the stranger's gentle snoring. I stood, still as one of the marble statues in the captain's house, for five minutes, ten, unsure of what I was even listening for. A mosquito bite on my ankle began to itch, and as I reached down to scratch it, I lost my balance and fell against the doorframe with a thud. I straightened up quickly. Had I woken her? I listened again. Nothing.

Then, suddenly, a sound.

No. Not a sound.

A *word.*

"*Hi-jalp.*" Softly and groggily; the tone of a sleepwalker. Then louder. "*Hi-jalp. Hi-jalp.*"

I pushed against the door to see if it would open on its own so I could peer in the crack. But it was latched.

Again that word. "*Hi-jalp. Hi-jalp.*" Then a long pause. Then again. "*Hi-jalp, hi-jalp.*" The word became a moan, almost frantic. "*Hi-jalp. Hi-jalp. Hi-jalp.*"

I started to turn the doorknob. But abruptly the talking stopped. Had she woken up? I froze.

A minute passed, then two. There was no sound of the stranger stirring, and no more words. She must have been talking in her sleep. I stood for a few more minutes, then crept back to my room.

I sat in bed on top of the covers, absolutely awake.

Hi-jalp.

What could it mean? Or did it mean anything at all? I got up again and retrieved the language book from downstairs, then sat at my desk poring over it in the murky light of my little stained-glass lamp. The book was 851 pages long. The chances that I'd find the words the stranger had spoken—assuming I'd understood them correctly—were tiny. Still. I ran my fingers under lines of text in Crimean and Estonian and Faroese for hours, a headache slowly unfurling behind my eyes like a poisonous flower. I must have fallen asleep, because when I next blinked there was green morning sunlight streaming through the window and my cheek was numb from lying on the book.

I dressed quickly and went downstairs, ready to tell my

family about the discovery. Jesse was wrong. The doctor was wrong. The stranger wasn't mute. She wasn't a phony. She *was* a foreigner.

When I entered the parlor, I found the stranger awake and dressed already, wearing the same pale blue dress. She was sitting on the chesterfield with Fanny, their heads inclined towards each other like schoolgirls sharing a secret. On the coffee table in front of them was the little globe on the brown pedestal from Auggie's room. The stranger was jabbing with her index finger at the globe, and Fanny was nodding vigorously.

"Good morning," I said. Both of them looked up, startled. They'd been so involved they hadn't noticed me.

"Millie!" said Fanny. "The girl picked up the world and is very excited."

"What's she looking at?" I asked, rushing over to sit down next to the stranger.

"Norway?" Fanny said, squinting at the globe. "Or—no—Sweden?"

The stranger looked up at me, her pale eyes glowing with an excitement I hadn't seen before.

"What is it?" I asked. "Did you find your home?"

The stranger jabbed her finger again. The globe was so small—barely bigger than a muskmelon—that it was difficult to see exactly what she was touching.

"Sweden," I said, peering at the small shape beneath her finger, just south of the Arctic Circle.

I looked at Fanny. She looked back at me. "Is this where she's from?" she asked.

"I don't know. But I heard her talking last night. The same word over and over. Maybe it was Swedish?"

Fanny raised her eyebrows. "Talking?"

"Yes. I think she was asleep, though. Sleep talking."

"Jesse does this sometimes, speak while sleeping," Fanny said thoughtfully. "About the pickles, mainly. But in the morning, he has no memory."

Perhaps the stranger had had some sort of shock that had caused her to forget to speak, but she still remembered it in her dreams? I thought again of that horrible pink slash on her stomach.

The stranger was caressing the outline of Sweden on the globe with the tip of her finger, and her lips were moving as if she were trying to say something, though she wasn't making any sound.

"The book!" I cried suddenly. "Let me get the book!"

I ran back to my bedroom, where the book lay in a pool of sunlight on the desk, its open page slightly crinkled from where my cheek had lain. I flipped to "Swedish," all the way on page 733.

Swedish: Originating from the Old Norse, the language belongs to the East Germanic group of . . . I scanned down the page to the section of "Useful Phrases."

Hello: Hej

Please: Snälla

I'm sorry: Förlåt

Help: Hjälp

Wait. *Hjälp. Hi-jalp.* "Help."

Help.

The stranger had been moaning for help.

I rushed back downstairs and sat down again on the chesterfield, laying the heavy book open on my knees.

I looked the stranger in her gray eyes. "*Hej*," I said carefully, hoping I was pronouncing it correctly. *Hello.*

The stranger looked back at me quizzically. Then her face

broke into an enormous smile. "*Hej*," she said to me in a soft voice.

"*Hej!*" I said again.

"*Hej*," she said back, smiling even wider.

I know this sounds silly, but in that moment I felt a sense of relief in my body, like I'd been wearing a heavy jacket that suddenly vanished. I'd figured it out! I'd solved it! I'd done it! I looked at Fanny, who was grinning too. Then I looked down again at the book, searching for another phrase to use. "*Förlåt*," I said finally. *I'm sorry*. "I'm sorry for whatever has happened to you." The scars. The camera.

"*Förlåt*," she said back to me.

"You have nothing to be sorry for," I said, reaching for her hand and squeezing it. She squeezed back.

Suddenly I had a thought. "Benji's assistant at the fishmonger's," I cried. "He's a Swede, right?"

Fanny wrinkled her nose. "The mean little man with yellow hair?"

"That one."

Fanny shrugged. "I try not to speak to him."

"I'm almost certain," I said. "Bea said he'd been working on one of those foreign fishing boats out of Morehead City that follow the oysterfish, and he was so irritating they left him on shore and sailed away. He turned up at the Middle Street docks with empty pockets, and Benji hired him out of pity."

The room darkened. I looked up to see my mother standing in the dining room doorway, her square shape blocking the window behind her. "You want the breakfast to get cold?" she said.

Either the stranger smelled the food or had learned the word "breakfast," because she was up and across the room before I had a chance to close the book and put it on the side table.

"Millie has figured out the mystery, perhaps!" Fanny announced to my mother. "The girl may be a Swede."

"Oh?" My mother raised her eyebrows and leaned against the doorframe, folding her arms. I thought again of what Jesse had said, his ugly accusations.

"She was speaking last night, in her sleep, in her native tongue," I said.

"What did she say?"

"'*Hi-jalp.*'"

"'*Hi-jalp*'?" my mother repeated with a scoff. "That sounds like nothing. She was probably just sneezing."

"She wasn't sneezing!" Of course my mother couldn't acknowledge that I'd done anything right. "It's a real word. It's Swedish. It means 'help.'"

"Help? Why would she need help in the middle of the night?"

"I don't know," I said. "It seemed like maybe she was dreaming. I'm going to ask Benji. His assistant is from Sweden, we think. He can translate."

My mother looked doubtful. "The one whose apron is always filthy?"

"That one."

The stranger was eating in her usual way, head bent over the plate at a ninety-degree angle, shoulder hunched forward as if she were protecting her food.

Hi-jalp. Help.

From what? From whom?

AFTER BREAKFAST, FANNY went to Benji's shop to see if the Swede was working, and my mother went to help Mrs. Lieb with her weekly baking. The stranger and I sat in the parlor, paging through the newspaper. Just thinking of Jesse's smug face and the way the stranger had reared back in terror at the camera made me so angry my teeth hurt, but I had to see the ad for myself.

Britain Conducts Air Defense Tests; Baseball Game to Be Televised in World First; US Scientist Hails Nazi Racial Purity Program at Eugenics Expo. The ads on the back page could have served as a membership list for Chester B'nai Sholom Synagogue. *New Fall Attire at Lipinor's Men's Furnishings. The Finest Fresh Fish at Fineman's Fine Fish. Affordable Luxury from Meyer's Jewelry.*

There it was. Once I'd spotted it, I couldn't help but read it, the way you can't help looking at a possum that's been run over by a car, even if it makes your stomach turn.

> *Found: White woman, young, average size, short blond hair. Wears flower brooch with red stone. Doesn't Speak. Call 751.*

I wondered how many nearby papers Jesse had placed the ad in. There was no photo, at least. Hopefully no one would recognize her.

Hearing my own thought, I felt a pang of embarrassment. What was wrong with me? Wasn't I trying to help reunite her with her family? I could imagine Jesse smirking, saying, "That girl was the most exciting thing that's happened to old maid Millie in her damn life."

But the embarrassment didn't stop the voice in my head. *Not yet,* it said. *I haven't even finished telling her my story.*

"Come on." I motioned to the stranger. "While we wait for them, let's take a little walk."

Chapter 13

1936

It felt like a train was bearing down on me, and I was only keeping ahead of it by a single step, running with all my power as its screech and smoke grew louder and thicker. I had to help Auggie. I had to get him the Coley's toxins, quickly, quickly! But how?

That night, I sat at the Silverbergs' big mahogany dinner table, not eating, but waving my fork to illustrate my points. Doctors didn't know everything! There were more treatments! We just had to find the right person to help! I saw Mrs. Silverberg give my mother a look and put a hand on her shoulder. Finally, Mr. Silverberg interrupted me. "I wonder," he said, "if you ought to talk to Abraham Klein. He's at Duke too, but he's a chemist, not a doctor. He might be able to . . . offer advice?"

A chemist! It all fit together now. Auggie was planning to study chemistry at Duke. Of course it would be a chemist who could help. It all made sense, the threads of the story coming together at last. Auggie would tell this story to his grandchildren, how we'd searched and searched and fought against all odds and finally, finally the solution appeared, glowing like magic, and the grandchildren would gasp in amazement. How close they came to never being born! But Auggie pulled through, like he always did, bent the world to his will with a smile.

He's no ordinary man, your grandfather, I'd say.

Laurence Silverberg dropped me off in front of the chemistry department amid the solemn row of gray buildings on Duke's West Campus.

"Are you sure you wouldn't like to go home for a while, get some rest?" he said, his sweet round face creased with concern. "Or I could skip my afternoon class and we could get a sandwich?"

I was already halfway up the stairs.

The chemist's office was at the end of a corridor that must have backed up against an airshaft, as the light there was murky and gray, like being underwater. The floor was worn and the paint on the walls smudged; nothing like the gleaming new halls of the hospital. I knocked on the frosted glass door, which read PROFESSOR ABRAHAM KLEIN, CHEMISTRY. A voice directed me to enter.

Professor Klein was hunched over a table, peering through a microscope. All I could see of him was the top of his bald head. When he finally raised his face towards me, he had raccoonish red rings around his eyes from pressing too firmly into the microscope. He didn't speak, only raised his thick gray eyebrows.

I explained who I was, and why I was there. Imagining what Auggie would do, I tried to be charming, telling the professor that rumors of his brilliant research had reached far and wide. I could tell I was talking too fast, but I couldn't stop. There was so much to tell, so much to do, so many moving parts!

"How quickly could you treat my brother with Coley's toxins?" I said, nearly gasping for breath. "We have so little time."

The professor looked at me for a moment without speaking.

My words hung suspended like dust motes in the air. I could hear my heartbeat in my ears, the ragged sound of my own breath.

"I'm so sorry," he finally said in a soft voice. "That's not possible."

I felt like I'd been punched in the stomach. Nausea. Pain. Fury. This wasn't what was supposed to happen. This wasn't how the story went. "But why?" I cried. "Look!" I shoved *The Cancer Problem* in front of him. "See!"

Professor Klein was quiet again for a moment. Then he looked up. "Millicent—is it all right if I call you that?"

"It's my name," I said angrily.

"Millicent, that's a very old book. Prewar, I think."

"And so?"

"Coley's toxins did seem promising, a generation back," Professor Klein said, rubbing his eye. "I'm old enough to remember that. But in the end, it didn't work. Science and medicine are full of disappointments like this."

I stood there for a moment, swaying, my jaw opening and closing as I attempted to find some argument, some combination of words that would make this right.

"But the little girl with the tumor on her throat?" I said finally.

"It was probably an ordinary infection. Not cancer. Cancer doesn't disappear without surgery. It simply doesn't. Someday—perhaps within a decade, even—we'll have chemical treatments that truly help. We've learned so much from the war—the effects of mustard gas on certain malignancies, for example. Researchers at Harvard and elsewhere have been doing some wonderful work. But it's not ready yet. Not in time for your brother. I'm so sorry."

He did look sorry. He looked tired and sad and sorry. Sorry was more than any other doctor had given me. But it wasn't enough. It wasn't nearly enough.

"You're wrong!" I spat, turning and slamming the door so hard the glass rattled.

I flew out of the chemistry building and into the quad, nearly colliding with a group of laughing students in letterman jackets. The great lawn was full of boys—boys reading, boys tossing footballs, boys drinking bottles of Coke. The azaleas were blooming. The sky was perfect blue. Auggie should be sitting here in the sun with a textbook.

Instead, he was up in the hospital ward growing weaker and weaker, with no one to help him. No one but me.

I'd find a way. I had to.

I just needed to talk to Auggie. To tell him the plan.

A strange energy rippled through my body, like I was filled with electricity. I turned and ran across the quad and down the slate path until I got to the main entrance of the hospital. There, sitting on a bench, was my mother. There was someone with her. A man. He had round silver glasses and wore a yarmulke. They held a book between themselves, and the man was pointing out something on the page.

I strode over to them. "What are you doing?" I demanded, aware of how mad I must look, red-faced and frantic.

"Millie!" my mother said, looking up at me.

I noticed, with some shock, how much older she looked. The skin under her eyes was purplish and hashed with wrinkles. I'd seen her just this morning, sitting at the Silverbergs' breakfast table, but I realized now that I hadn't truly looked at her in months.

"What are you doing?" I demanded again.

The man sitting next to my mother closed the book and looked at me. I saw Hebrew writing on the book's cover: a prayer book.

"Millie," my mother said, "this is Rabbi Fried, from the Silverbergs' synagogue."

"Why's he here?" I said, aware I was being rude and not caring, knowing all too well why the rabbi was there but not wanting to know.

"Millie," the rabbi said, his eyes owlishly magnified by those silver glasses.

"I'm tired of people saying my name," I said under my breath. "I'm just so tired of it."

"I'm sorry," the rabbi said. "It's time for Auggie to say his *vidui*."

"No."

"I'll sit with him and give him the chance to say his final atonement himself," the rabbi went on. "If he can't say the words, don't worry, he can say the prayer in his heart, and God will forgive him, of course."

"Auggie has nothing to be forgiven for," I shouted, the words roaring from my mouth like flames. "And he's not going to die—there are more treatments." I turned to my mother. "How could you just give up like this? What kind of mother are you? Why am I the only one who's actually trying to do something?"

"Millie," said my mother, her face white.

I looked at her, trembling with rage, and screamed: "What did I tell you about saying my name?"

Then I turned and, once again, I ran.

Chapter 14

When the stranger and I got back home, Fanny was sitting on the porch steps, twisting her hands together, looking one way down the street, then the other.

"There you are!" she called, spotting us.

"What's going on?"

"He's here," she said breathlessly.

"Who?"

"Benji's man. The Swede. He's very rude; he says again and again that he will leave if you don't come soon. I've had to give him three slices of poppy seed cake already!"

I felt like the air had been sucked from my lungs. *He's here? Now? Already?*

I straightened my back. "Oh, good!" I said as brightly as I could. I turned to the stranger and glued a smile to my face. "Come on. The Swedish man is here. Hopefully he can help you."

She followed me inside like a calf follows its mother.

The Swede stood in our parlor, smelling of fish. He wore a wrinkled undershirt and had an impatient expression on a narrow face with a sharply sloping forehead and the invisible eyelashes of a white rabbit. "Is her?" he demanded.

Benji, sitting on the chesterfield, stood up and tried to make a proper introduction—"Millie, this is Gustaf Gustafson; Gustaf, this is—"

The Swede cut him off with an impatient flip of his hand. Cut off Benji, his employer! "Which one is girl?"

Benji, cowed, pointed at the stranger. "I'll be going back to the shop now," he stammered.

Gustafson strode across the room and looked at the stranger with narrowed eyes the color of the dirty ice at the bottom of the icebox. "*Är du svensk?*" he growled.

The stranger nodded, looking down at her feet.

Gustafson barked a series of slushy-sounding words, and the stranger hesitated. Then she took a step towards him, and beckoned for him to lean in. Gustafson inclined his greasy blond head towards her, and she whispered something in his ear.

Gustafson's eyes grew even narrower and his mouth twisted in a curious way. Then he nodded and straightened up. "She wishes to speak alone."

"Alone?" I exclaimed. "But why? We don't understand a word of Swedish."

Gustafson shrugged. His shirt was stained with something dark and greasy.

"Yes," said Fanny, standing up. She took my arm. "We'll be in the kitchen."

I looked back over my shoulder, uneasy. I should be there, shouldn't I? Leaving the stranger with this thoroughly nasty little man seemed inadvisable, even if they were just in the other room. Plus, I was desperate to hear her voice, even if I wouldn't understand.

Fanny put the kettle on. "It's fine," she said, as if she was reading my mind.

"I know," I said. Though it didn't seem fine to me.

"Sit down," Fanny said, and I obeyed. I so wanted to push

the door open and peer into the parlor, but I forced myself to look the other way. My foot telegraphed my nerves, tap-tap-tapping on the linoleum. I felt like I might vomit, or faint.

When the kettle whistled, Fanny poured two cups of tea and sat down across from me. She noticed my tapping foot and gave me a funny look. "Drink," she commanded.

I picked up my blue-and-white cup and took an overlarge sip, scalding my tongue. I put it down more roughly than I intended, and hot amber liquid sloshed onto the wax cloth. I went to wipe it up, and as I did I noticed that Fanny's teacup was filled with something different, some sort of pale liquid with bits of pink fluff floating in it. "What is that?"

Fanny looked embarrassed. "It's . . . I'm not sure the name. The little plant that grows on the edge of the garden, with the pink flowers like a circle. The bees always eat it."

"Clover?" I gave her a look. Fanny, with her garden, would sometimes introduce us to things we hadn't tried before—she was very fond of broccoli, which she learned about from the Italians she worked with at the soap factory in Baltimore. But drinking clover tea was new to me.

She brightened. "The girl—the woman—she made it for me the other day. I think she understands about my—my problem."

"Your problem?" Oh, the baby problem. "But how would she possibly know?"

"The other day, she saw me holding Aaron, and, well, sometimes when I hold one of the babies I start feeling a bit sad," Fanny said, lifting her cup of clover tea to her lips. "After, she took me by the hand and led me to the yard to where the flowers grow, and she picked some. Then we came inside and she showed me how to chop them up small and mix with hot water like this. She makes a motion to rub her belly like this—" Fanny drew an invisible round belly in the air in front of herself.

"She just *knew*. She's very . . . What's the word for someone who sees things? Not only sees, but *sees*."

"Observant."

"Observant!" Fanny smiled. "She is very observant."

I thought of the way the stranger's eyes followed me in Auggie's room, lighting on this and that.

"It's so selfish of me, I know this," Fanny said. "Being sad about babies when there are so many worse things in the world."

"Fanny, you're allowed to be sad, even if other people have problems too," I said.

She patted my hand. "Thank you. You are good at saying your feelings out loud—I admire this."

Admire! Absurd. Being unable to hide my emotions was one of my many failings. Still, I smiled at Fanny. "I hope the tea works. You'll be a terrific mother."

Fanny looked away. "It's all I've ever wanted." She took another sip of tea and grimaced.

"Bad?" I asked.

"Like grass," she said. "Though better than the calf's foot Mrs. Lefkowitz cooked me." She sighed. "Anyhow, I will not complain, even if I am allowed. I got another letter from my cousin Shmuel in Hamburg."

"Oh? What did he say?"

"The situation is worse than ever." Fanny rubbed her temples with her fingers. "I just don't understand. How can America not allow him to come?"

"Maybe he'll get off the waiting list soon?"

Fanny shook her head. "Do you know how long the list is? They say years. Years and years. It's all because of that law, the one for protecting the 'white race.'" She snorted. It's rare to see Fanny angry, but America's refusal to take in more Jews puts her in a fury. I don't understand why the government is acting like this either—haven't we been good citizens? Haven't we done all the things Americans are supposed to do—work, buy homes, start families?

"I'll write to our senators and lodge a complaint," I said.

Fanny looked at me and we both burst into laughter, bitter tinged and slightly hysterical. One of our state's senators speaks regularly on the superiority of the Anglo-Saxon, while the other recently called for a ten-year ban on all foreigners entering the country for any reason whatsoever.

We were still laughing when the Swede appeared in the doorway. I startled. The conversation had done its job; I'd almost forgotten he was there. Immediately my heart hammered in my throat.

"Finish," he said.

I rose. "And?"

Gustafson gave a long wet cough. "She is Svensk."

Fanny and I looked at each other. "Svensk?" I said.

Gustafson narrowed his dirty ice-colored eyes. "Ehh, Swede, you say."

"From Sweden? Like you?"

"Yes," Gustafson agreed. "From Sweden."

"So what did she tell you?"

Blood was rushing into my ears. I didn't know what I wanted him to say.

He cleared his throat with a phlegmy sound. "Her family, very rich. They have a . . . some family problem—mother and father sick, they die, father's brother try to steal money that should be for girl. He try to kill girl so he have money instead. She go on ship, to America, like . . . what do you say? Person who hides on ship?"

"A stowaway?"

"Yes. Stowaway. She stowaway to America, but the sailors,

they find. Girl is fear, she jump, she swim. Svensk people is very good at swim. And *ppff*." He raised his hands as if to say "end of story."

I opened my mouth and closed it again, unable to think of a single thing to say.

Fanny looked at me quizzically, likely wondering if she'd just heard what she thought she heard, or perhaps she'd missed something in the translation.

"So she's the daughter of a rich Swede who escaped being murdered for her inheritance and stowed away on a ship to America?" I said.

"Yes," said Gustafson indifferently.

"What does she need? How can we help her?"

Gustafson shrugged. "She cannot return to Sverige. Perhaps you send her to somewhere—New York?—where she can get job, find man. I cannot take, I have wife."

"No one was asking you to 'take'!" I exclaimed.

Gustafson shrugged again. "She need money, of course. For start new life."

I nodded.

"You have money for me?" Gustafson asked. "For speak to girl?"

"Certainly not!" I cried. "Demanding money for helping a poor lost countrywoman—what kind of person are you? I have half a mind to—"

Fanny interrupted me. "Here you go, Mr. Gustafson. Thank you for your help." She shoved something into his hands. I recognized it as a cold tongue sandwich she'd been saving for Jesse, wrapped in a napkin.

Gustafson grunted and nodded. He turned to leave.

"Wait!" I said.

He turned back around and regarded me with his bored, heavy-lidded eyes.

"What's her name?"

"I ask," he said, and disappeared back into the parlor. A moment later, he reappeared, saying only, "Elisaveta."

He turned and left without another word.

I looked at Fanny. "Elisaveta," I repeated. "Elisaveta. What an elegant name. It fits, doesn't it?"

Fanny looked unsure. "I suppose."

"Wait until I tell Jesse," I said, imagining the look on my brother's stupid face.

Back in the parlor, the stranger—Elisaveta—was sitting very upright on the chesterfield, staring vacantly at the stairs.

I sat down next to her. For a while we were both silent. Then I spoke, my voice trembling with emotion I hadn't expected. "I'm so sorry about what happened," I said. "How awful. Perfectly awful. I'm so glad you escaped."

Elisaveta looked down at the floor.

"It must have taken all your strength," I said. "It must have been terrifying. And lonely."

An image flashed through my mind, of those moments on the Lucky Strike tower. The conviction that I was the only person in the world. Lonely, and frightening too.

"I hope Mr. Gustafson helped," I said. "Though I know it takes more than a common language to make someone worth speaking with. Now that we know who you are and what language you speak, we can find you someone better to help. I'll make some telephone calls after the wedding, find a better translator. A professor of Swedish, perhaps, or—"

I noticed something then. She was no longer wearing her odd gunmetal gray brooch with the red stone.

"What happened to your special brooch?" I asked, pointing at my own chest.

Elisaveta's hands flew to her throat. Not finding her jewelry there, she looked startled. Then she seemed to remember, and her face relaxed. She pointed at the stairs.

"Oh, it's in your room," I said. "I wish I'd told Mr. Gustafson to ask you about it. It's so interesting. It must have belonged to your family?"

Elisaveta gave her customary noncommittal nod.

"I need to go pick up the tablecloths for the wedding from the laundry," I said. "You can stay here with Fanny. She'll make you a snack if you're hungry."

I left Elisaveta sitting on the chesterfield. As I walked away, I had a distinct memory of her sitting there earlier that morning. She'd been wearing the brooch then, hadn't she? She always wore it.

But memory is not always reliable.

Chapter 15

Smash!

The napkin-wrapped glass shattered under Morris Kaplan's shoe.

"Mazel tov!" cried everyone in the sanctuary.

Elisaveta gasped. She reached over and squeezed my shoulder.

"It's all right. It's a Jewish wedding tradition," I whispered.

Her hand relaxed.

Someone began clapping and singing "Siman Tov U'mazal Tov," and a moment later everyone was standing up, singing along and cheering. It was loud enough to fill the synagogue, almost like the old days, when there were twice as many Jewish families here in New Bern.

Violet and Morris paraded down the aisle, beaming. Violet's dress, with its puffy sleeves and smocked bodice, really did make her look like a little girl in a nightgown. I managed a small smile as they passed.

The reception was across the street at the community hall of the Presbyterian Church. I knew the Jews of Baltimore or Atlanta would have looked askance at a Jewish wedding reception in a church hall, but in New Bern we didn't have much choice. My mother and I had come earlier in the day and made sure the portrait of Jesus that hung above the buffet table was hidden behind the stand for the faux wedding cake.

Though everyone in Jewish New Bern had heard about Elisaveta by now, there were still plenty of stares as we made our way across the reception hall to the table. Mrs. Lieb, looking hot in a long-sleeved plum dress—yes, indeed the one she'd worn to Fanny's winter wedding—stuck out her long neck to gawk. Elisaveta seemed to take it in her stride, smiling and looking straight ahead as she parted the crowd, very much like you'd imagine a princess walking among her subjects.

Is that what her life had been like, back in Sweden, a girl from a family so rich someone would want to kill her over it? Grand balls and smiling and waving to adoring commoners? I could see it easily, Elisaveta with her elegant walk and her perfect posture, her demure smile. She'd probably had tutors, governesses. Imagine what she must think of our muggy, brackish-smelling little town.

We made our way to the table designated for my family, to the right of the buffet. My cousins had made decorative fans for the tables—Violet had seen something similar in a film, of course—and I'd positioned ours such that Elisaveta could be shielded from curious eyes.

I got two glasses of punch and sat down. To deflect anyone coming to speak to us, I chattered effusively to Elisaveta, hoping we'd look deep in conversation despite her not responding.

"There's Zeke—you've met him, of course," I said, watching Zeke looking bored and antsy by the door. He probably wanted to get back to his workshop. "He and Auggie were best friends when they were boys. His parents are going to send him to Atlanta to find a wife at the Ballyhoo this December—that's a big fancy party at a Jewish country club, with people coming from all over the South. My mother didn't make me try that, thank goodness."

Zeke would be miserable at the Ballyhoo, but dollars to doughnuts he'd come home with a match. He was handsome in his strange, angular, birdlike way, with his bright eyes and his way of leaning his head towards you when listening. And, unlike so many men, he's kind. The only problem would be finding a woman with patience for a husband who's so busy tinkering he forgets to eat dinner. And, of course, finding a woman content to live on Zeke's railroad salary, barely eight hundred dollars a year (like I said, there are no secrets in Little Jerusalem). Women wanted men like Sam Cohen or Johnny Lipinor, men who would one day own their fathers' shops, who talked big about expanding to Wilmington or Kinston or Goldsboro. Men who would buy their brides new homes with real refrigerators instead of iceboxes.

Elisaveta took a sip of the punch, and her face puckered.

"It's rum," I said, making a hand gesture to mime drinking from a liquor bottle. "Violet insisted. Normally we'd just have spiced grape juice and little glasses of cherry cordial, like in the old country."

Elisaveta pushed her glass to the far side of her plate.

The door opened and Sophie swanned in on Sam Cohen's arm. Ugh. Even I had to admit that Sophie looked terribly elegant. She wore a peach satin dress, which showed off her lithe figure, and a pair of matching heels with little pom-poms on the top of the toe. She had the same long strand of pearls draped in a fashionably haphazard way around her slim neck.

"There's Sophie Cohen from the dress shop, and her husband, Sam," I said. "I wouldn't tell anybody but you, but in elementary school Sam used to pee his pants practically every day. In first grade, he'd be standing at the blackboard and—whoops!—there'd be a puddle at his feet. He'd die if he heard me talking about that."

Everyone in New Bern talked about Sophie's return as a success—she'd gotten an education *and* made a good match with a local boy; her college degree hadn't ruined her after all. But I wondered, watching her glide through the room, if Sophie thought of it the same way. Sam Cohen was rich and good-looking, yes, but hadn't Sophie wanted something else? What had happened to her dreams of being a fashion designer? What about all those parties on boats on the Hudson River, those weekends in country houses with everyone who was anyone in New York?

Or maybe I was the only one childish enough to think those kinds of dreams still sounded wonderful. Perhaps when you grew up properly, a life of marriage and children and a new electric washing machine was all you could possibly want.

Harry Morgenthaler walked in with his new wife, a tiny woman with the pushed-in face of a Pekingese dog. He looked over and spotted me, then pretended he hadn't, turning quickly towards Uncle Abe and giving him a hearty slap of congratulations on the shoulder. Acting as one of the men, now that he's married, ha!

Harry had been, I could admit, fun to kiss. Back when I thought I was at the very beginning of life's adventure, when I thought there would be endless boys to kiss, books to write, cities to visit.

Violet and Morris stood next to the front door, greeting guests. Violet kept a pincer grip on Morris's arm, looking like the cat who ate the canary. I guessed now her next competition would be to try to have more babies than her sisters.

The arriving guests tucked little white envelopes into a crepe-paper-covered box on a table next to Violet and Morris. The envelopes were full of money, what people could afford to express their warm wishes. Violet and Morris would probably save it towards a house, though I knew Violet was sore she couldn't spend it on a honeymoon to Miami Beach.

"But it's the sharpest town for honeymooners these days," she'd whined.

Someday I'd take Violet firmly by the hand and lead her to the hobo camp by the train yard. I'd let her have a good long look at the boys with their starved-sharp cheekbones and their sores that won't heal and ask if she still felt like whining about Miami Beach.

Clink, clink, clink. A knife tapped against a punch glass. It was Uncle Abe, standing in front of the buffet table. As he droned on about his "baby," I let my mind wander back to Elisaveta's predicament. I'd contact a Swedish translator as soon as possible, and then—what? Would she want to return home to Sweden? Was she still in danger? Did she really just want some money to start a new life in a bigger city? If she did, surely she'd need someone to come with her, at least for the journey. Perhaps I could accompany her to the Swedish embassy in Washington, DC? Would I get a medal?

A deep blush rose from my chest as I caught myself in the fantasy. *Stupid little girl.*

Finally, the speech was over and it was time to eat—roast chicken with potatoes and carrots, Benji's herring, loaves of fresh-baked challah. Elisaveta and I were joined at our table by Lizzy and her husband, Pete, and Benji and Bea. Pete was unshaven and irritable looking, as always. He's a door-to-door vacuum salesman, and he saves his good face for customers. Benji sat next to Pete, silent and miserable. Bea, next to him with the coiled energy of an animal ready to pounce, wore a sailor dress that tented over her huge belly; she looked more like the ship than the sailor. Her long, naturally curly black hair had been carefully lacquered with setting lotion and pinned behind her ears. Lizzy has the same curls, but she believes married ladies should keep their hair sensibly bobbed. She wore a powder blue ruffled dress that hugged her hips and bottom, and the same heels she'd worn at her own wedding, dyed with a packet of Rit to match the dress.

"So, Gustafson says the lady's some kind of princess or something?" Benji asked, watching Elisaveta plow through her plate of chicken like a lumberjack.

"Not a princess," I said, "but the daughter of someone quite wealthy and important back in Sweden."

Benji whistled through his teeth. "Wow."

Pete gulped his glass of punch and checked his watch.

"So what are you going to do with her now?" Bea asked, taking a prissy little bite of chicken. "My mother said that your mother said she wanted to go to New York?"

"We're not sure," I said quickly. "I'll have to contact a proper translator, maybe the embassy."

Bea raised her eyebrows.

"What?" I snapped.

"Nothing," she said insincerely. "It's just *such* an amazing story. Like something from a book!"

Before I could say anything back, the violinist drew the first note of "Hava Negilah" and a hora circle began to form. Violet and Morris were hoisted up in chairs and guests began to dance around them, singing and kicking their legs. "*Hava negilah! Hava negilah!*" The music and singing grew louder, the dancers sweatier. The men holding the chairs were red in the face but kept their expressions manfully stiff. "*Hava negilah!*" Violet and Morris bobbed up and down like boaters on a wave, Violet's updo almost touching the low ceiling with each rise.

I saw Sophie dance by, arms linked with Sam's. Our eyes met, and I looked away. Harry danced by with his Pekingese-faced wife.

The music grew even louder, and I saw that Joe Nathan, Louise's husband, had joined the fiddling. Now Aunt Zora and Uncle Abe were being lifted up, the men heaving under their weight. Zora gripped the edge of the chair and was borne away past the buffet table. "*Hava negilah!*" My mother was next, then Lizzy. The dance went on and on, growing louder and more frantic, the dancers sweatier.

Suddenly I looked up and saw Sophie standing in front of me. Her face was flushed and her hair had come free from its pins. She flopped down in Benji's empty chair.

"Phew, I'm hot," she said.

I nodded stiffly and took a sip of my drink.

"Why aren't you dancing?" she asked.

"I'm not much of a dancer," I said.

"You used to be," she said. Her voice was loose and warm, and I realized she'd probably had more than a few glasses of punch. "Remember our senior class dance?"

I saw an image of myself at eighteen as if in a photograph. Smiling in my new dress, arm linked with Sophie's. Eager, carefree, expecting the future to open wide. Another person entirely.

"I used to be a lot of things," I said.

"You should try it again," Sophie said. "You might have fun."

"Fun?" I narrowed my eyes. How dare Sophie talk to me like this, like we were still best friends giggling together on her canopy bed, as if nothing had happened? "You mean, fun like New York City?"

"Well, maybe not *that* much fun," Sophie replied, smoothing her hair and picking up Benji's half-drunk glass of punch.

"If it was so fun, why didn't you stay?" I asked, hearing the meanness in my voice.

Sophie didn't seem to notice. "I had to get married, silly."

"No one has to get married. It's not a law." Now I sounded like a child again, the same way I am with my mother.

Sophie laughed. "When a man like Sam Cohen agrees to marry a woman like me, you don't say no."

I thought again of Sam Cohen at seven, standing in front of the classroom in a puddle of pee. She must have known a million better-looking, more successful men in New York. Why Sam? Why come back here?

"I know what you're thinking," Sophie said. Again, that familiar intimacy in her voice. "You're thinking how stupid I am, how could I do such a stupid thing, ruin everything?" She threw back her head and laughed mirthlessly.

"Marrying Sam?"

Sophie huffed that same hollow laugh and took a gulp of Benji's drink. It was a bit frightening, seeing her this way. She'd always been so in control. I glanced at Elisaveta, but she was still watching the dancers with fascination.

"No, silly, the thing before that. The reason I had to marry Sam."

"I'm not sure what you're talking about."

Sophie gave me a sharp look and made a sputtering sound. "Did you not read my letters?"

I felt my face grow hot. "You mean the ones you sent while I was in the hospital, about the wonderful gay time you were having in New York? No, Sophie, I didn't read them. I was a bit too busy having my 'nervous breakdown.'"

Sophie stared at me. "So you really don't know what happened to me?"

"What happened to *you*?" I said, my voice rising. "What about what happened to *me*? What about what happened to Auggie? Did your letters mention that? Or were you too busy talking about all the fun you were having?"

Sophie drained the glass and set it down on the table with a thud that sent the silverware juddering. The music was even wilder; my cousins went bobbing past on chairs. The thud had attracted Elisaveta's attention; she was looking at Sophie curiously out of the side of her eye.

"You're not the only one who's suffered, Millie," Sophie said. "But the difference between us is that I've tried to get past it and make the best of things, and you're determined to . . . to wallow in it. Like a pig in muck."

"A pig!" I cried, standing up. "Are you calling me a pig?"

Sophie stood too and began to turn away, as if to return to the dance floor.

I couldn't let her. My entire body was hot and itching with fury. Sophie Zucker calling *me* a pig in muck. Sophie, who grew up with a canopy bed and a maid to make her rice pudding. Sophie, whose hair curled into perfect ringlets. Sophie, who got to go to Sweet Briar and to Paris. Sophie, who swanned around New York until she got bored with it. How dare she tell me I should "make the best of things"! I wanted to hit her.

So I did hit her.

My hand swung out as if by its own volition, though it was less of a punch than a swat. She was already moving away, and my fingers barely grazed her neck. It wasn't enough to hurt her. But it was enough to catch her strand of pearls.

The thread snapped as it gave way. At first slowly, then all at once, the pearls began falling to the floor. A cascade of pearls. A waterfall.

Sophie screamed.

The music stopped.

Pearls bounced across the dance floor and pinged in every direction—under the buffet table, beneath the feet of the suddenly halted dancers. Pearls hit the baseboards and ricocheted, like marbles. A pearl landed in the punch with a delicate splash. Everyone turned to stare.

Suddenly I was back on the street in Durham, kicking my legs and screaming as people stared. The faces of the people all turned towards me, like sunflowers, gawking.

My face and body burning, I turned to Elisaveta. She was already standing. She followed me as I stalked across the room to the side door and pushed it open, not turning to look at the gawping guests.

Madwoman Millie, I could practically feel them thinking. *Old maid Millie. Just as crazy as we thought.*

AS SOON AS the night air hit my face, I began to sob.

I felt a hand on my back. Elisaveta, silently patting me.

I turned, wiping my nose on my sleeve.

I felt momentarily guilty. Elisaveta had her own uncle try to kill her, had to flee her country. Other people did have it worse than me. Not Sophie, obviously, but other people. I took a deep breath.

"They'll probably lock me in the attic now, like the crazy woman in *Jane Eyre*," I said. I laughed, a mad-sounding cackle. "At least I won't have to go to a wedding ever again."

We began to walk, ambling along the riverside on Front Street, past the bridge and the captain's house, then up into Riverside, where the rail yard and the factories were still and silent. The heat had finally broken, and the haze around the moon was gone. The sky was a crisp black, with a sprinkling of clean white stars. Even the muddy river stink was gone, replaced by a fresh, salty-smelling breeze from the ocean. As we passed the rail yard, a car slowed and the driver, his face obscured by the dark, gave us a long look, but otherwise we saw no one.

"I guess I ought to tell you the rest of the story," I said, sniffling. "I haven't told anyone before."

Elisaveta looked back at me serenely.

"All right, then," I said.

Chapter 16

1936

The words of the rabbi echoing in my ears—*It's time for Auggie to say his* vidui—I ran across the Duke campus, aware that students were stopping to stare at me, but not caring. I ran past the campus's stone walls and out into a wide street. The air was thick as milk. My lungs burned and sweat stung my eyes. I ran through a neighborhood of stately homes, and the thought of the happy, healthy families inside made me want to scream and never stop. The sun was large and white and burning overhead. I staggered on, growing hotter and hotter, into the tobacco warehouses of downtown Durham, and the sweet smell of drying tobacco leaves made me gag. A bell rang, and a moment later the street was flooded with factory workers. "You all right, missy?" said an old Negro man, his cheek bulging with chewing tobacco. I stopped for a moment, breathing heavily, and looked into his kind-seeming eyes, dark and crinkled with concern. I wanted to wail, *No, I'm not all right! Auggie is dying and no one will help!* Instead, I turned and fled down an alley. Finally I stopped and looked up.

I was underneath the Lucky Strike tower. The water tower with the cigarette logo on it, the tallest thing by far in Durham.

My mind was full of fuzz, like radio static. I slumped and

laid my cheek against the tower's cool metal leg. It was shady here and quiet. I looked up. A ladder with infinite-seeming rungs disappeared into the shadow above.

Suddenly, I understood what I had to do. A jolt of purpose propelled me upright, despite my exhaustion.

Researchers at Harvard have been doing some wonderful work with chemical treatments for cancer, Professor Klein had said.

Harvard! I needed to get Auggie to Harvard!

I'd make them understand. I just had to get their attention.

I tied my skirt in a knot and began to climb.

I'd make them listen.

I hadn't spoken urgently enough, hadn't managed to make them feel the freight train barreling down on us. I'd been too polite, too circumspect. I should have screamed at the top of my lungs from the very beginning. I should have stood in the lobby of the hospital and screamed and screamed and screamed.

I'd make them understand. I'd make them listen!

It was hot at first, and my face burned. But the higher I went, the cooler it got, a breeze whipping through my sweaty dress. It grew quieter as the chatter of the after-work crowds faded away. Somewhere far away, a church bell tolled. I kept climbing, hand over foot, like this was what I had been born to do. Eventually I came to a platform with a small square opening. I climbed through the opening and stood on the narrow balcony encircling the water tank. Up close, the texture of the paint on the Lucky Strike logo was rough, like tree bark.

Someone ought to be coming soon. Maybe they couldn't see me? So to make myself more visible, I climbed up on the rail. I dangled one leg over the side, then the other. It was a good thing I was wearing a red dress; surely they'd be able to see me all the way from Mr. Silverberg's office, if not farther.

What's the opposite of a lucky strike? I wondered, looking down.

My mother had prayed without stopping since Auggie got sick. But what had it gotten her? I'd spoken to God too, promised I'd do whatever he wanted if he would just make Auggie better. But God had remained silent.

Auggie didn't believe in God. He was a materialist, he said, which meant nothing existed except matter. Nothing that couldn't be explained by the laws of science. No above, no below, no beyond.

If there was a God, surely he wouldn't punish a boy for disbelief?

I was so lost inside my own mind that I didn't hear the police until they were nearly through the trapdoor.

"Miss," one of them called.

I turned and there they were, three of them, huffing and sweating in their blue uniforms. My plan was working!

"Miss," they called again.

They were standing with their hands extended, to show they weren't going to get too close.

"I need to get my brother to Harvard," I called out. "You must arrange a special train for him. Do it now, or I'll jump!"

"It's all right, miss; we'll do whatever you want, just don't do anything hasty," called one.

"I need a special train, like the one Nellie Bly's publisher arranged for her," I said. "You know, on her journey around the world." Surely it could be done. Surely it could be done. I just had to make everyone understand the urgency, the utter urgency.

The officers nodded slowly.

"All right? You'll do it? You'll arrange it?" I said, aware that I was speaking much too fast.

"Whatever you need, miss. Just let us help you down."

Too late did I see the rope behind their backs.

I SCREAMED MY throat raw as the ambulance drove and drove and drove. I tried to bang on the stretcher, but my hands were too firmly tied. Eventually we stopped. The doors opened and two faceless attendants in white slid me out like a cake from the oven. I had just enough time to glimpse the outside of the towering brick building before they pushed me through a pair of double doors and left me lying in a hallway beneath a very bright light. "Help!" I screamed. "I just need to get my brother to Harvard." I realized on some level that, to someone who didn't know me and Auggie, this request sounded insane, but at the time I was certain that *if I could just explain*, someone would help me.

I'd soon learn that I was now the kind of person no one would ever listen to seriously again.

Somewhere behind me one of the attendants was speaking to someone, a doctor, I presume. I tried to turn, but I was firmly restrained by a thick strap across my chest. I heard the words "attempted suicide."

I bucked, feeling like my rage could break the straps, but I barely moved an inch. I started to scream, *I just need to get Auggie to Harvard!* But just then, I felt a sting in my arm and saw a figure in white withdrawing a syringe. I opened my mouth, but my tongue was too heavy to speak. The light overhead gleamed maliciously, then winked out.

WHEN I WOKE up, I was lying in a bed in a bright ward, sunlight streaming through the windows. I tried to sit up, but my wrists were bound to the bed with some sort of soft restraint.

"*Shhhh*, it's all right, *shefele*," a voice said.

I turned my head. It was Aunt Zora. She was sitting at my

bedside. Her large square face was wet with tears. She reached for my hand.

Shefele, she'd called me.

I knew then.

While I was in the loony bin at Dix Hill in Raleigh, Auggie had died.

IT'S JEWISH TRADITION to bury the dead within twenty-four hours. While I'd been unconscious and strapped to a bed, Auggie's body had already been washed, placed in a pine coffin, transported by train back to New Bern, and buried next to my father in the Hebrew Cemetery, under the oak trees dripping Spanish moss.

He was gone.

I had let the train hit him.

He was the person I loved the most in the world, and I'd failed him.

Why was I even here?

My memories from the next two months are blurred, like they're smeared in Vaseline. My body was like mud, my soul ash. Eating was impossible; food stuck in my mouth like shards of broken pottery. Morning felt like the middle of the night. My eyes made tears continuously, even when I wasn't crying, until my cheeks were red and chapped and my throat burned with thirst. It hurt to swallow. It hurt to talk.

So I stopped.

Chapter 17

I stopped. I'd been so deep in the past, I hadn't noticed we'd wandered all the way up Pasteur Street, and now we were standing alone in the crushed-oyster-shell lot of the pickle warehouse. The same place I'd found Elisaveta.

I took a deep, raggedy breath and found I was, somehow, dry-eyed and calmer than I'd felt when we'd left the wedding. Calmer in fact than I'd felt in a long, long time.

"Well, now you know," I said. "Now you know why everyone around here thinks I'm a madwoman, why I'm afraid of heights, why I don't have a degree or a job or a husband."

Of course she didn't know, didn't understand.

"And now I've ruined Violet's wedding. Every Jew in the South will have heard about this by tomorrow afternoon, I'm sure. Maybe the matchmaker will give up on me for good now, at least."

I sighed and looked out at the silent dark stretch of the Neuse River. Besides the moon, the only light was the yellowish glow of the streetlamp by the Felix's Famous Pickles sign.

"I'm sorry, I shouldn't complain so much, not when you've had such an awful time—"

Elisaveta gasped.

I whirled around. Her normally serene face stretched into a white mask of terror. She was staring past me. I turned to follow her gaze.

A figure stood just outside the cone of yellow light from the streetlamp, so I couldn't make out any details, but there was something strange about its size and posture. Too tall. Too thin. Too many angles. I thought, childishly, of the stories my grandfather told of the golem, a man made of clay, with no mind but unnatural strength.

The figure moved. It stepped forward.

Elisaveta took a step backwards. I heard her breath catch in her throat.

The figure stepped into the light.

It was a man. A tall, extremely thin man. He wore pants several inches too short above a pair of old-fashioned brogues like the poorest farmers wore. His hair was cut straight across his forehead like a little boy's. His shirt was also too short, revealing long pale thin wrists and enormous hands.

Elisaveta whimpered.

The man was staring at Elisaveta, smirking.

Oh God. It was one of the men from her home. They'd found her. Now he was going to kill her.

The man began to walk towards us with fearfully long strides, his brogues making a crunching sound on the oystershell gravel.

I looked back at Elisaveta. She was backing away towards the wall of the pickle warehouse. Her hands were raised defensively in front of her.

"Stop!" I called, in my stoutest voice.

The man kept coming.

I looked around desperately. Riverside was empty on a Sunday night, with all the factory and dock workers gone. Still, I spun in a circle, looking for someone, anyone—a fisherman, a hobo, a rail yard worker walking home. But there was no one. And the nearest houses were blocks away. No one would hear me if I screamed.

I screamed anyway. "Get away!"

He kept coming, moving with his unnaturally long steps, that hideous leer on his pale narrow face. Maybe he didn't understand English either.

I began to back away too, into the shadow of the pickle warehouse's brick wall. With growing panic, I looked left and right for something I could use to hold up as a shield, something that would tell the man "stop" even if he couldn't understand my words. Almost before I registered what it was, I felt the wood handle of the mallet Baxter and his men used to secure the lids of the pickle barrels before they loaded them into the trucks. I closed my fingers around the handle. It was solid and warm beneath my hand.

The man was still coming. His face was long and bony, its expression a hideous mix of mockery and menace.

I raised the mallet. The man was nearly upon us. I heard Elisaveta moan.

Then the man spoke.

"Hey there, Cecilia," he said. "That's a real pretty dress." He reached out a huge, spiderlike hand towards Elisaveta.

"No!" I screamed, rage and fear flooding through me. With all my strength, I swung the mallet like a baseball bat. It caught the man on the side of his long bony head.

For a moment, he stood absolutely still. His mouth opened and closed silently. Blood began to spurt alarmingly from his scalp just above his ear. Then he swayed and toppled over like a felled tree. His face hit the gravel with a meaty thud, bringing up a cloud of dust.

I dropped the mallet and turned to Elisaveta, stunned.
She was staring down at the man's body.
Slowly, she raised her face towards me.
She was *grinning.*
"Now you done it," she said.

PART TWO

Chapter 18

CECILIA

Sure, I smiled when Matty Barnwell toppled over dead in the dirt. You might think that's proof for sure I'm bad and low, just like they said I was. But if you knew about Matty Barnwell, you'd know he deserved that hammer as much as anyone's ever deserved anything in this life.

I do feel sorry it was Millie who hit him and not me. Girl's tender. Not crazy, no, not a lunatic like she's scared everybody thinks. Just tender, the way you get when you grow up in a house with a parlor and food all the time and people who try their hardest to protect you from all the badness in the world.

Back home in Tobacco Run, we'd start the 'backer plants in seedbeds, under linen, to protect them from the cold. Come April, once the frosts were past, we'd dig them up and move them to the fields. But first, we had to harden them: we'd leave the linen cover off every evening for a few hours, then a few hours more. If you didn't harden them enough, they'd get cold shocked and wither in the field. Hardened right, even a late icy snap couldn't hurt them.

I reckon I'm like a seedling that got hardened off good and early. Ain't nothing can kill me now.

Millie, though, she was protected under linen for most of

her life. The bad stuff didn't hit her till she was grown, and she wasn't ready for it.

But you know what? I don't think she's gonna wither. I reckon she's gonna grow. She's just a little cold shocked right now.

I do wish it was me who hit Matty. After what he did to little Ruthie, I would've loved to feel his head split like a watermelon under that hammer.

Chapter 19

MILLIE

Wait. Wait. Elisaveta *spoke*. She spoke English. She spoke English with the same accent as any Craven County farm girl. I tried to form a question, but my mouth just opened and closed like the tall man's had. The tall man who had called her "Cecilia."

"We better hide him quick," Elisaveta said, squatting next to the tall man's still body in her poofy blue dress. "I'll get his hands, you get his feet."

Speechless now, I just followed her directions and picked up the tall man's skinny ankles.

With surprising strength, Elisaveta yanked the tall man's body towards the row of pickle barrels lined up against the wall awaiting their pickup. "You reckon he'd fit in the big one?" she asked, inclining her head towards the largest of the barrels.

I stood dumbly, holding the man's ankles.

"C'mon now," Elisaveta said. "We don't hide him good, we'll get the electric chair."

My head was buzzing. I couldn't think. I just obeyed and lifted the tall man's ankles as Elisaveta kicked over the barrel. Pickles and brine sloshed onto the gravel.

"Legs first," she said, and we did an awkward do-si-do, spinning the tall man's body around so his feet were pointing towards the barrel's sideways mouth. His ankles flopped limply, and I felt hot, vinegary bile rise in my throat. "In he goes," Elisaveta said, and together we sort of folded the tall man into the barrel, his knees bending towards his chest. His blond head, which was now half-darkened with blood, didn't fit at first, but Elisaveta pushed on his neck until it slumped between his knees. "Heave-ho," she said, and we strained to pull the barrel upright. She picked the lid out of the gravel and laid it on top of the tall man's head, just as casually as if the barrel was really full of pickles. She gave the lid a thump with her fist. "When do these get picked up? Where do they go?"

I opened and closed my mouth. "M-M-Monday," I managed. "They go all over the Southeast."

"Someone'd be right surprised when they pried this one open," she said, cackling. She looked down at herself. "Goddamn it, Matty Barnwell, you ruined my pretty dress!"

The blue dress was wet with pickle brine. A trail of something darker stained the bodice. I didn't dare look down at my own dress.

"We'd better push him in the river, then," she said. "It goes into that ocean yonder? He'll be halfway to China by the morning."

"China's the other way," I said dumbly.

Elisaveta rolled her eyes. "I know where China is. They might call me a moron or feebleminded, but I ain't. Not even close, all right?"

"All right," I repeated. My mind was so frozen it felt like I'd been the one hit in the head with the mallet.

"So c'mon, let's hop to!" She reared back and gave the barrel a hard kick until it rocked enough to tip over. "Help me roll it."

Again, I obeyed, and the two of us rolled the barrel across the crunching gravel lot. We stood at the top of the embankment leading down to the ink-dark Neuse River. It was low tide; reeds silhouetted by moonlight swayed in the breeze. Was I really here? Was this a dream? Was I having another nervous breakdown?

Then Elisaveta gave the barrel a hard push and it rolled down the embankment and into the river. I heard the splash, and the barrel was gone. Had it sunk to the bottom? Or was it just blending in with the dark water?

My head went swimmy. "I need to sit down," I said, collapsing into the muddy grass.

Elisaveta looked at me scrutinizingly. After a moment, her face softened. "Oh, don't feel sorry. He deserved it."

"Who deserves *that*?" I cried, covering my face with my hands. Oh God. I *was* going to get the electric chair.

"*He* did," Elisaveta said darkly. "Matty Barnwell."

I lifted my head and looked up at her. In the moonlight, her entire face seemed transformed. Her nostrils were flared, her mouth hanging slightly open. She looked wild and hard, not at all like the peaceful silent companion I'd grown so used to.

"You're not really Swedish," I said.

"And you're not the queen of England," she said.

"I never said I was the queen of England!"

"And I never said nothing at all."

"But . . . but, but the Swede said—" My head was pulsing. "But I don't understand—" I had a thousand questions, all pushing against each other.

"C'mon, let's go home and get cleaned up before that

wedding's over." She reached out her hand to help me up. "I'll tell you the real story of how I got here. I know you like stories."

I stared up at her. A drop of blood had landed on her jaw. It looked like a beauty mark.

I took her hand.

Chapter 20

CECILIA

Tobacco Run, North Carolina
1938

I was standing in the yard, stringing 'backer leaves, when the lady from the Casteen Training School showed up at the end of the road. Knowing what I know now, she should have looked like a witch or a goblin from one of Mrs. Randall's fairy-tale books, all warty and growling and evil. But she just looked like a normal old lady.

Call me Auntie Sybil, she'd said.

It was the end of the 'backer harvest. All the 'backer would be shipped out to the factories in Durham in a week or two, then I could get back to school. I couldn't wait. I always loved school. Loved it. The other kids in my family quit going when they were ten or twelve, but not me. My teacher, Mrs. Randall, gave me cheese sandwiches and let me sit by the radiator in the winter, just reading. I'm a great reader. Later on, at Casteen, they said I was a "high-grade moron," but clearly that ain't true. I was reading books for grown-ups by the time I was ten. My favorite ones, though, were the Chalet School books, about a school for girls in the mountains over in Europe. I read all of them, and when a new one came out, Mrs. Randall ordered it special for me. She's from England, Mrs. Randall, a war bride.

Her husband spun her a fancy tale about his beautiful farm in North Carolina where the corn was so high it was like a forest. Then he went and got himself crushed dead under his tractor, and now poor Mrs. Randall is stuck teaching a bunch of dirty-footed kids.

The Chalet School girls—Jo and Juliet and Grizel and the rest—were always getting into adventures, like falling into pits or water as cold as ice. Nobody ever got real mad at them, though; they just got put to bed early with hot water bottles. But my very most favorite part of the books was the food: for breakfast they always had sweet rolls and coffee with milk and pots of plum jam. I imagined those rolls tasting just like heaven.

My own breakfast was usually corn mush, when Mama could be roused. She was dog-tired most of the time—weak blood from having all the babies. When she couldn't get up to cook mush, we'd have leftover cornbread, cold and greasy. There wasn't never plum jam. Can't say for sure I know what a plum looks like. We've got a tree at the edge of the farm that grows the tiniest, most sour apples you've ever tasted. Eat more than one and you'll get the trots, though that never stopped my brothers, when they were hungry enough.

Maybe it was reading all those Chalet School books that made my ears perk up like a rabbit's when Auntie Sybil started talking about the Casteen Training School near Kinston town. She was a "field agent" for the school, she told Ma. She traveled all over Lenoir County and even farther looking for "suitable students." She said they'd told her about us down at Big Sproul's General Store, and that me and my little sister, Jean, would be perfect for it.

That should have been a warning too. The Sprouls wouldn't never have said anything nice about my family. Just the week before, old Willard Sproul screamed in my face for getting sweet with his grandson Jimmy behind the cheneyberry tree. Jimmy's the only good-looking one of the bunch, and I'll kiss him if I want to, Willard Sproul.

Me and Jean were the oldest two still at home. Luelle, the real oldest, had gone off to Wilmington the year before, to find work as a housemaid. Virgil, the second oldest, walked off into the 'backer rows and disappeared one day. Didn't say a word to nobody. Must have hopped on a farm truck and gotten far, cuz none of us never saw him again. I like to imagine he's off in some big city, working in a factory maybe, eating city food. But I know in my heart he's probably working in a field just like the one we grew up in, or worse.

Once Luelle and Virgil left, it was up to me to mind the young ones and keep the house. After Barney, the littlest, was born, Mama couldn't barely leave bed. I've wondered lots of times why she had so many babies when she couldn't barely even feed her own self. But maybe she didn't know what I learned later from the older girls at Casteen, about how you can stop a baby from happening by putting Lysol up your lady parts. Or maybe they didn't sell Lysol at Sproul's General?

With ten of us in the house—Mama and Pa and the eight of us kids—even after Luelle and Virgil left, there wasn't barely enough room to breathe. Our little tin-roof house was like a tiny boat on an ocean of 'backer stretching as far as you could see. Not that I knew what an ocean looked like back then. Back then I didn't know hardly anyone who didn't have dirt floors and grease-paper windows. Didn't know people who lived in houses with *parlors* and carpets with flowers on them. My pa rented the house and the land from Big Sproul's brother Fred. Fred got fifty percent of what we grew, which seemed a good deal for Fred and a raw one for us. But that's life, ain't it?

In the summer we slept outside. We'd lay out on quilts in the dirt yard, the air so still the sweat just sat on your face and didn't dry. Everything smelled like spicy green 'backer leaves and the mint plant we burned to keep off the skeeters, their whine so loud it'd find you even in your dreams. We'd fall asleep slapping at skeeters and wake up in the small hours soaking wet from the thunderstorms that rolled in from nowhere. One time a copperhead came sliding out of the 'backer and bit little Ezra right on the face. His cheek turned blue and bubbled up in blisters, and everyone thought for sure he'd die, but he didn't.

Winters, we lay buried under those same quilts on the scratchy corn-husk mattresses, crushed together like a litter of puppies, the house smoky from the wood fire Mama burned to keep us warm. The smoke made the young ones cough something terrible, and we'd all wake up with red eyes and chilblained toes.

If you crossed the 'backer fields and walked down the dirt road for a mile, you'd get to the crossroads with a few old buildings. Tobacco Run, North Carolina. Big Sproul owned the general store—the Sprouls owned everything in our patch of Lenoir County—and he was always sitting outside, spitting dark patches in the dust. We tried to stay away from the store. It was dark and stunk like the oily round of hoop cheese Big Sproul kept on the counter. Flypapers swung from the ceiling, with flies still moving their little hairy legs, trying to escape, not knowing they were good as dead already. Big Sproul would always run his eyes down the neck of my dress when I came to pick up a parcel of flour. Once he tried to pinch my bottom, and I stomped his foot with my heel so hard he yelped like a kicked dog.

Across from the general store was a filling station and post office. One or another Sproul brother was always sitting outside, just staring into the distance like a frog on a log. They looked like frogs too, with their big wide mouths and eyes too far apart. Past the filling station about a half a mile was the church, where on Sundays the Sprouls sat in the front pews and the rest of us sat in the back while the preacher preached and us kids tried not to fall asleep. Beyond that was the Bottoms, where the Negro families lived.

That was it. That was Tobacco Run. All of it circled by 'backer fields with no end. Strangers didn't come around too often. Which was why we were so curious when Auntie Sybil came along.

If only I hadn't read those Chalet School books. If only I hadn't been so full of *want* for coffee and sweet rolls and mountains and oceans.

If only. The two most useless words in English, ain't they?

Some girls have a good pa to protect them, but not me. The moonshiners—Sprouls, all of them—used to give out their liquor for free, to pay back later. Pa would borrow and borrow. He'd come home from Johnny Whitrock's house, across the fields, weaving and singing stupid old love songs. The whole house stunk like his breath on those nights, like rotten fruit and sick-up. Then he got a bad batch of moonshine, and everything really went to hell. I reckon they didn't know what they were doing, them moonshiners. Or maybe they did it on purpose, who could say? Pa went drinking one night and came home sicking-up blood. He lay there for two days, somewhere between dead and alive. When he finally got up, he was blind in one eye and his hands shook. His head wasn't right after that neither. Dizzy. Angry. Couldn't barely work.

The hot summer morning Auntie Sybil showed up, he lay on the mattress, one eye open, stinking and moaning. There was still 'backer to harvest, but you could tell he wasn't gonna help none that day.

I can see Auntie Sybil now like a photograph in my head,

picking her way down the dirt road in her town lady shoes. Beauty, our hound, barked and ran against her chain so hard she almost pulled the stake out of the ground. All the fur on the back of her neck was standing up.

That should have been a sign too.

The lady looked so sweet and harmless. She was old, maybe even fifty. Gray hair all in a roll, like the librarian in the Chalet School books. Wore a black dress with a flower pin at her bosom.

Me and Jean and Floyd were all set in a row with our thread, stringing the 'backer leaves onto a pole to cure, while the little boys played around in the dirt. We watched the lady, our eyes all big, as she moved towards us.

"You reckon she's a nurse here about the hookworms?" Jean whispered.

"Reckon so," I whispered back.

The summer before, one of them nurses had come out to the farm and gave us all a dose of some nasty-smelling medicine to take the worms out of our blood. Said we needed to wear shoes, cuz the ground itch we got in summer was the worms sneaking into our feet. Imagine!

"Hello, girls," said the woman, when she got to the bottom of the porch steps. She had a sour face she tried to cover up with a sweet one, like someone pretending not to smell the big old fart you just laid in church. "Is your mama home?"

She had a square black leather bag, which I found out later was full of papers about Casteen. Course, my pa was too drunk to read, and my mama couldn't read much better than a kid. Not because she's stupid, Ma. Later, at Casteen, they would tell me I was a moron because my mama was, and her ma before her and on and on. But that ain't true. Mama wasn't stupid, she just hardly got to go to school because her own ma died trying to have a baby, and Mama had to raise up the young'uns for her pa.

Since I was the oldest, I answered the lady. "She's inside with the baby."

"Thank you, dear," the lady said.

Well, me and Jean and Floyd looked at each other and went right to stand by the grease-paper window so we could hear what the lady was saying. She was talking in a quiet voice, but I could hear some.

"The Casteen School has structure and professional care for young women in need of guidance," she said. "Your daughters will get Christian teaching, instruction in the trades, plus three meals a day and a comfortable dormitory with their own beds. There's hot water in the bathrooms."

She was quiet for a moment, probably letting Mama have a good long think about our corn-husk mattress and our crooked privy.

"I see," Mama said softly. "But they're good girls."

"Good girls go bad so easily in an unwholesome environment, don't they?" asked Auntie Sybil.

Now, my mama and pa didn't know words like "structure" or "dormitory." But you know what words they did know? "Eggs and fresh milk." That's what Auntie Sybil promised next. Eggs and fresh milk every day. Every day.

Mama signed up me and Jean that very morning, the *S* in "Sarah" turned round the wrong way.

Her wobbly signature was good enough for Auntie Sybil. She came the very next day in a car to take us away. I was seventeen. Jean was fourteen.

Sometimes I wonder how she could have done what she did, my mama. Give us away like that, without even asking a single question. But then I think about that promise about eggs and fresh milk. It was a bad harvest that year, and a bad one the last. Pa wasn't barely working, just sitting in the corner of the house all glassy-eyed in the dark like a raccoon. We didn't even go to church anymore; Mama and Pa were too sick or too ashamed.

And me and Jean wanted to go. We were so excited we couldn't barely sleep the night before. It wasn't but twenty miles to Casteen, but it felt like we were going to Europe or something. The only time I'd ever rode in a car was when I broke my leg falling off the roof and Mama begged a Sproul to drive me to the clinic in Fortner. Can't say that was a ride I enjoyed much.

Auntie Sybil's car was long and black and smelled good: fresh and spicy. She wore a pair of white gloves to drive. Driving wasn't ladylike, she told us, so you had to at least wear gloves to be proper about it. We stopped at a filling station and Auntie Sybil bought us a chocolate bar to share. A real chocolate bar!

Then we got to the school, and my jaw just about fell off my face. It was the biggest building I'd ever seen in my life. All fancy brick with lots of windows. Me and Jean were squealing and grabbing each other's hands like we'd won a prize. We couldn't wait for those eggs and fresh milk. I remember feeling sorry for the rest of the kids back home, missing out.

We followed Auntie Sybil inside.

I want to scream at that girl that was once me. *Don't go in!* I want to holler at her. *Turn around! Run!*

But she can't hear me. She's already inside.

Chapter 21

CECILIA

1938

Those heavy doors closed behind us and we were standing inside the biggest and whitest room I'd ever seen. White walls, white tile floor, a long white hallway lined with white-painted doors. It was quiet—too quiet. What kind of school was this quiet?

"Follow me, girls," said a lady in a nurse uniform with a bright white cap, her arms stiffly at her sides like a soldier about to march.

We followed her through one of the white doors, which opened without a sound; when I turned around to look for Auntie Sybil, she was already gone.

The door hid a staircase, also white, but more gray looking because the light was so poor. As we walked downward it got colder, till Jean and I were both shivering. It was summer, and we wore our short-sleeved feed-sack dresses, the ones we used to wear to church—mine a blue and red check, Jean's white with tiny yellow flowers.

At the bottom of the stairs was another hall, even darker. The walls down here were some kind of cold gray stone, dripping with wet. At the end was a door with a sign that said SANITIZING. Inside was a room covered in tile—tile floor, tile walls, tile ceiling. In one corner was some kind of stove—brick, with a black iron door, same as our stove at home, just twice as big.

"Remove your clothes," said the nurse.

Jean and I just looked at each other. Take off our clothes? In front of a stranger? For what?

When we didn't move, the lady came over and yanked the hem of Jean's dress right up and over her head, like shucking an ear of corn. Jean shrieked, but the lady didn't seem to notice.

I started to take off my own clothes, to show her it was all right. Maybe this was just a part of it. Maybe the girls at the Chalet School had to get undressed in the basement before they got their pinafores. I didn't rightly know what a pinafore was, but it sounded pretty.

But as soon as we were naked as blue jays, the nurse lady picked up our dresses, pulled open the door to the stove, and shoved the dresses inside. I could hear the crackle as they caught fire.

"Hey!" I yelled. "Why'd you do that?" I'd sewed those dresses myself.

The nurse didn't say anything. She reached into the pocket of her dress and took out a pair of scissors.

"Be still," she said, coming up behind me.

I froze up. I heard the blades snicker-snick and I felt suddenly lighter around the neck. My neck felt cold too.

I knew then this place wasn't gonna be nothing like the Chalet School.

She'd cut off my hair.

She'd cut off my gosh darn hair.

Now, you gotta understand this: I'm not a vain girl, but my hair was so pretty. I didn't have no good dresses or no jewelry. I never wore rouge. Hadn't even heard of it—that's another thing I learned from the other girls at Casteen. My one pretty, fancy thing was my long, long hair, yellow-white like the tassels on the corn. Mama used to brush it at night with a brush that once belonged to her own grandma, who had the second sight and could cure any sickness with herbs. When she finished my hair would shine like moonlight. Neither of my sisters had hair half so pretty, even Luelle, who was the looker of us three.

My hair. How dare she!

I got to howling and turned on the nurse, while Jean tried to run for the corner. But suddenly Auntie Sybil was back, and she snatched Jean by the elbow with long pincher fingers. "Shut your mouth and sit down," she hissed at me.

She held Jean down while the nurse lady cut her curly red hair. By then Jean was quiet and limp like a rag doll, tears making rows down her cheeks.

When the nurse was done, Jean and I both looked like boys. Our hair was no longer than a thumb's length and sticking up in all directions. I felt something warm on my forehead and reached up to feel it. My hand came away bloody. The nurse had cut my scalp with her damned scissors.

"What did you do that for?" I demanded.

The nurse ignored me, like I hadn't even spoken.

"Mark 'defiant' on her chart, Nurse Chilcott," Auntie Sybil said.

Well, I didn't know what that meant, but I didn't like it none. I didn't like none of this.

"Where's our eggs and fresh milk?" I hollered.

"Mark 'intemperate' on her chart," Auntie Sybil said.

I gave Jean a look to say *Don't worry, I'm gonna fix this.* But of course I didn't know how to fix nothing. All we could do was follow Auntie Sybil and the nurse into the next room. It was bigger than the first and also covered in tile. Cold, slick, white tile. In the corner of the room was a tub. It was a big round tin tub, not that different from what our mama used to give us our Sunday bath. But, while at home our water had to be carried in from the well pump in buckets and heated on the stove, this tub had a faucet, like the bathroom at school. Jean and I were thinking the same thing: let it be nice and warm, at least.

Well, what do you think? Was it nice and warm?

Ha.

Jean and I wrapped our arms around our bare shoulders and stood hip to hip, shivering. Without a word, the nurse picked up Jean like she was a piglet and dumped her into the tub. From the sound of Jean's scream, I could tell it was cold as ice.

"Hush now," Auntie Sybil said.

"It stings!" Jean cried.

I sniffed the cold air. There was a funny smell. Soapy and sharp. Then I noticed the metal shelves with bottles on them. Rows and rows of brown glass bottles with labels on them. BLEACH the labels read. GERMICIDE AND DISINFECTANT.

"What is that?" I asked. "What's that smell? What did you put in the bath?"

Auntie Sybil said nothing.

The nurse smiled a nasty smile. "Delousing solution," she said.

"The lord only knows what diseases and vermin these creatures are harboring," Auntie Sybil said to the nurse. "I heard one of the girls on the second floor—couldn't be more than eleven—was rotten with syphilis. Can you imagine? Claimed she was a virgin too." She laughed. It was a horrible sound, like bones rattling in the wind.

"We're not dirty," I said. It was true. We always had our Sunday bath, except for when it was too cold. I washed our clothes myself, pumping the water from the well and rubbing the cloth against the washboard until my knuckles were raw. Weren't none of us dirty.

Both ladies pretended they couldn't hear me. The nurse kneeled down and began scrubbing at Jean with some kind of brush.

"Look at these breasts, Nurse Chilcott," Auntie Sybil said. "Girls of low moral character often show early development."

"Interesting," the nurse said. She started scrubbing Jean's head.

Jean shrieked.

"Can't you tell you're hurting her!" I hollered.

This wasn't nothing like school. I knew school. I'd been going since I was six or seven. School meant sitting at desks and doing writing and arithmetic and reading from books. At boarding school like the Chalet School, the kind where you lived, you had meals in a dining hall and kind teachers and libraries full of books. This wasn't school. Something was very wrong.

My angry feelings began to be covered by a kind of creeping fright, a blackness swirling into my mind like a storm cloud. This was bad. This was very, very bad.

Then it was my turn in the tub of bleach.

When they were done, the nurse pulled rough smocks over our heads. We were still wet underneath, and Jean was shivering so hard her teeth clicked.

The nurse looked at Auntie Sybil. "We should give her a cup of warm water, at least, so she doesn't catch her death," she said. "You remember what happened to that mountain girl, Miss Leigh."

"Nonsense," said Auntie Sybil. "Cold is healthful for girls like this. We can't treat them with delicacy; their systems aren't made for it."

I wondered then what "girls like this" meant. What kind of girls were we?

I was about to find out.

THE NURSE DISAPPEARED, and Auntie Sybil made us follow her up three flights of stairs and into a hallway. There was a window at the end of the hall, and I could see treetops beyond the glass. I had the burning feeling in my belly that I needed to leave this place, to get outside, to run.

Instead, I followed Auntie Sybil into a room with a red cross on the door. The basement had been dim and gray. This room was so bright it hurt my eyes. It had black-and-white floor tiles that felt cold beneath my bare feet, and walls painted a strange pale green. The ceiling was hung with rows and rows of square-shaped lights. Along one edge of the room were beds. In the middle was a table like I'd seen when I went to the hospital with a broken leg: metal, covered with a white sheet.

Jean whispered my name. I turned to her and saw her looking fearfully at one corner of the room. I followed her look. In the corner was something awful: the bones of a person. I felt my heart thud against my chest, but I kept quiet. I had to be brave for Jean. The bones had been tied together with wires and hung from a hook in the ceiling, so it looked like the person was standing. The teeth were smiling at us, and the eye holes were black as coal lumps. I thought of the bones of rabbits we found under the porch, after the hounds had got to them. There'd be dried brown bits of skin and meat still hanging on. These bones were pure clean white.

"It's not real," I whispered to Jean.

"Oh, I can assure you it's very real," said a deep voice.

A man had come into the room. He was tall and puffy, like a regular man had been blown up with air. His face was huge and square, with big slabby cheeks and a long white beard like Santa Claus. His hands were as big and pink as the country hams that hung from the rafters in Sproul's store and he wore a white coat.

"It's from Eastern Biological Supply," he said, walking slowly over to the bones and reaching out to stroke the top of the head bone like you'd pet a cat. "Cost a pretty penny. A male. A prisoner, most likely. Died of tuberculosis, as we can see from the scarring of the zygomatic bone." He tapped the skeleton's face with one of his big sausage fingers. "Never got to finish paying off his debt to society, so he's paying now, by serving science."

I reached for Jean's hand. She clutched on to mine.

The man turned to us, again moving slowly. He gave us a long look. I could feel his eyes moving up and down my body. I wanted to wash his look right off my skin, like it was mud.

"Where do they come from?" he said after a long time.

"Not far," said Auntie Sybil. "Lenoir County. Sharecropper's daughters. Living in squalor."

"You're a marvel, Miss Leigh," he said, smiling. His lips were thick and dark, like raw chicken liver. "These have to be—what?—your twelfth and thirteenth recruits of the year?" He looked over at Jean. "Step forward, girl," he ordered.

Jean's fingernails dug into my palm. I could feel her fear coming through her hand. She wouldn't move.

The man nodded towards Auntie Sybil. She stepped forward and grabbed Jean's arm. "Come forward. Don't be silly," she said, pulling.

Jean pulled back, moving towards the wall.

"What are you doing?" I cried.

Nobody answered.

"It's all right, girl. I'm not going to hurt you," the man said. He kneeled down so his face was the same height as Jean's. His eyes were a strange color, a cloudy green. "I simply need to ask you some questions."

Jean whimpered and looked down. I looked down too. A sudden puddle was spreading on the floor between Jean's legs. She'd peed herself. They hadn't given us any underpants to wear with the smocks, so the pee just went straight down.

The man stood up, a disgusted look on his face. His livery lips were all twisted. "No point in the intellectual examination," he said. "She's clearly an imbecile, or perhaps the lowest grade of moron. We'll examine the sister."

I could have fought. I could have screamed and thrashed like a wildcat. But I could see that wasn't gonna work. They weren't just gonna let us go. My mind was working, thinking ahead.

So I stepped forward. I looked the man right in the face, to show him I wasn't scared.

He looked back at me with those weird dead-fish eyes. "Let's begin with the Binet Test," he said.

Auntie Sybil took a box off a shelf. She took the top off the box and began taking things out and putting them on the desk. Some of the things I knew—a pencil, a clock. Others were strange. There was a little tin filled with shiny red-and-white-striped discs. There was a wooden box with a handle on top. There was a large feather, larger than from any bird I could even imagine.

"Sit down," she said, pointing to the desk chair.

I sat.

"Now, name these objects," she said.

"Pencil, clock, flower, key," I said. What the heck kind of test was this?

"All of them," she said. Her mouth was set in a straight line, like it had been slashed on with a pencil.

"Uh, box with a handle," I said.

"But what is its name?" she said.

What kind of stupid test was this?

"Wooden box with a handle?" I tried.

Auntie Sybil made a snorting sound and marked something on the paper. "And this?" she said, pointing at the tin full of red-and-white discs.

"Tin?"

"But what's inside?"

"Little red-and-white circles, 'bout as big as pennies."

She made the same snorting noise and wrote something down.

The angry feeling was starting to rise up in me again. I tried to push it down. I should listen now, I told myself, do what they said. Later I'd have a chance to get away. Not now. Later.

Next, she pointed to the feather.

"Feather," I said.

"Feather what?"

Feather what? I thought again of all the birds I knew. None of the birds in Lenoir County were very big—chickens and robins and sparrows. Sometimes a seagull that must have got lost. "Turkey?" I guessed. Sometimes we saw a wild turkey crossing the fields. They were pretty big, at least twice as big as chickens.

Auntie Sybil laughed, that ugly, rattling sound.

"She shows almost a cleverness of thought," said the man. He took a pipe out of his shirt pocket and lit it, his loose, wet pink mouth turning into an O as he blew out smoke.

Auntie Sybil raised her eyebrows. "A girl who can't identify a feather duster, a coffee grinder, or a simple peppermint candy?"

"Yes, but she does know her words, and she combines them interestingly."

Of course I know my words, I thought. I'm seventeen years old, not three! But how was I supposed to know what a coffee grinder looked like? I knew what coffee was—the girls in the Chalet School drank it every morning, with milk and sugar. But my mama and pa didn't. They had chicory, sometimes, or just hot water. We sure didn't have no coffee grinder. And peppermints? I knew those too. They sold them in Sproul's, but they were shaped like sticks, not circles, and we never had no money for them anyway.

"Do you have the familial inventory?" the man asked Auntie Sybil.

"Yes, it's in here," she replied, opening her bag and pulling out a brown envelope. On the outside was written AIKEN. She cleared her throat and started to read: "'Evidence of hereditary feeblemindedness. According to the local business leaders I interviewed, the mother is indolent and nearly illiterate. Father is given to dipsomania and criminality. Eldest sister is a common prostitute. The older girl, Cecilia, has been showing signs of lewdness herself. She's been consorting with a local boy of a higher class, which is quite unacceptable to his family.'"

"What did you say about me?" I hollered. "What did you say about Luelle?" I wasn't too sure what "prostitute" was, but I knew it wasn't nothing nice. "My sister's a housemaid. In Wilmington!" And what was she talking about, local business leaders? *Consorting?* "If you talked to the Sprouls, they ain't nothing but liars!" I ain't done nothing but kiss Jimmy Sproul; I told him if he wanted more he'd have to get me a ring and a proper house in a city and a stove that worked with gas, like the one in his ma's kitchen.

"Don't worry, girl," the man said, speaking to my face for the first time. "We're simply trying to understand your genetics—the pieces of the puzzle that make you who you are."

"She's been in school," said Auntie Sybil, still looking at the papers. "Her mother claims she can read well."

"Really?" said the man. "Let's try her." He went to a bookshelf against the wall and pulled out a book. It was a McGuffey Reader, just like we had at school.

I began to feel a little better. Surely if I could show him how I could read, they wouldn't think we were stupid.

The man put the book in front of me, blowing a thick cloud of pipe smoke in my face. "Can you read this?"

I read. "'Can you fly a kite. See how the boy flies a kite.'" This was baby stuff. I kept reading until the man interrupted by talking to Auntie Sybil.

"Interesting," he said. "Do take notes, Miss Leigh." He began to speak slowly as he walked around the room, his hand on his chin, stroking his beard. "This case here is a classic example of a high-grade moron," he began. "Of low parentage in Eastern North Carolina, she can read at a basic level, yet lacks ability to identify common objects. A weak moral character can be discerned from her facial shape and characteristic ear formation. This type of moron is especially dangerous if allowed to go free in our society, as she is clever enough to manipulate. Indeed, her beauty and charm might allow her to marry into stock superior to her own, thus introducing her degeneracy into a higher stratum of society. We must prevent this. I prescribe vigorous physical activity to tame her baser impulses and perhaps teach her a trade—the sewing room or the market garden should do. Avoid beef, eggs, and other foods that could excite her nervous system."

I didn't know exactly what he was saying, but as he talked I could feel the color rushing into my face. He was calling me some kind of idiot. He was saying I was bad, bad right down to my bones. What I did understand perfectly well was the word "eggs." No eggs? I felt my teeth itch with anger. "Auntie Sybil promised us eggs and fresh milk!" I cried.

"See how she lashes out," the man said, paying me no attention. "Lack of self-control is characteristic of her type. As for the sister, dress her in the imbecile uniform and follow the soft foods protocol. You may room her with the older one; it will be easier for the warden that way."

Auntie Sybil nodded, writing this all down, her pencil flying across the page. "Shall we do the measurements, Dr. McDevitt?" she asked, looking up.

"Oh yes," the man said. There was a strange and awful gleam in his dead fish eyes. My brother Virgil used to catch bream in the old Sproul millpond and carry them home strung to a stick. Their eyes looked just like this.

What kind of doctor was he? There wasn't nothing wrong with me or Jean that we needed a doctor! We needed to go back home to Mama and Pa. I began backing towards the wall where Jean stood.

The man drew something from the desk drawer. It gleamed in the light like a sword. Jean began to sob.

I decided then that my plan to be good and listen wasn't gonna work. I was gonna have to fight. I was gonna have to protect Jean from whatever the gleaming thing was. I turned my body stiff and ready to spring, the way Beauty would get when a stranger came near, straining at the end of her chain.

Turns out, it was something called a "caliper." It was for measuring your head and your ears and your arms and even your parts down there. It was cold as ice, and even when you fought—even when you thrashed and screamed so loud the doctor called you a she wolf—you couldn't keep it away from your flesh. You couldn't do nothing at all.

You know the worst bit? After all that measuring, they did

finally let us eat. But it wasn't no eggs and fresh milk. It was mush. Corn mush. The same damn corn mush I ate every damn day of my life in Tobacco Run. Wasn't even salted. I'd have rather they hit me full in the face.

I will die before I ever eat a damn bowl of corn mush ever again.

Chapter 22

MILLIE

1939

The stranger—*Cecilia*—paused for a moment and picked up the cookie tin. She began munching on a piece of shortbread with a casual air, like we were just friends gossiping over tea.

We were sitting in the kitchen of my house, though I couldn't remember walking home. I felt queasy and hot, like I'd stepped off a carousel at a carnival.

Lenoir County. Lenoir County. That was just the next county over, butting up against the western end of Craven.

"You grew up not thirty miles from here," I said flatly.

Not only was she not foreign, she was just an ordinary Eastern North Carolina farmer's daughter. How could I have been so fooled? Why did she want to fool me? What had she gotten me into?

"Sounds about right," said Cecilia, licking shortbread crumbs off her fingers.

"Why did you lie to me?"

"You would have helped me if you knew the truth?"

"Of course!"

Cecilia laughed, and a hot red fury bloomed in my chest.

"C'mon, Millie—if you'd have known I was a runaway

moron with low morals from the Casteen Training School, would you have gone and bought me a fancy dress and let me sleep in Auggie's room?"

The sound of my brother's name on her lying tongue felt like a slap. I stood up and leaned over Cecilia, who had started in on another piece of shortbread. "Yes, I would have helped you, if you'd have just told me the truth. Now you've gone and gotten me tangled up in something horrible. That man . . ." I heard the crack of the mallet hitting his skull, the sound of the barrel splashing into the river, and felt a wave of vinegary nausea.

Cecilia went still and, for the first time that I could remember, looked angry. "Right. Sure. You'd have helped me if I'd *just told you the truth*." She turned to me, her pale eyes gone dark, and shook her head. "I'll tell you, Millie, that ain't been how it's gone for me so far."

Chapter 23

CECILIA

1938

The main building at Casteen had a west and an east side, which they called wings, like a bird has. The east wing was the cafeteria, the classrooms, the infirmary, and Dr. McDevitt's office. The west wing was the dormitories, which is a fancy word for rooms where you sleep. There were three floors. On the first floor were the imbeciles, who mostly seemed regular enough to me, but couldn't learn. On the second and third floors were the rest of us. Bad girls. Wayward. Degenerates. Girls who do any old thing they think girls shouldn't. That's what Auntie Sybil meant when she said "girls like this."

We were eight in our dormitory on the third floor. Four beds on one side, four on the other. In the bed nearest the door was Jacy, from Ocracoke Island, where you could only get to by riding a mailboat for half a day. She talked with a funny kind of accent almost like Mrs. Randall, my English war bride teacher. Jacy, though, she says she talks normal and it's the rest of us "offlanders" that talk strange. She came to Casteen after she had a baby and it died. At nights when the wind blew from the east she'd sit by the window and try to smell the ocean. She said it reminded her of home, and of her baby boy. He was born smelling like the sea, she said.

Sally and Vera were twins from Red Town, not far from Tobacco Run. They looked just alike—both of them fat with small dark eyes pushed into their round pale faces like holes poked in dough. They sometimes even talked at the same time—one of them starting a sentence, the other one finishing it. Their mama had died and their daddy sent them to work as maids for a rich man in Goldsboro. The man said they stole his silver candlesticks; that's how they got sent to Casteen.

"Did y'all do it?" I asked them once.

"Yes," said Sally, at the exact same time as Vera said "No."

Bertie Lou was a skinny, sour-faced girl from a hog farm outside Raleigh. She got caught in the hayloft with a Negro farmhand. Bertie Lou kept sayin' he was gonna come for her, and they'd run away together. The other girls rolled their eyes at that. "Bertie Lou's brothers strung that boy up a tree," Jacy whispered to me. "Made her watch too. Only now she plays like she don't remember."

The oldest third-floor girl was Mollie, who was near thirty. She came to Casteen when she was my age, during the Great War. She'd been a floozy at the army camp in Charlotte—that meant she let soldiers get up under her skirts for money—and the police told her she had to go to Casteen or prison. When you got Mollie talking, she'd go a mile a minute, telling stories about the time she went to Florida on a train with a rich man, and the time she flew in an airplane. Most of what she said wasn't true, I'd find out later. But some of it was. She scared me, Mollie. She was a full grown-up, but she was still here. I'd never let that happen to me, I swore to myself. Never.

Little Ruthie was me and Jean's favorite. She was twelve, but tiny as eight. Most of the time she seemed like a regular little girl, but every now and again she'd get staring spells. You'd wave your hand in front of her face, and she wouldn't even blink. Ruthie's grandma had thought the spells were from the devil. She'd tried to beat that devil out of Ruthie with a hot iron one morning back in Duplin County. After that, Ruthie came to live at Casteen. One side of her face was a mess of burn scars, like curdled milk.

Ruthie and Jean were thick as thieves right away. They even looked alike, if you saw Ruthie from her good side, both of them with freckles and hair orange as carrots. They'd whisper to each other during meals and Jean would even laugh sometimes, which was a rare thing at Casteen. At night, if the warden wasn't around, they'd clap Miss Mary Mack, softly, since they didn't have marbles or nothing to play with.

After prayers, they liked to crawl into bed with me and I'd tell them stories about the girls at the Chalet School and all their great big adventures in Austria. I'd tell them about how Madge Bettany, the headmistress, was once an orphan without a pot to pee in, and now she ran a whole dang school. They liked that. Pretty often Jacy or Mollie would creep up close and listen to the stories too.

"Where's Austria?" Jacy asked, and I had to say I didn't know.

We'd lie there in the dark and I'd tell about how Jo and Grizel and Simone and Robin rescued Rufus, the puppy, and escaped a flood, and put on "theatrics" and went to a holiday music show. Mostly, though, the third-floor girls wanted to hear about the food: the rolls and jam, the ham with cooked fruit, the raspberries and blackberries with fluffy sweet cream, the cold salad. None of us knew what a salad was, except Mollie—she said it was like vegetables, but raw, which didn't sound too good to the rest of us.

We would have eaten it, though. We would have eaten anything if it was only different than what they served us at Casteen. Mush, mush, and more mush. Sometimes biscuits, sometimes peas, sometimes a bit of salt pork.

When we heard the scratching of the night warden's key in the dormitory lock, we'd scatter like mice, else we'd get a red mark on our charts. Too many red marks and you'd get the strap, or worse.

By October, there was silver frost on the ground in the morning. The school had big radiators along the walls, with their peely silver pipes that turned on with a roar and got so hot they'd scorch your hand if you touched them. But they only came on sometimes, and the heat never warmed the room past the edges. Sleeping together helped keep us warm, just like it had done back in Tobacco Run. At least there Mama had kept the woodstove lit all night when it got coldest.

In the mornings they'd wake us up with a bell. That sound of that dang bell still rings in my ears every morning at six, no matter that I'm miles and miles away. I wonder if it'll ring in my head till the day I die.

We'd get dressed from our nightgowns into our smocks, which were barely any different. We all wore brown bloomers underneath—you could wear blue ones if you were an Honor Girl, which meant you were a snitch. Nobody in our dorm was ever an Honor Girl. Then we'd go downstairs to the cafeteria. Breakfast was mush, of course—salted mush on the regular days, sweet mush on Sundays. Once I asked about eggs, and the dining lady just laughed.

We had about ten minutes to eat, then it was time for classes. Only they weren't regular classes like you'd think of at a school. The first hours after breakfast were for sewing. We'd sit in a big room with long tables, each of us behind our own sewing machine, while the teacher, Mrs. Black, told us the lesson for the day. For the first few months, the lesson was always hemming sheets. I'd never sewed with a machine before—I'd never even seen one—but hemming sheets is something my pa could do half-drunk with his good eye closed.

"When do we learn something new?" I asked Mrs. Black.

"When I decide you're ready," she said.

Mrs. Black was a tall lady with the face of a horse—long nose, long teeth that her lips didn't quite close over. She had a funny accent—a Yankee accent, the other girls said. When she got mad her face would go pink. She was all right, though. She wasn't the worst. Not by a lot.

It never made sense to me, hemming the sheets for our lesson every single day. At regular school, back in Tobacco Run, when we'd worked out one lesson we got to start on a harder one. But not in Mrs. Black's sewing class. It was hems, hems, hems for week after week. It got to where I dreamed about hemming sheets at night, and when I woke I could still feel the hum of the sewing machine in my fingertips.

After a few weeks of me asking, Jacy finally rolled her eyes and leaned over to whisper to me. "We'll learn something new when we've finished stocking the warehouse with sheets," she said, patting my arm.

That's when I understood. The sewing lesson wasn't about us learning. It was about us making sheets for Casteen to sell. Casteen sold everything we made at a shop down in Kinston town—the sheets from sewing class, the milk from the dairy barn, the cabbages from the fields. This didn't seem to bother the other girls. "They've got to have money to keep us," Jacy said.

But they weren't hardly keeping us, not as far as I could tell.

After sewing was mush for lunch. Jean and Ruthie would

make me tell them stories while we ate, till the warden hollered she'd take away my food unless I shut my mouth. Then we'd have Behavior.

Behavior was more like a regular class than sewing, but it still didn't make much sense to me. The teacher was Miss Pritchard, who had a little girl's high voice and a little girl's meanness. The other girls said Miss Pritchard had gone to school at a university, which meant she was smart. But she sure didn't do much to show it. In Behavior, she mostly made us practice sitting—knees together, backs straight. Sometimes that's all we'd do, just sit and sit until our sides ached from holding us up so long. "Proper posture and proper morals go hand in hand, girls," she'd say.

Sometimes Miss Pritchard would make us stand in front of the class and smile, and then she'd tell us what was wrong with our smiles. "Too sassy." "Provocative." "Insincere." Sometimes Auntie Sybil would show up and stand in the back of the class like a black shadow, watching. When she wasn't off stealing girls from their families, she lived in a dark little cottage near the front gate, like a witch in a fairy tale, and would creep in and out of the main building whenever she pleased.

When it was my turn, I smiled like I normally do, and Miss Pritchard shook her head. "Showing teeth is brazen," she said. "Girls like you cannot—must not—give men the wrong idea."

I felt that old mad red feeling starting down in my chest and rising up my front. It wasn't none of Miss Pritchard's business how I smiled! So just to make her mad I gave the biggest, most tooth-showing smile I possibly could, a smile so big it made my cheeks ache and squeezed my eyes shut.

"You laugh, Cecilia," Auntie Sybil said from the back of the room. "But you won't be laughing when you've been ruined like Jacy was, will you?"

Poor Jacy just sat there staring at the wall.

Why do they say a girl like Jacy is ruined? She ain't broken. She laid with a boy she wasn't married to, but that's just a regular sin. Don't God forgive the sinners, let them get on with it?

When she got tired of having us sit and smile, Miss Pritchard would read to us from a book called *A Ladies' Guide to Household Management*. She said some of us might work as "domestics" one day, and we'd need to know how to polish forks and scour pots. As soon as she started talking my mind would go dead and I'd just stare out the window. The Behavior classroom was small and faced west, so it got warm in the afternoon, even during that freezing cold fall and winter. My eyelids would get so heavy I couldn't help closing them softly—*just for a moment*, I'd tell myself. If I fell asleep, I'd get sent out in the hallway to stand on one foot as punishment.

Now, that don't sound so bad, right? I could stand on one foot for an hour, easy.

It ain't standing on one foot that's the problem. The problem was that there was always someone slinking around the hallway, someone tall and skinny with arms like the branches of a dead tree, jingling the janitor's key ring from his spider fingers.

Matty Barnwell.

Matty Barnwell was what they called an "orderly." He ran errands for Dr. McDevitt, who we called "Dr. McDevil"—carrying papers and dropping off medicines at the room with the big red cross on the door where they'd measured me and Jean. The "infirmary," they called it. He kept a big ring of keys on his belt and he liked to jingle them as he walked around. But mostly Matty Barnwell spied. You stuck your head around any corner in any hallway at Casteen and there he'd be, his long pale face smirking back at you. It was almost like he could be in two places at once. Ruthie used to close her eyes whenever she saw him, like he was a bad dream she couldn't wake up from.

When I was little, my mama would tell us stories about Tommy Rawhead. He had the body of a tall skinny man, but his fingers were claws and all the flesh was torn off his face. He lived in the pine trees on a pile of bloody bones from all the naughty children he'd taken away in sacks in the night. If you didn't mind your manners, if you didn't pick enough 'backer or corn, if you didn't go to sleep when Mama said, then old Tommy Rawhead would come get you. When you closed your eyes and opened them again, he'd be right in front of you, grinning his bony smile and breathing his raw meat breath into your face.

Mama would sing: "Rawhead and Bloody Bones, / steals naughty children from their homes. / Takes them to his dirty den, / and they are never seen again."

I used to be so scared of Tommy Rawhead I sometimes peed myself instead of going to the privy on a dark night. Later, I saw he was just a tale Mama told to make her life a little easier.

Now I know he's real.

No, there ain't no man with claw fingers and no skin on his face. But there are men just as scary.

When I said Matty Barnwell deserved what Millie did to him outside the pickle warehouse, I meant it.

Chapter 24

CECILIA

1938

It snowed the day Ruthie woke up feverish. Winter had come hard that year, and by the end of November there was a good coat of snow on the ground. That ain't normal for Lenoir County. I could count on my fingers the times I'd seen snow, and then only a little white powder, like sugar on a hoecake.

The scar side of Ruthie's face was always white, but now the other side was just as pale, and her eyes were too shiny. We tried our best to get her dressed and ready for breakfast, but she kept flopping back down on her bed. "Just let me sleep," she said. "I'm just so cold."

Ruthie felt the cold more than anybody. She was small, and during the time I knew her she only got smaller. The rest of us shoveled down our horrible mush like starving dogs, but Ruthie would stir hers around with a spoon until it got cold. The only thing worse than hot mush is cold mush. Even on days when we'd have something half-nice to eat—cornbread, or biscuits with sugar—she'd slip most of it to Jean, if greedy old Mollie didn't snatch it first.

Jacy thought it was for the best. "You don't eat, you won't grow, you know," she said.

"Shouldn't you want to grow?"

"Problem is, when you grow taller you grow in the bosom too. It's when your bosoms grow that the men commence to mommucking you."

"Mommucking?" Sometimes Jacy used those Ocracoke words I didn't understand.

"Bothering. The bosoms give the men a feeling in their nethers, and then they're slinking around you like hound dogs all day and night. They only want one thing."

I thought of old Mollie, who said it was better to just give a man what he wanted, cuz he'll take it anyway. Might as well get a couple dollars and an ice cream from it, she said, in her scary-bright voice.

"You want the men to quit mommucking, you got to get skinny enough that your bosom shrinks down," Jacy told me in a motherly sort of way. "Your monthly will stop, so that's good too."

Now, I had only started getting my monthly the year before, and I didn't much like it. What's the good of having to spend a week waddling around with a towel between your legs and pains like someone's trying to tug your guts out with a hot spoon? My mama would give me red clover tea to help, so I could be well enough to work the fields, but it only half worked.

"How skinny do you have to get for your monthly to go away?" I asked.

Jacy shrugged. "Mine stopped for a while during that bad summer a few years back, when the mullet didn't run. We had to dig for oysters and eat nasty old turnips and I got so skinny you could put your hands around my waist." She gave a sigh, but a happy-sounding one, like it was a good memory.

After that, I watched Ruthie and tried to wheedle her to eat. Not having bosoms was all well and good, but that winter she was getting so skinny I worried she'd freeze. Most days they made us go outside for a few hours to wash cabbages or squash from the farm and ready them for market. On those days we'd get cloaks to wear, but they weren't much good. Ruthie would near about turn blue. Once she got so stiff she couldn't walk, and Jean and I had to carry her back, each of us holding one elbow. We didn't want the barn warden to see how bad off Ruthie was, or she might have got sent to the infirmary.

Nothing good happens in the infirmary, the girls all said. That was Matty Barnwell's patch. He slept on a cot behind the nurse's desk. If you got sick enough, they'd leave you there overnight, and you'd be alone with him and his big hands and long fingers. There were girls who had stories, Jacy said, and not the kind of stories in books.

On the morning Ruthie got sick, we did everything we could to warm her up. I gave her my nightgown to wear under her smock, then me and Jean laid next to her for the body heat.

"C'mon, get up, Ruthie," I wheedled. "You'll feel better if you eat a little."

"I'm just so tired," Ruthie said, not opening her eyes.

When Miss Grieve, the house warden, showed up to take us to breakfast, Ruthie was still laying there with her eyes closed, a blaze of pink on her good cheek.

"Oh dear," said Miss Grieve.

She was the nicest of them, Miss Grieve, a short little pigeon-shaped lady with a voice like syrup.

"I'll go get the nurse," she said.

Well, Nurse Chilcott took one look at Ruthie and ordered her to the infirmary. Matty Barnwell came to carry her there. Watching him circle her little body in his long skinny arms made my guts go cold.

"She don't weigh no more than a sparrow," he said, his long finger stroking her good cheek.

I asked the nurse if I could go too, to help take care of her. But she just laughed and said, "Get yourself down to breakfast."

So I went.

Ruthie stayed in the infirmary all that day and the next. Us third-floor girls tried to find reasons to go past the infirmary, so we could stand on tiptoes and wave at her through the window in the door. She looked all right. Sleeping peaceful as a baby.

Mollie said the beds in the infirmary were the best beds at Casteen. "Real chicken feathers," she said, smiling to herself. "I was in there for two weeks when I had my appendix. It was real, real nice. Almost as nice as the bed in the Hollywood Hotel."

All the other girls rolled their eyes at that. We knew old Mollie hadn't never been in no Hollywood Hotel, but she did have a big pink slash of a scar on her stomach. I wasn't too sure what an appendix was, but I hoped I never got one.

On the third day they let two of us visit Ruthie. Me and Jean went. When Ruthie saw me, she grabbed my hand. The color was back in her face, but her mouth was tight and white. She was scared.

"Tell them I'm ready to go back to the third floor, Cecilia," she said. "I don't want to spend another night here, I can't."

"Mollie says the beds are the nicest in Casteen," I said, trying to make her feel better.

"It ain't the bed, it's"—she dropped her voice to a whisper—"it's *him*."

Nobody was around, but I knew who she meant, of course I did.

"He's not trying to . . . do things, is he?" I asked. Even after all those months in Casteen there were evils in the world I couldn't quite imagine. Like touching a girl as little as Ruthie.

"He says he's comforting me," she whispered, her eyes shiny with tears. "But it don't feel like comforting."

Anger leapt up through my body like tongues of fire. I took a deep breath; I didn't want to scare Ruthie. "You tell him if he so much as lays a finger on you, Cecilia will kill him dead."

Ruthie nodded miserably.

Just then the nurse came and shooed us out. "She's better, ain't she?" I said. "She can come back to the dormitory?"

The nurse gave a sharp little laugh. "We'll decide when she's better. Out with you!"

So we went. If only we'd been able to take her with us.

If only. If only. If only.

Two most useless words in the English language.

JEAN WOKE ME late that night. She always slept lighter. I rolled over and saw her face, pale and worried, in the moonlight.

"I hear a girl crying," she said.

I heard it too. But "crying" wasn't the word I would have said. "Screaming" was more like it. Is there a word for screaming that's worse than screaming? "Howling," maybe.

I could tell right away it was Ruthie.

Jean and I ran down to the second floor in our bare feet and nightdresses. The door to the infirmary was open and the lights were on. The nurse and Dr. McDevitt were bent over Ruthie's bed. Matty Barnwell stood with his back against the wall, his eyes shifting back and forth.

Ruthie screamed again. Jean and I ran to her bed.

"Stop them," said Dr. McDevitt.

But it was too late. We'd seen.

Ruthie's nightdress was rucked up around her hips. There was a smudge of blood on the nightdress and I thought maybe she'd started her monthly and was scared and that's why she was carrying on. But then I saw that her legs, from the knees down, were the red of raw pork heart. She arched her back and screamed, her eyes screwed shut.

"What the heck!" I screamed. "What did you do to her?"

"There's been an accident, girls, but we're taking care of it," Dr. McDevitt said.

I tried to pick up Ruthie's hand, but the nurse had waved at Matty Barnwell and he was already reaching out with his long arms to grab me away. I tried to kick him, but those arms wound around me tight as wires.

I saw then that he was wet. Water dripped from his pants and made a puddle on the white tile floor.

"Quit your fighting," he whispered. "It won't do you no good."

I screamed Ruthie's name, but Matty Barnwell had me out the door in a flash.

"Just go back to bed if you know what's good for you," he said, pushing me up the stairs. "And don't go telling no tales. It was an accident, that's all."

Jean and I sat up in bed all night, holding each other. I rubbed her hair the way our mama would do when we were little, but it didn't calm her down none. In the morning, Miss Grieve opened the door wearing a long sad face.

I took one look at her and started to cry.

IT WAS AN accident, they all said—Miss Grieve, Dr. McDevil, all the teachers. They said it over and over again. An accident. A sad accident. Ruthie had wet herself in the night and had wandered into the infirmary bathroom to bathe herself. But she'd turned the water on much too hot and scalded her legs.

It wasn't the scalding that killed her, Dr. McDevil said. It was the shock to her system, which was weak from being so skinny.

A terrible accident. But it wasn't no accident. Not a single girl on the third floor believed that. It was Matty Barnwell with his long fingers, doing the things Jacy said men did. Ruthie must have screamed and carried on, and he tried to wash away the proof with hot water.

Like I said, he deserved what he got.

They buried Ruthie in the little cemetery behind the school, where none of the gravestones had names on them, only numbers. I asked why she didn't get buried back home in Duplin County and Mollie said her family must not have wanted her.

They made all us third-floor girls gather round the grave while Dr. McDevil stood there with a Bible and went on about the Good Lord Jesus's comforting embrace and Ruthie being in a better place now. Matty Barnwell stood behind him in his black coat with the sleeves too short, holding a shovel.

"That bastard," Jacy whispered, squeezing her hands open and shut. "That bastard."

I just stood there, barely breathing. It was cold out—you could see Dr. McDevil's breath—but I didn't feel it. Inside I was lit up hot with anger like a woodstove. I should have known. I should have done something. I should have protected her.

I wanted to scream. I wanted to howl so loud that every dog in Lenoir County would howl back. But I stood still as a statue as Matty Barnwell shoveled wet clumps of dirt onto Ruthie's tiny plain wood coffin. In that moment, I swore to myself and to every girl at Casteen and to the Good Lord Jesus with his comforting goddamn embrace that I would never let nothing like this happen again.

Chapter 25

MILLIE

1939

I was crying.

Poor little Ruthie. To die in pain, alone and unwanted, surrounded by hateful people.

I hadn't been with Auggie when he died, but my aunt and mother were there, holding his hand. He wasn't alone. He wasn't in pain—that much my aunt has sworn to me. He just slept more and more deeply, swaddled in a thick blanket of morphine, until he was gone.

"Was there an investigation after Ruthie died?" I asked.

Cecilia made a raspberry sound. "What do you think?"

"Is there no oversight, no board of directors?"

"You and your fancy words," Cecilia said. "You gotta understand—Dr. McDevitt is like God at Casteen. What he says might as well be the Holy Bible itself. No one would have believed us against him. That's why I had to do what I did."

I wiped my eyes on the back of my hand and felt the anger in my chest well up again. How could a man be so evil? All the bad things that had happened in my own life were no one's fault. But what if they had been? What if Auggie had died because someone had done something evil and twisted and sick to him on purpose? I'd want that person dead too. Anyone who did such a thing to a little girl deserved to rot in a pickle barrel bobbing down the Neuse River. I wished it hadn't been me who'd done it. But I understood.

"All right, then, tell me," I said to Cecilia. "How did you get away?"

Chapter 26

CECILIA

1938

At Christmas you could almost believe that Casteen was a real school. On Christmas Eve, the ladies from the Baptist Church came with a special supper: turkey and mashed potatoes and sweet cooked apples. We all ate so quick we hardly took time to breathe.

"They're quite the little savages, aren't they?" I heard one church lady whisper to another.

How would you eat when you hadn't had nothing but mush and old biscuits for months and months? I wanted to ask them. But I kept quiet. My plan was almost ready. I couldn't get in trouble or get sent to isolation, or everything would be ruined.

On Christmas morning, families from another church came with presents wrapped up so pretty and bright, with ribbons and everything.

"It's just socks," Jacy whispered to me. "But if you act real sweet, they might give you some candy too."

So when a lady came up and asked me how I liked living at Casteen, I gave her a little smile—modest, just like Miss Pritchard told us—and said, "Oh, ma'am, I'm just so grateful to be here."

Jacy was right—the lady patted me on the head like I was a dog and gave me a whole bag of horehound drops.

The preacher back in Tobacco Run always said lying was a sin, but I could see now it was better to be a sinner with a bag of candy than an honest girl with nothing but mush to eat. Telling the truth hadn't gotten me nowhere so far.

Those horehound drops were just about the nicest Christmas present I'd ever had. Back home, us kids would hang our old socks on a nail on Christmas Eve and in the morning we'd shake out an apple and a penny. Of course, we all saw Mama putting the apples in, though we squeezed our eyes shut and pretended we didn't. You can't believe in Santa Claus in a two-room house. When I was little, Mama used to make us corn husk dolls as well, but later on she was too tired for that, and there were too many little girls. So Christmas was apples and pennies, then a lunch of roasted peanuts and hominy with ham. A whole bag of candy—now, *that* was a Christmas present. As soon as the lady wasn't looking, I passed the candy to Jean. We were trying to cheer her up. She hadn't been the same since Ruthie died. She barely ate and just stared out the window like she was waiting for someone who never came.

After the presents, the church kids sang some carols. I pasted a pretend smile on my face as I watched, but inside my guts were boiling. Their parents must have told them they were doing a good deed, bringing Christmas to the poor, ruined, feebleminded girls at Casteen. *We're just as good as you*, I wanted to scream. But I kept my mouth shut tight. Back in the dormitory on the third floor, under my bed, a sack of hard-dried biscuits squirreled away from the cafeteria and an extra cloak I'd nicked from the barn were hiding, waiting for the right moment. I soothed myself with the thought. I'd be gone from here soon. Then I'd come back for Jean and we'd leave this place forever. We'd get to Wilmington, find Luelle, get jobs as maids too. All three of us would share a little house by the ocean. We'd eat whatever we wanted.

The girls at the Chalet School called the day after Christmas "Boxing Day" and said it was the most "jolly" day of the year. They'd go tobogganing, which meant riding a cart down a snowy mountain, and they'd drink hot cocoa and have special cakes for teatime.

At Casteen, "Boxing Day" meant sweeping up the cafeteria and cleaning all the windows, then an early supper of mush and bedtime in our cold dormitory. I cleaned so well Miss Pritchard said if I kept on being so good they might make me an Honor Girl and let me wear the blue pantaloons and have chicken on Sundays.

I smiled at her with my best Behavior class smile.

Everyone was tired and sad that night. Christmas had been the one nice thing all year, and now it was back to sewing and mush and thinking about poor Ruthie. But tired was good, because it meant everyone went to sleep right quick.

I hadn't told anyone my plan but Jean. She lay in the bed next to me, her eyes shining in the darkness.

"I'm scared," she whispered.

"Don't be scared," I told her. "Just tell them you didn't know I was gonna run away, that you're just as surprised as anybody. As soon as I get home, we'll all come get you."

But in my own secret heart I was as scared as I'd ever been. No part of the plan was for sure. Anything could happen. I could break my ankle jumping out the window. I could get hit by a car and squashed flat as a frog. I could get lost. Then what would happen to Jean?

Hush, I told my mind. *Don't think like that. You can't.*

There was no clock in the dorms, but I knew the night

warden came by about two hours after lights-out. I lay curled up in the dark, listening to the night noises. Old Mollie snored like a hog. The twins talked in their sleep—broken, mushed-together pieces of words. I could hear soft sounds from downstairs, where the imbeciles lived: crying and snuffling, and every now and again a sharp snap from one of the night wardens—"Quit it," or "Hush."

When I heard the night warden's step on the stairs, I lay still on my back and let my eyelids flutter. Through my lashes I watched the warden walk slowly around the room, pointing her flashlight at each girl's sleeping face. When she shone the light at me I gave a sleepy little moan and said "whaaa" in a sleep-talky way, like the twins. I was pretty proud of that. I ain't never seen a film, but I reckon I'd be a better Hollywood actress than old Mollie.

After the warden was gone and her footsteps had quieted, I sat up and slipped on the cloak I'd hidden beneath my bedsheets. I was wearing socks too, plus the extra pair I'd gotten for Christmas. I looped the bag—an old feed bag, pinched from the barn—over my shoulder and grabbed my boots. I gave Jean a kiss on the cheek.

No use dragging it out. My heart was slamming in my throat as I climbed onto the windowsill and pushed the window up.

Now, the windows at Casteen had bars, of course. But I'd reckoned I could just slip through the last bar at the edge, where the window was sorta bent outwards. Then I'd shimmy on down the drainpipe like it was a cheneyberry tree.

Now I was on the window's edge, holding my shoes in one hand and the sack in the other. I had to do it now—if I didn't go and let Jean close the window, the cold air would wake up one of the other girls. I put one arm through the bars and let my boots drop. Then I dropped the sack. No going back. I looked at Jean and whispered, "See you soon." Then I slipped sideways between the last bar and the edge of the window.

My hips stuck. My brand-new hips, flat as a little girl's not half a year before, dug into the bars. I pushed. My flesh screamed back at me. I pushed more. I felt a flash of hot pain, and one hip popped past the bar. I tugged to get the other free, and as I did I lost my balance.

I went bottom-down like a sack of cabbages. Just before I hit the ground I saw Jean's little white face in the window, her mouth a circle of surprise.

Thud.

A jolt of pain shot from my rear all the way up to my head. I heard a whining sound in my ears and tasted blood, hot and metal-y like the smell of the radiator. I'd bit my tongue. I pushed myself up to sitting. Nothing broken. I was lucky there was so much snow, or I might have really got hurt.

I found my boots poking out of the snow and laced them up over my wet socks, my toes already starting to sting with cold. But where was my sack? It was a white sack, and in the dark snowy night it was hidden like a brown owl in a brown tree. I scrabbled around for a minute, then got scared. The grounds warden walked around the buildings with a flashlight all night long. At any moment he might come round the corner, whistling, and I'd be done for.

So I ran.

I ran across the yard and into the west field. I stood for a moment at the edge of a field against a tree trunk, looking back at the main building. I could still see Jean's face in the window. *Get to bed*, I said to her in my head. If they found her staring out the window and me gone, they'd know she was in on the plan. Then she'd get sent down to isolation, or worse.

Not seeing the grounds warden's light, I ran as fast as I could across the west field and into the shadows of the barn. I could see the warden now, by the front gate. I reckoned he couldn't see me there in the dark, so I stood as still as a deer until he'd disappeared behind the other side of the main house. Then I ran again.

At the edge of the west field was a stand of scrubby pines. We knew there was a road on the other side—sometimes we heard trucks screeching their brakes while we were in the field, loading cabbages—but we didn't know how far it was. I got to the edge of the pines and stopped to catch my breath. I looked backwards again. The sky over the west field was an angry-looking purple-gray. It was gonna snow again. I stepped into the forest.

It was darker than I thought it would be, and suddenly everything seemed loud. My breathing. My heartbeat. The snow crunching under my boots. Wings flapped over my head, almost making me scream—a bird. A twig snapped somewhere in the dark. A squirrel, I told myself. I tried to calm my breathing. Wasn't nothing out here worse than what was in there.

Lucky for me, the forest was shallow, and it wasn't but ten minutes before I came out the other side. I was standing by the edge of a road. It was black tar, dark as water. Not a few feet away was another road crossing the first one, thinner but just as black.

As I stood there, it started to snow: big, fat, wet snowflakes that melted right away on my hair and slid all shivery down my neck. I reckoned it was about midnight. Would cars come by this late? I hadn't thought about that. Maybe I should start walking. Standing still made my feet ache with the cold. But which direction?

I understood then, with a sick feeling in my stomach, that

there was lots of things I didn't know, things I should've thought of but didn't. How far was Tobacco Run? I reckoned we'd spent about an hour in Auntie Sybil's car on the way here, but I wasn't too sure. And I hadn't figured on there being more than one road.

The snow started falling harder. What would Jo in the Chalet School do? She'd probably do eeny, meeny, miny, mo and go marching off in whatever direction she landed on, brave as a tiger. I thought of all the times Jo had been in danger—the flood, the blizzard, the time she fell in the frozen lake. She'd always been fine. I straightened my back.

"Eeny, meeny, miny, mo," I whispered to myself, shivering.

I wasn't done with the rhyme when I saw the headlights. They were blurry and yellow in the falling snow, moving slowly. I moved closer to the edge of the road and began waving my arm back and forth. The headlights got closer and closer, and just when I thought they were gonna go right past me, they stopped. Then the door opened.

"Are you all right, girl?" said a man's voice.

I leaned down and poked my head inside of the warm car. It was so dark I could barely make out the man's face, but I could see a big black doctor's bag on the seat next to him, just like the one Dr. McDevitt kept in his office. He must be a doctor making a late call to someone sick, I reckoned.

"I just need a ride towards Tobacco Run, please," I said. Inside my head I was cursing that I hadn't come up with a good story to explain why I was standing there on the side of the road in the snow in the middle of the night.

"Where?" The man leaned towards me, and now I could see his face. He was older than my pa, with silver hair and a long nose. He looked me up and down. "You're running away from the training school," he said.

"No, sir," I said, pulling myself back.

He grabbed my wrist. His hand was cold and dry. "Get in, girl. I'll take you back. It's much too cold for nonsense."

For just a moment I thought about it. I could go back and slip into bed with Jean and get warm. Maybe they wouldn't even know I'd been gone.

No.

No.

I tore my arm away. I slammed the car door so hard and quick it must have hit the man in his long nose, cuz I could hear him yelp like a kicked dog.

Then I ran. I ran right across the road and into the field on the other side. I couldn't hear nothing but my own breath and the crunch of snow under my boots. I ran until my lungs burned. I didn't stop till I came to a barn. Almost ran right into it; I couldn't hardly see what with the dark and the snow.

I stopped and looked around. There was a farmhouse about a hundred paces away, with one light on in a downstairs window. I watched it for a few minutes, but I didn't see nobody. Then I looked back at the barn. It had a big door, barred with a piece of a wood. This was a fancy barn, fancier by a mile than what Jimmy Sproul had. I tried to lift the wood bar, looking back over my shoulder to make sure nobody was coming out of the farmhouse. My heart was beating so fast I felt dizzy. I better not faint. I'd freeze to death before anyone found me.

I heaved with all my strength, but I couldn't lift the wooden bar. In the faint light of the stars, I saw there was a chain around one end. Damnit. I crept around the side, looking for other ways in. On the back, opposite the main door, was a smaller door, with a pane of glass and a regular knob, like the door to a house. I tried it. Locked.

I felt around in the snow with my stinging fingers until I

found a rock. Looking around me again, I threw the rock against the door glass. It broke without hardly a sound. Carefully, I stuck my wrist through the opening and turned the knob from the inside.

The barn felt warm at first, compared to the outside. It was dark as ink and smelled sweet and dusty like hay. I felt my body relax. I crept forward with my hands in front of me. I'd find a corner to curl up in and wait out the snow. Maybe there was even a blanket or work coat hanging on a peg, which I could snatch to wear. Without the wind blowing, it was very quiet. My feet bumped into a pile of hay bales. I felt around to make sure there was no pitchfork or nothing else sharp sticking out. Then I sat down.

Oh, it felt so good to be sitting in a warm barn after running across the snowy fields for the past hour. Right away my eyelids began to fall. I tried to pry them open. What if I didn't wake up before dawn, and the farmer found me sleeping in his hay? But it was no good. At Casteen, my body had learned to sleep even when my mind was scared or angry. If it hadn't, I'd never have slept a wink. My eyelids settled shut.

Phrrrrrraawwww!

A loud wet rumbling sound in the darkness, not a foot from my head. I stood so quickly I fell right over. A scream stuck in my chest. I scooted my body behind the hay, shaking and shivering with the fear. What the heck?

Phrrewww!

Wait a second. I knew that sound. I stood, slowly, and crept forward with my hand out in the direction of the noise. A moment later my fingers touched the warm soft nose of a horse.

Of course there was a horse. That's who lived in barns. My shoulders fell and my body went limp like a rag, all that fear melting. I leaned against the stall door, stroking the horse's nose in the dark, for a good while. I imagined the horse was a girl and her name was Peaches.

"This is a nice barn," I whispered to Peaches. "I hope they treat you real nice here."

Peaches snuffled and I could feel her hot breath on my cold neck. I imagined she was a beautiful creamy white with a heart-shaped spot on her flank.

"I'm just gonna lie down for a minute if that's all right," I said to her. I slid down the stall door until I was sitting. I reckon I was asleep before my eyes even shut.

Chapter 27

CECILIA

1938

I roused to Peaches snuffling and stomping around her stall. I jumped to my feet, ready to fight any person that had come into the barn.

But there wasn't nobody there. Blue dawn light was seeping through the cracks of the barn walls. Now I could see that Peaches wasn't creamy white with a heart-shaped spot, but an ordinary dark brown. I could also see, as she sent a steaming rope of piss into the dust, that she wasn't a girl either. Oh well.

"Thanks for waking me up, Peaches," I said.

I did a quick look around the barn and saw—yes!—a jacket hanging from a peg on the far wall. Even better, there was a paper sack on the bench beneath the jacket, and when I opened it, I found it was full of dried apples. I wrapped myself in the coat, which was as big as a dress on me, and stuffed the sack in the coat pocket, after grabbing a handful to cram in my mouth. I gave Peaches one last pat on his shiny brown nose and crept out the back door of the barn.

I kept my eyes on the farmhouse as I backed away towards a stand of trees. But no one moved in the windows. The light was still on. Hidden snug in the trees, I looked all around. There was the farmhouse and barn on one side, and fields on the other two. I must have come through one of those fields, though my footprints were covered up by all the new snow that had fell in the night, so I couldn't tell which one. The snow shone cold and blue in the pale light. I hadn't never seen so much snow, and it gave me a bad feeling. The sky was gray with low clouds. On the far side of one of the fields there was a gray line. A road?

Keeping inside the trees, I made my way along the edge of the field. As I got closer to the gray line, I saw it wasn't a road. It was a creek. Goddamn it. Cussing at my bad luck, I got near enough to look over the edge. It was partly frozen over, but I could hear the water moving under the thin skin of ice. Though I was sore it wasn't a road, at least this meant I was going in the right way—away from where I'd come from—cuz I hadn't crossed no creek before. I looked back towards the farm. Nothing moved. Okay. I was gonna have to get across the water.

But how? The creek was shallow, so shallow some of the small rocks weren't even all the way covered. But it was too wide to jump. I looked around for some rocks or sticks to make a little bridge, but everything was covered in snow. Then I saw the tree.

It was a big live oak, with branches all twisted like an old person's fingers. One of the branches stretched out most of the way across the creek. If I climbed up and scootched across the branch, I could hop down on the other side.

I never had much cause to climb trees before. Like I've said, there was mostly just scrubby little pines down in Tobacco Run, with skinny trunks and branches that didn't even start till twice my height. But I reckoned I could do it. Using a knot as a step, I pushed myself into the lowest branch, then hooked my leg over the next highest, pulling myself up thataway. When

I came to the branch that crossed the creek, I got on my belly and started scootching. The cold rough bark, covered with a thin coat of ice, scraped at my belly even through my cloak. I wished I had a pair of dungarees like my brothers got.

I was halfway across when I did a fool thing. I looked down. It wasn't that high, but seeing the water below made me feel sick. Feeling sick made me grip the branch harder. Gripping the branch harder made my hands slide. The rest happened slowly, then all at once. My hands came away, and I slipped around the underside of the branch and hung there by my legs, like a possum. The apples fell out of my pocket and into the water.

For a moment I just looked around at the upside-down world. There was the barn, its weather vane now pointed downwards. The white field was the sky and the gray sky was the ground. Snow was falling again, and I felt flakes land inside my nose.

Then, for the second time in less than a day, I fell.

It was lucky, I reckon, that I landed on my back and not my head. There I lay, the creek water soaking the back of my coat and smock, so cold it felt like fire. I stood up, and a gust of snowy wind hitting my wet body almost made me scream.

This was bad. In one of the Chalet School books, Jo and Maureen fall through the ice in the big lake and get rescued by Gottfried. They have to get hot baths and hot blankets and something called schnapps to drink, and they're sick almost to dying for weeks and weeks anyway.

My feet were already losing their feeling. When I tried to take a step I almost fell. It was like walking on tree stumps.

Damnit.

I was gonna have to go to that farmhouse. There wasn't no other way. I didn't know what was on the other side of the creek; it could be miles and miles of fields. I wouldn't make it but ten minutes before I toppled right over. I had to go knock on the door. I had to.

Getting from the creek back to the farmhouse was the hardest thing I've done in my whole life, and I've hauled sacks of 'backer in summer suns hot enough to fry your neck since I was five years old. My legs were so senseless I had to swing them forward without bending my knees, the way a baby walks. I must have looked a ridiculous sight, swinging my legs like that in the snow. I hadn't gone but halfway when I began to feel tired like I'd never felt in my life. Tired like Jo must have felt when Dr. Jem gave her the ether gas for her tonsil operation. Like a big black nothing was surrounding me and pulling me into it. Maybe I could just take a rest. The snow looked soft. It didn't feel so cold at all, suddenly. I could just rest for a minute.

Then I saw Jean's face in the window. Her mouth was opening in a little circle. No, she said, though I couldn't hear her voice. No.

No. No. I couldn't lie down here. I wouldn't wake up. I thought of Ruthie in the graveyard behind the school, no marker to say who she'd been. If I died, they'd bury me there too. I thought of Dr. McDevil's bulgy fish eyes and imagined him saying, "Poor girl, probably best for society that she's gone, though." The thought made me so hot it shocked me into moving again. I wasn't gonna let that bastard win.

One of my legs was so frozen I had to use my hands to lift it to take that first step. I couldn't stop. I had to keep going. I kept my eyes fixed on the farmhouse's downstairs window, where the yellow light still shone. I'd count down from a hundred. When I got to zero I'd be there.

Ninety-nine. Ninety-eight. The skin of my cheeks felt like someone was peeling it off with a paring knife. I reached up to touch my face, sure there'd be blood on my hands. But there wasn't no blood, just my fingers, stiff and white as candlewax. Sixty, fifty-nine.

I reached the farmhouse porch before I got to twenty. I stared up at the steps. There was six of them, all covered with a perfect white layer of snow. Nobody'd been outside yet. Strange. Didn't someone get up in the morning to feed Peaches? I felt a panicky fear start in my chest. What if nobody was there? What if it was cold inside, with no hot bath or hot towels or schnapps to revive me?

I started on the steps, but I couldn't swing my frozen legs high enough to get up. My foot slid in the snow and I fell to the ground. It took a mighty effort to get back up. This time, I didn't try the steps, but just sort of pointed my body onto the porch itself and rolled. I lay there for a minute, staring up at the porch ceiling. It was painted pale blue—haint blue—the color folks rich enough for paint used to keep the ghosts away.

I must look like a ghost myself, I thought, with my frozen white skin and the snow in my hair. I wriggled towards the door and used the very last bit of my strength to knock.

For a long time there was nothing. No sounds. No footsteps.

"Help," I tried to shout, but the word came out a whisper.

If I died right here I was gonna haunt this farmhouse, haint blue paint or no.

Could ghosts feel cold? Did ghosts get to eat?

I was still wondering when the door opened.

"Oh my word," said a voice.

That's the last thing I remembered for a good long while.

WHEN I WOKE up I thought for sure I was dead. I tried to remember what the preacher used to say about going to heaven. Something about how we'd go up in the clouds to "meet the

Lord in the air." This must be it: heaven. I couldn't even feel my body. Was I an angel already? I'd never cared much for church, but I guessed the preacher was right all along. Was there food in heaven?

"Are you awake, sweetheart?" said a voice.

My eyes popped right open.

I wasn't dead. I wasn't an angel. My arms and legs were right there in front of me, covered up with a quilt. "Where am I?" I tried to say, but my tongue felt thick and heavy. I turned to the side and looked around.

I was laying in a big, beautiful bed in a big room. A pale bit of sun was shining through lace curtains. Sitting next to me in a rocking chair was an old lady with long white hair pinned up with a comb.

The old lady reached out and patted my shoulder with a hand all knotted like the tree I'd climbed. "You were frozen stiff as a board," she said. "Lucky my brother got here to tend the animals just in time. Vanda and I would never have been able to get you upstairs on our own."

I moved my arms. The bed I was laying on was so soft, that's why I couldn't feel nothing. I could tell I wasn't wearing my old smock or the barn coat no more. I had on something clean and warm. I raised an arm out from the covers to look—it was a white nightie with pale pink ribbons.

"Don't worry, Josiah turned his head while we got you dressed," the old lady said.

Is that what she thought I was thinking? That her old brother might have seen me bare? I almost laughed, then stopped myself. *Don't be rude*, I told myself sternly. You gotta make her like you.

"Thank you for saving me," I said, my voice coming out as a funny little croak.

"Well, it wouldn't have been very Christian to let a girl freeze to death on my own porch," she said.

I opened my mouth to speak, but she shushed me.

"It's all right," she said. "Let's get some warm broth in you first." She turned and called out the door. "Vanda! Some broth!"

A minute later a Negro lady in an apron came into the room carrying a tray. On the tray was a white bowl filled with steaming liquid. She put the tray on the table next to the bed. "Ma'am?" she asked.

The old lady raised her hand to wave her away. "Can you sit up enough to eat, dear?" she asked.

I pushed myself upright. Broth in bed! Just like in the Chalet School!

The old lady took the bowl and held a steamy spoonful of soup in front of my face.

Right away I felt silly. Nobody had ever fed me like a baby before. Probably not even my mama when I *was* a baby. In my house, by the time you were weaned you sat on the steps and gnawed an old biscuit like everybody else.

I leaned forward and slurped the broth. It was delicious. Maybe the most delicious thing I'd ever ate in my whole life. I forgot about feeling silly and just slurped and slurped that hot salty soup.

"Feel better, now?" the old lady said, putting down the spoon in the empty bowl.

I nodded. Now that I was revived, I took a better look at the lady. She was as old as anyone I'd ever seen. Her hair was pure white, and her pink scalp shone through it. Her eyes were cloudy blue and her face was wrinkled as a walnut. Her head drooped forward a bit, like a flower at the end of summer. She wore a thick black velvet ribbon around her neck. Attached to the ribbon was a silver circle with a picture inside, carved in white stone. It was a picture of a man, looking sideways so you could see the shape of his nose and chin.

The old lady saw me staring and reached her wrinkled hand to her throat. "You're looking at my cameo," she said. "That's my husband, Captain Pattishall, God rest his soul. He served at Fredericksburg."

I nodded. I reckoned she was talking about a war, but history wasn't never my best subject. Too busy reading.

"He's been gone near about twenty-five years," she went on. "That's what happens when a girl of seventeen marries a man of forty. She spends the last years of her life alone." Her pointy chin trembled, almost like she was gonna cry.

I looked around the room. The walls were covered in a pattern of big yellow roses—this must be what they talked about in books when they said "wallpaper." A gold mirror hung across from the bed. There was a dresser of a rich dark wood with a carved box and a silver brush on top. I'd never seen nothing like the room in my life, and that bed—oh my word—felt so good I might never stand on the floor again. Sure, it was sad that this lady's old husband was dead, but how bad could you feel when you lived in a house like this?

Be nice, I told myself. "I'm sorry 'bout your husband," I said. "He must have been a real nice man."

She nodded. "Thank you, dear," she said. "'Nice' is perhaps not the word many would have used about Captain Pattishall, but no one could dispute he was the best shot in all Lenoir County." She turned to look at me with those cloudy blue eyes. "Now, tell me, dear, how did you come to be on my porch on the coldest morning I can remember in my rather long life?"

Chapter 28

CECILIA

1938

Why didn't I lie?

I should have said I fell off a traveling circus train. I should have said I was a half orphan from New York City looking for my long-lost pa. I should have said I was a sleepwalker who wandered off from her house in the middle of the night. I'd read enough books. I knew how to make up a story.

But the old lady's milky blue eyes looked at me so trustingly, and the bed was so warm. My mind was slow and sleepy. Surely I could tell the truth. I'd tell her how Jean and I had been taken from our parents by lies. How we were being held prisoner in a terrible place by cruel doctors who said we were degenerates and made us eat mush and sew sheets till our fingers ached. For sure she'd want to help me then?

So I told her. That I was a girl runaway from the Casteen Training School. That I wasn't supposed to be there. That my sister was left behind, and I needed to rescue her. I told her about Matty Barnwell and his long arms and poor Ruthie.

When I was done talking I could feel tears starting in my eyes. I hadn't cried since I got to Casteen, but now I was weeping like a little baby.

The old lady reached out and patted my back. "There, there, dear—what a difficult time you've had."

I wiped my nose on the nightgown sleeve before I remembered I was supposed to be using good manners. "So you'll help me?" I asked. "Can you get the sheriff?"

"I'll go speak with him right now, dear," she said. "And I'll send Vanda up with something more solid for you to eat."

That made me cry even more. It was like once I started I couldn't stop. "Thank you," I sniveled.

The old lady stood up slowly and picked up a walking stick, which had been leaning against the bed. I hadn't noticed it before. It was wrapped in strips of brown leather and had a gold knob on top. Something about it made me shiver. I don't know why.

I lay back down against the fluffy pillows and looked at the big yellow roses in the wallpaper. When I had a big house one day maybe I'd have wallpaper too, I thought. Wouldn't do yellow, though. It doesn't suit me. I could see now, looking close, that the wallpaper was peeling at the edges and there were faint little smudges of black mold along the top, near the ceiling. Looking at the ceiling itself, I could see bulgy spots in the plaster, like blisters.

A few minutes later the Negro lady came back with another tray. This one had a plate with a slice of buttered bread and a slab of pink ham. In a little bowl was some cooked apples. Just looking at it made my stomach growl so loud I laughed.

The Negro lady didn't laugh. In fact, looking at her face, I noticed she looked . . . what? Not scared, exactly. More just uneasy like.

"You best eat quick," she said in a low voice.

Well, I was planning to. I always do. "Thank you," I said as she set the tray down on the bed next to me.

I expected her to leave, but she lingered, not looking at me. Finally, she turned. She opened her mouth to speak, but as she did there was a creaking on the stairs. She whipped around quick as a squirrel and was out the door.

The old lady came back in. Behind her was an old man. There was no mistaking that he was her brother. He had the same milky blue eyes beneath big, bulgy eyelids, and the same long neck. He wore a work jacket just like the one I'd snatched from the hook in the barn. A smell of animal came off him. He must have been out feeding Peaches.

Both of them stood at the foot of the bed, looking down at me. Made me feel strange. Reminded me of the way Dr. McDevitt looked me up and down in his office on that first day at Casteen.

"Hello," I said.

They didn't answer.

"Well, what do you think, Josiah?" said the old lady after a minute.

"Hmm," said the old man.

Whatever this was, I didn't like it. I drew my feet up towards my bottom, so I could spring up if I needed to.

"My brother is a man of few words," said the old lady, speaking to me. She turned to him. "Is that a 'yes'?"

The old man looked at me for another few seconds. The skin on my neck began to prickle. Finally, he nodded.

The old lady smiled for the first time. Her teeth were very long. "Good, good."

"What's going on?" I asked.

The old lady nodded to her brother, and he left the room. She hobbled back to the rocking chair and sat. "My brother and I have a proposal for you."

"A proposal?"

"A question."

"I know what a proposal means," I said, hearing the peevishness in my voice. I couldn't keep being polite if these people were gonna act so strange!

"My brother, Josiah, lives just over the field yonder," she said. "Beautiful house—the first one our great-grandfather built when he settled here back in 1801. He used to own all the land for miles around. Till the war, of course." Her face grew sour and even more shriveled. "Josiah's getting on in years, as you can see, and can't cook or clean. Vanda helps out, but she's got her duties over here, and she's getting on as well. I believe what Josiah really needs is a girl."

"A girl?"

"A girl." The old lady looked at me hard, and her blue eyes didn't look so milky all of sudden—they looked sharp and clear.

"You want me to work for your brother? Like a maid?"

I thought of Sally and Vera back at Casteen, how they'd worked as maids for the rich man who said they stole his candlesticks. Sally and Vera were lazy, but I was a hard worker. I didn't steal. Not when I didn't have to, at least. I'd be a good maid. But what about Jean? Would they let her come? I was about to ask, when I saw the old lady was shaking her head.

"It wouldn't be proper for a young white girl to be living with a man," she said. "You'd have to do it properly."

"Properly?"

The old lady laughed, a sound like bare branches scraping together. "You'd have to marry first, my dear."

I blinked. Marry that man? He was older than Dr. McDevitt! Was she joking? But I could see from her face she was not.

The old lady must have noticed my surprised look, because she said in a gentle voice, "Be reasonable, dear. Josiah is seventy-eight. His heart is poor. You wouldn't have to bear it very long. Not like I did. Captain Pattishall was forty when we married, which seemed very old to me back then. But I had to bear him for thirty years."

My jaw just hung open like the moron they said I was. Then I thought of Bertie Lou, who'd gotten in trouble in the hayloft with the Negro farmhand. She always said they were "engaged to be married," even though that was against the law.

"I'm engaged," I said quickly.

"Oh!" said the old lady. "To whom, may I ask? I didn't realize engagements were allowed among residents at your . . . your . . . institution."

"A boy back home," I said. "John."

"John?"

"John Spencer. His family works the plot of land next to ours."

As I talked I could see this John Spencer rise in front of my eyes. He had wheat-colored hair and a friendly smile with a little gap between his two front teeth. We would walk in the evenings around the edge of the 'backer field and talk about baseball. Sometimes his little brothers would tag along after us, giggling. I smiled to myself, imagining John Spencer.

"I see," said the old lady. "Does John Spencer own his own home? Has he prospects for the future?"

I felt a little bit sore for John Spencer, even though he wasn't real. "He's gonna build me a nice house," I said. "With a shingle roof."

"Oh, a shingle roof," said the old lady, her mouth twisted in a mean little smile. "Well, by all means, I won't come between you and a shingle roof."

"Sorry," I said. "Your brother seems real nice."

"It's fine, my dear, I'll go tell Josiah, and we can figure out your situation." She stood up and hobbled out of the room on her walking stick.

I should have wondered why it took so long for the old lady to come back. I should have paid heed to Vanda when she said to eat quick and gave me a hard look. Instead, I just lay there enjoying my warm bed.

(But can you really blame me? I hadn't never felt nothing like it in my life.)

I must have fell back asleep, because I woke up to a new voice. A man's voice. A voice that I knew so far down in my soul that my whole body ran cold before I'd never opened my eyes.

The room got darker as his big body filled up the doorway and blocked the light from the hall.

"Hello, Cecilia," said Dr. McDevitt. "You've had a little adventure, haven't you?"

Chapter 29

CECILIA

1938

The drive back to Casteen was so short it made me ashamed. I hadn't gotten any farther than a squirrel could run.

Dr. McDevitt stopped the car at the gate and opened my door. "We're going to put you in the jacket," he said, "so the other girls can see what happens when someone runs away."

"Don't you even dare." My body filled with an anger that felt both hot and cold at once. I'd seen the jacket. It had long sleeves that tied behind the back so you couldn't use your hands. I once saw a poor girl fall over while wearing one and bust her nose so bad blood sprayed on the cafeteria wall.

Dr. McDevitt nodded at Matty Barnwell, who was standing by the side of the car. Matty Barnwell smiled. He came at me, holding the jacket.

I pulled back my leg and kicked him square in the throat. He fell back, his hands scrabbling at his neck. I thought for a second I'd killed him, and I felt nothing but glad. But he wasn't dead, just angry, and he got up and came flying towards me. The jacket was over my head and my arms were tied up in ten seconds flat.

"I'mma make this extra tight, stop you acting like a bitch in heat," Matty Barnwell whispered as he pulled me out of the car.

Then they marched me into the main building and into the cafeteria. It was dinnertime, and everyone was sitting down, eating their mush and biscuits. When they saw me, everyone started to whisper till the warden thumped her hand on the wall and shouted, "Hush up!"

"Just wanted everyone to see that we've got Cecilia back safe and sound," Dr. McDevitt said. "We'll be taking her to have a nice long rest while she calms down."

Even worse than the jacket was the look on Jean's face when she saw me standing there. Her dark eyes got so big and sad. She could see that I'd failed. I hadn't gotten help. I'd only gotten us further from ever getting away from this place. She started to come towards me, but Miss Grieve stepped up and put a hand on her shoulder.

His long fingers on the back of the jacket, Matty Barnwell pulled me towards the staircase. Isolation. The basement. Whatever. I didn't care no more. I'd slept in a barn and walked soaking wet through the snow. The basement wasn't gonna hurt me.

But they didn't take me to the basement. They took me to the infirmary. Matty Barnwell propped me up like a rag doll on the bed under the window—the same bed where Ruthie had laid, screaming—and tied the sleeves of the jacket to the bedpost. Then he left.

I lay there for what felt like an hour or more, my hands crossed over my chest. My ankle itched something terrible, but I couldn't move to scratch it. I should have lied to that old lady about where I'd come from. I should have said I'd marry her shriveled-up corn husk of a brother. I could have gotten away later. But I'd told the goddamn truth, and now I was back here tied to a bed. I'd failed. I'd failed Jean. The fury of it all made my ankle itch worse, and I wanted to holler, but didn't want to give them the satisfaction.

After a long while, Dr. McDevitt came in. He was still wearing the black suit he'd worn to come get me, though he'd tucked the tie inside the shirt and had his white coat on over it. His face was especially red and he wore a jolly little smile above his beard.

It scared me, that smile.

"I had a little talk with Miss Leigh, Cecilia," he said, coming closer. I could smell the sweet, burnt smell of the pipe he kept in his pocket. "We agreed that your behavior has become an unacceptable risk, not just for you but for society."

"I didn't do nothing to that old lady!" I shouted.

He laughed. "No, no, I'm sure you charmed her. But that just shows the danger, Cecilia. What if you ran away again and met someone less morally upright than Mrs. Pattishall and her brother? What if he had been a different kind of man, or a younger man, and had accepted your wanton entreaties?"

"My what?"

"Fortunately, we have a way to help, Cecilia." His voice was warm and twinkly, but his words made me colder and colder. "A way to protect you, and to protect society from you."

I felt ice in my stomach and drew my knees towards my body. "A way to help?"

"Yes, Cecilia." He nodded, his fish eyes scary bright. His mouth looked very wet and pink surrounded by that snow-white beard as he spoke. "I've been lucky enough to study with Dr. William Allan at the North Carolina Medical College in Charlotte. He's pioneering an exciting new method to improve the bloodlines of our nation. It's very simple, really. You're a farm girl, right, Cecilia?"

I nodded. My heart was beating so hard in my throat it felt like it might come out my mouth.

"Tell me, then, when there's a weak or lame animal on the

farm, do you allow it to breed? Or do you use your strongest stock?"

"We grow tobacco," I whispered.

Dr. McDevitt gave a big cheery laugh and sat down on my bed. I could feel the heat coming off his heavy body like it was one of them radiators. "I'm sure you can grasp the principle, nonetheless. If we allow degenerates to breed, they simply produce more degenerates. Weak-minded, promiscuous, idle, unable to care for themselves and their children. You see, Cecilia, this is for your benefit as well—imagine you trying to care for a child! It would be a catastrophe."

I wanted to say I'd cared for my little brothers and Jean since I was barely tall enough to reach the water dipper. I wanted to say I'd picked tobacco from sunup to sundown with nothing but a grease-soaked biscuit to eat. I wanted to say I'd never known an idle day in my goddamn life. But I couldn't make my mouth move.

It was then that I saw Matty Barnwell had come back into the room, quiet as one of the daddy longlegs that crept along the walls of our privy in summer. Dr. McDevitt nodded, and he sidled forward. He wasn't smiling, but his eyes were bright, like a child about to get a present.

"Ah, Matty, we're just waiting on Nurse Chilcott," Dr. McDevitt said. He had something in his hands. It was a bottle. ANESTHETIC ETHER, the label said. HIGHLY FLAMMABLE.

I couldn't have told you what "anesthetic" or "ether" was, but the words put a fear into me like nothing I'd known before. The air felt heavy and strange the way it does before a thunderstorm. Something was about to happen.

"I'm sorry," I whispered. "I'll be good."

"Yes, Cecilia," Dr. McDevitt said. "You will be now."

The nurse came in with a tray, and suddenly Dr. McDevitt was holding something shiny and metal.

"No." I tried to raise my arms, but of course they were crossed over my chest and tied down.

Matty Barnwell took another step forward. His head blocked out the ceiling light, like a giant blocking out the sun.

"No," I said again, but I'm not sure I made any sound.

"Restrain her in the usual way," said Dr. McDevitt.

Matty Barnwell's spider hands pushed my forehead down hard against the bed. I struggled against him, but I couldn't move an inch. Dr. McDevitt licked his pink lips and leaned over me. He held out the shiny thing the nurse gave him: it was a little mask made of wire, like you'd put on a mad dog. A whining sound came up from somewhere deep in my body, and I felt my bladder go in a hot gush. Dr. McDevitt pressed the mask over my mouth. He put a white cloth on top, then dropped a bit of liquid from the anesthetic ether bottle on the cloth.

I held my breath for as long as I could. I saw little Ruthie, her fingers digging into my hand, begging me to take her back to the third floor. *I don't want to spend another night here, I can't.* I saw Jean, her eyes wide and disappointed.

No.

No.

But everybody's got to breathe sooner or later. I gasped and sucked in warm air smelling like rotten fruit and kerosene. The room went hazy, the way the 'backer fields look on a boiling August afternoon. I heard buzzing like a mosquito in my ears. I don't remember nothing else.

THE NEXT THING I knew, I was on another bed in the infirmary. My head ached and my middle felt funny, heavy and stinging. I tried to sit up, and the room seemed to tilt like it was shoved on its side. I gagged.

The nurse shoved a metal pan in front of my face. "Don't mess the sheets," she said.

I sicked up a bit of green water into the pan, and the sicking up made my middle explode into pain so bright I saw yellow stars. It was like someone had made me a belt of barbed wire and was twisting it tighter and tighter. I reached down to touch my stomach, to make it stop, but the nurse grabbed my hand.

"You'll spoil the stitches," she said.

"The what?" My voice was all wobbly, like Pa's when he'd been on a tear with the moonshine.

The nurse didn't answer.

I fell into a strange sleep with strange dreams. A snake as big as a man slithered out of the 'backer and bit my middle. Mrs. Pattishall stood by my bed and raised her gold-topped walking stick like Moses about to part the Red Sea. Tommy Rawhead smiled and his mouth was full of blood.

I think I screamed, but maybe I was just dreaming.

It wasn't till some hours later that I was alone and awake enough to pull my gown up. When I did, I almost sicked up again. There was a big white bandage from one hip bone to the other. It was wet with some kind of yellow liquid, and spots of dark red blood showed through here and there. The pain was hot and sharp and throbbing and sick making all at the same time. I'd never felt the like of it, not even when I broke my leg.

I thought of Mollie and her raggedy pink scar.

"Did I have an appendix?" I asked Nurse Chilcott when she came back later.

She smiled at me with too many teeth, her eyes dark and dead like the infirmary skeleton. "Yes, but Dr. McDevitt fixed you up properly."

IT WAS JACY who explained it to me, when I came back to the dormitory after two weeks. I was still walking funny; if I came down too hard on my heels, the pain shot through me and I had to stop and lean against the wall to gather my breath. But I was so glad to be out of the infirmary; I'd been sleeping in the day and staying up all night to make sure Matty Barnwell didn't creep anywhere near me.

"They took your womb," Jacy said plainly, sitting down on the edge of my bed. "You won't get no monthly anymore, so that part's good."

"But ain't the womb where the baby grows?" I asked. You don't watch your mama have half a dozen babies without learning something.

"It's all right," Jacy said, patting my arm. "Girls like us don't make proper mamas. It's better like this."

I lay down and folded my arms across my chest like a dead person. I couldn't talk. I couldn't barely think. *They took my womb.* They pinned me down to a bed and smothered me with ether and cut me open and took my womb.

I don't know if I would have wanted babies one day. It never looked too good, the way my mama did it—a newborn mewling and sucking at her breast, another baby in shitty diapers at her feet. But that wasn't their choice to make! That was my choice. They had no goddamn right.

If we allow degenerates to breed, they simply produce more degenerates, McDevil had said.

What the hell did they know. My babies—if I'd have had them—might have been presidents or doctors or even run their own schools. They might have had my pretty hair. They might have loved the Chalet School books. They might have curled up next to me at night and said, "Read just one more page,

Mama." And, heck, they might have been dumb as Jimmy Sproul, but I'd have loved them anyway. *If* I'd have had them. If I'd have wanted them. If I'd have decided. Me.

I thought I'd known anger before. When they cut my hair. When they measured my parts with the caliper. When they fed us mush instead of milk and eggs. When they killed Ruthie.

But when I learned what they'd done to me in that infirmary, it was like all those angers came together into a power as big and bright as the sun. Like if I opened my mouth, I'd scream so loud every window in the building would bust into a million pieces. Like if I raised my hands, fire would come shooting from my fingertips. Like if I stomped my feet, I'd crack the world apart.

But I couldn't stomp my feet. I couldn't barely move. I just sat in class with the cut on my middle prickling like someone was twisting the barbed wire, and Miss Pritchard still fussing at me to sit up straight.

I sat up straight. I pulled my face into a mask.

I couldn't show my anger. Not here. Not now.

I was gonna have to escape again. This time I wouldn't make the stupid mistake of telling the truth. I'd thought the old lady in the farmhouse would hear my story and want to do the right thing. But I'd been wrong. From now on, I'd need to reckon that everyone who met me only saw what Dr. McDevitt saw: a "degenerate," nobody worth helping.

I'd need to become someone else.

Chapter 30

MILLIE

1939

"Eugenics," I said, the word heavy and ugly in my mouth. "Sterilization. I've read about that."

"What?"

"What Dr. McDevitt told you, about being prevented from breeding. They're doing that in Europe too. Mr. Hitler, the leader in Germany, he's made a policy of it. Sterilizing the 'unfit.' Fanny says it's quite disgusting, that what he really wants is to have a country full of blond-haired, blue-eyed Christians by any means possible."

"You don't say! Guess I'd fit right in there," said Cecilia, cackling. "Funny, huh, that I ain't worth a damn here, but they'd like me over there just cuz of my hair. People are just plum stupid."

"How can you laugh?" I said, the words coming out harsher than I'd expected.

"Oh, what, I should sit here crying boo-hoo I can't have no babies?" Cecilia said. "Wouldn't do me much good, now, would it?" She turned to the window and was quiet for a moment.

"Wouldn't mind reading the Chalet School books to a little girl one day, though. Even if she wasn't mine."

I thought again of what Sophie had said at the wedding. That I was wallowing in my grief. That wasn't right, exactly. A pig enjoyed wallowing in mud. I didn't enjoy anything about my situation. I just felt entirely stuck in it, like a fly drowning in a pickle vat, beating its wings but going nowhere.

Cecilia had been through something unspeakably awful, yet here she was, upright, smiling, making plans. I wasn't sure if I admired that or found it suspicious. Perhaps both.

I thought about my time in the hospital at Dix Hill. Surely many of the women in the ward would be deemed "unfit" to become mothers. If I'd been less fortunate, if it had been another kind of facility, if I hadn't had a family who'd shown up every day at my bedside, could I have been tied up and ethered too, marked forever as bad, unworthy, insane? Nellie Bly had found that the asylum itself drove people mad—fed rotten food, forced to sit in the cold surrounded by rats. It didn't matter if you'd gone in perfectly sane; you'd come out cracked.

I shook my head to remove the image. "So when you decided to pretend to be someone else, rather than tell me your true story, how did you come up with the particulars? Do you speak Swedish?"

Cecilia leaned back against the kitchen counter in a leisurely way and laughed. She shoved another cookie into her mouth before answering through a mouthful of crumbs. "I made it up in bits and pieces as I went along, but y'all helped."

"Helped?" I felt irritated again, being wrong-footed by Cecilia like I was another enemy.

"You and Fanny and your cousins, y'all kept on about 'the bad Swede this,' 'the bad Swede that.' I was playing mute, not deaf! I listened, and I reckoned: Now, here's a foreigner who speaks a foreign language who don't mind lying. Here's someone who will help me, if I just give him something he wants."

Suddenly it was perfectly clear. "The brooch."

"The brooch. I told him it was my rich old aunt's, worth a bundle. Pretty sure it's just tin, though, ha!"

I *had* noticed that she'd been wearing the brooch before she saw the Swede and that it was gone after. Why had I ignored my own eyes?

"And how did you create the story about your rich father, the uncle who tried to kill you?"

Cecilia smiled. A proud smile. "Chalet School book number three. *The Princess of the Chalet School.* My very favorite one. It's where a princess from Belsornia comes to the Chalet School, but nobody knows she's a princess—she's keeping it a secret, cuz her uncle's after her, trying to kill her so he can be king and have all the money. But she and Jo get him good!"

"Belsornia?"

"Yeah, I looked at your little globe ball and couldn't find it neither. Reckon it's a made-up place. But princesses—they're real."

"Well, yes, in some places."

"It's a funny old thing, princesses," she went on, starting in on another cookie. "You get to be a princess because your parents are kings and queens. It's in your blood. Dr. McDevitt said I was wayward and degenerate because my parents were bad, low people and I shouldn't have no babies, because my babies would be bad and low too. But a princess, a princess is someone good by nature. The opposite of me, right? I know there ain't princesses in America, so I didn't say that part of the story. But I liked imagining it, imagining being someone like the princess at the Chalet School—someone so good by her blood that nobody could ever say nothing different."

"What was her name, the princess character in the book?" I asked.

"Reckon you can guess, can't you?"

"Elisaveta."

"Elisaveta."

Chapter 31

CECILIA

1939

By the time the sweet corn was ready to harvest out in the west field, I knew it was time. I was ready. I had a new bag hidden beneath my bed—I'd spent weeks sneaking by the kitchen after supper, chatting with the poor lonely Negro girl who washed the dishes, telling big funny stories so she didn't notice me slipping apples and bits of salt pork into my pockets. I also had a new plan. I'd figured, by watching the delivery trucks coming and going from the third-floor window, which way was Kinston town. The girl who washed dishes had said there was a train station there. I'd walk to Kinston, find the train station, and head towards Wilmington to find my sister Luelle. She had more sense than Mama; for sure she'd know how to help.

This time, I didn't jump out the window. Couldn't have, anyway—they'd put new bars on the ones in the dormitories, tighter than before.

This time, I knew I needed someone's help. I just needed to combine my words—as Dr. McDevil would say—in the right way to make them give it to me.

"Men only want one thing," Jacy had said.

I guess I'd find out if that was true.

I WAITED FOR a Sunday morning. Dr. McDevil didn't work on "the Lord's Day." Sometimes we'd see him driving past the building in his shiny green car with tires the color of fresh milk, his wife beside him, her face hidden by a big church hat. When everyone else was walking to the cafeteria, I slipped out of line and hid in the stairwell while they passed. Being Sunday, breakfast would be extra-long, since the preacher would be there to read from the Bible and tell us stories about Jonah and the Whale and Daniel in the Lion's Den like we were little kiddies. I'd have plenty of time.

I hadn't gone near the infirmary since my "appendix," and just getting near the door with the big red cross on it made my heart beat faster and my scar throb. I opened the door real slow, feeling sweaty and cold and hot all at once.

Rawhead and Bloody Bones,
steals naughty children from their homes.

There he was, crouched like a giant spider on his little cot behind the desk, reading the funny pages. There was a plate sitting next to him, with a biscuit sandwich—ham and cheese, looking like—and two boiled eggs.

Goddamn Matty Barnwell got fresh eggs?

"Hi," I said.

He looked up and frowned at me with his wide ugly mouth. "What are you doing in here? Ain't it breakfast time?"

"I cut my knee on a nail in the barn yesterday, and Miss Pritchard says I should put ointment on it so I don't get lockjaw." I spoke in a soft voice, the way old Mollie imitated herself talking to the soldiers when she was a floozy.

"Dr. McDevitt's not here."

"I know. I thought you could help me."

Matty Barnwell looked confused.

"You know about medicine and things, don't you?"

And sure enough, Matty Barnwell smiled. "Well, I know a few things, course." He stood up, and all of a sudden he was at his full height, staring down at me.

I swallowed my fear and smiled back. "Thanks."

He pulled the key ring off his pants loop and unlocked the top cabinet. Inside I could see the bottles of ether, the glass winking in the light like an evil eye. I had to stop myself from shivering. He ran his long skinny fingers along a row of bottles—blue, green, brown, clear. He plucked out a little white tin and held it up to read. "This should do the trick," he said. He handed it to me.

I opened my mouth, then stopped. How could I get the words to come out without choking? Then I thought of Jean's face, of Ruthie's face, and forced myself: "I thought you could do it, Matty."

Matty Barnwell froze. For a second, I was scared he was going to start hollering about me being wanton and degenerate. But then he just raised his eyebrows and tilted his head and said blusteringly, "Course I will."

Instead of sitting down on one of the infirmary beds, I sat down on Matty Barnwell's cot. I pulled my bloomers down and raised my smock up over my knee. I had a feeling in my stomach like if I moved my head too fast I might be sick, but I took a big breath. Matty Barnwell sat down next to me, his eyes big and round in his Tommy Rawhead face. He opened the tin of ointment.

"Where's the cut?"

"Right here," I said, drawing the smock up higher.

Matty Barnwell bit his lip. "That ain't your knee."

I made myself look up at him through my eyelashes, made myself smile through the sick feeling. "Reckon it ain't."

I would have done whatever needed doing. I would have laid with Matty Barnwell the way old Mollie laid with the soldiers. I was ready for that. I'd just close my eyes and pretend it was me and Jimmy Sproul behind the cheneyberry tree back home. I could feel Matty Barnwell's hot stinking dog breath on my face as he opened the tin and scooped some ointment onto the tip of his long finger. He put the key ring down on the cot next to me. Then he dipped his hand under my smock. He moved his finger back and forth roughly like he was trying to rub an ink spot off a desk.

"Oh, that feels nice," I said, shifting to cover the keys with one leg. "You're good at that."

Men go crazy for it when you say, "Oh, you're so smart, you're so good, you're my big, big hero," Mollie had said. *Dumb bastards.*

Matty Barnwell's hand moved up. "Oh," I said, and I shifted again to push the keys into my smock pocket. Matty Barnwell made a sound halfway between a cough and a hiccup. A look came over his face like someone caught him on the privy. "Oh," he said, but it was a different kind of "oh." There was a dark stain at the crotch of his brown pants.

I looked away real quick, then jumped up and pulled up my bloomers. "Thank you, Matty," I said, and I made myself smile, hoping this would be the last time in my whole life I had to make myself smile when I really wanted to scream.

Matty Barnwell's mouth opened and closed again like a dead fish's.

I walked back to the dormitory just as slow and innocent as anything. I could hear the preacher's droning voice coming up through the stairwell. Good. I got my new bag from under the loose tile near the radiator. Then I walked down the back stairs.

I unlocked the side door, the one we used to go to the barn. The grounds warden was gone on Sundays too, for the Lord. I stepped outside. The summer sun was so bright it made me blink.

I was free again. This time, I'd do whatever it took to stay free. Whatever it took.

THERE WAS ONE thing I had to do before I left the grounds.

It was dark and cool inside Auntie Sybil's cottage, and there was almost no furniture, just a desk and an armchair in the front room, and a bed and dresser in the back. On the dresser was a small wooden box. I tried to push the latch open, but it wouldn't go. I picked it up and shook it. Nothing. I was about to smash it on the floor when I realized there was a small button on the latch. I pushed it, and the whole thing popped open and a strange tinkly song began to play. I was so surprised I almost dropped it.

Inside was that awful gray-and-black flower pin she'd been wearing the day she came to snatch me and Jean. There was also—yes!—a small wedge of folded dollar bills and a little pile of quarters. I stuck the pin and the money in my sack with the food. I put the music box back on the dresser. Someone, somewhere, sometime gave Auntie Sybil that box, back when she was a human and not a monster. I thought again of that day, one year ago almost exactly, when she'd appeared at the edge of our field, promising milk and eggs and real school. How trustful we were, getting into her big car, all excited to have a chocolate bar!

I'd die before I let anyone trick me like that again.

I slipped back out of the cottage and through the front gate. It was hot and pretty out, and the sky was a bright clear blue, but my insides still felt cold, like a part of me didn't believe I was really out of Casteen. I didn't want to walk on the side of the road in case someone saw me, so I stuck to the shadows of the trees along the edge of the fields. A few times I saw farmers among the crops, but I just kept walking, pretending I was on my way home from church or something. If I didn't look scared they wouldn't think anything. Nobody said a thing, and my body began to relax. After a while, I felt good, loose and happy in a way I hadn't felt in a long, long time.

I hadn't been walking but an hour when Kinston town appeared out of the 'backer fields. First there was a little grocery and filling station with a sign for boiled peanuts. Then a church and cemetery. Not five minutes later I was walking on a real sidewalk among brick buildings with painted signs. Fresh seafood! Finest tobacco! Auto repair! I passed another church, this one like a castle in a fairy-tale book, with big colored windows and towers with crosses on top. I could hear people inside, singing. I smiled. It was almost like the Lord was helping me out, keeping all those people busy.

On the other side of the street was the tallest building I'd ever seen—three times higher than Caswell, with a pointy red roof poking at the sky. HOTEL KINSTON said the sign in front. A man was standing beneath the sign wearing a funny little round hat and a jacket with gold buttons. I could feel his eyes running up and down my body in its Casteen smock and bloomers. I had a plan for this too. As soon as I passed a yard with laundry pinned to the line, I ran back and snatched the first thing I could grab. It turned out to be a white bedsheet and a pair of men's pajama pants, with a waist about twice as big as mine. That was just fine with me. I crouched down in an alley and shucked off my smock and bloomers, leaving only my undershirt, then pulled on the pants and knotted them at the waist so they wouldn't fall down. The sheet I draped around my shoulders and pulled it tight around my neck, like a cape. I pinned Auntie Sybil's brooch to the front, to keep it closed, and put the keys in the nice deep pajama pockets.

I knew I looked mighty strange. But I didn't look like a Casteen girl no more. As I walked out of the alley I could already feel myself standing taller than before.

I came to a corner where a man was selling newspapers. I dug one of the quarters out of my pocket. "A Pepsi, please," I said.

He pulled a bottle out of his ice chest and popped it open with a hiss. He handed it to me, along with two dimes.

"And can you tell me where to find the train station?" I asked, taking a drink. The cool bubbly sweetness felt so good in my throat after the long hot walk that I almost laughed with the pleasure of it.

"Down yonder about five minutes, miss," he said, pointing down the street.

Miss! Never in my life had anyone called me "miss." "Girl," maybe, or more like just "hey you." Now, wearing my strange bloomers and cape with my nose in the air, I was "miss." Just because I had a quarter in my pocket.

The train station was a long skinny brick building with a wide roof. I went to the window that said TICKETS and asked the girl sitting there when the next train came.

"You want the four thirty to Atlantic Beach, or the five o'clock to Raleigh?" she asked, looking up and down at my clothes with eyes bulging like a frog's.

"When's the one to Wilmington?"

The girl gave me a look. "This line don't go to Wilmington. You want Wilmington, you've got to go to Goldsboro, get the Coast Line. But the Coast Line's already left, so you'll have to wait till tomorrow."

"Is Atlantic Beach near Wilmington?" I wished now I'd

taken a rest from reading long enough to pay attention to Mrs. Randall's geography lessons.

The girl shrugged. "Near enough, I reckon. Both at the coast."

At the coast. I imagined Luelle walking on the beach, in the sand, like I'd read about in books. I'd never seen the ocean, never seen any water bigger than Sproul's millpond. But I imagined it perfectly in my mind. Big as the 'backer fields, blue as the sky.

"One ticket to Atlantic Beach," I said.

"Class?" the girl said, her froggy eyes all wide.

"Huh? I mean, *excuse me*?"

"First class? Second?"

"How much is it?"

"Fifty cents for second, a dollar fifty for first."

I reckoned I ought to save as much of the money I'd taken from Auntie Sybil as I could. But oh, those words—*first class*—filled me with so much want. I knew this was the kind of wanting that got me in trouble. The kind of wanting that said I deserved books and sweet rolls with jam and to kiss Jimmy Sproul's pretty pink lips under the cheneyberry tree even if his whole family thought I was nothing but field trash.

I looked up at the girl with what I hoped was a haughty expression. "Actually, I remembered that my fiancé already paid for a first-class ticket for me in Atlantic Beach," I said. "You're meant to give it to me here."

The girl gawped for a moment, then craned her neck around like she was looking for someone to tell her what to do. She stared again at my strange gown and my fancy brooch. Finally she just handed me the ticket without a word and stared as I walked onto the platform.

She does know her words, and she combines them interestingly, Dr. McDevitt said.

Well, I guess he was right. I *could* combine my words interestingly—I could use them to pluck train tickets out of thin air. I smiled to myself.

Chapter 32

CECILIA

1939

The train was wonderful and scary. It pulled into the station with a hiss like a big old cat spitting. Before it started to move, it blew a whistle so loud I jumped halfway out of my seat. But once it started going, it was the most amazing thing I'd felt in my life. All the 'backer and corn fields rushing past out the window so fast they looked like smears of green and yellow. There were houses too, little brown dots, nothing you could even keep your eyes on before they were gone. Was this what it felt like to be a bird flying over the farms of Lenoir County, all the people tiny little nothings below?

The first-class seats were soft dark green. The sun fell through the window and warmed my face, and my head lolled against those soft seats. Luelle would be so happy to see me. How long had it been? Two years? Or three? Barney, the baby, was still tiny; I remember him reaching out his fat little hands to pat her face before she walked out the door and down the dirt road that split the field. When we rescued Jean, we could all live together in a big house in Wilmington. I closed my eyes. Another minute, and I would have fallen asleep.

Thank goodness I didn't. Because just then the train stopped for what felt like a tick too long. My eyes snapped open, and I felt the hairs on the back of my arms stand up.

Then I saw them. Police. Two of them, sidling along the way men do when they're in no hurry because they know they're in charge. One of them held a club and was swinging it in slow lazy circles as they moved down the aisle.

I picked up a newspaper from the seat next to me and held it in front of my face. The police kept moving, closer and closer. I held my breath and made my body absolutely still, the way I used to play hide-and-seek in the corn. The police leaned over to talk to a man a few rows up, and as soon as their eyes turned I leapt up, walked fast as I could down the aisle, and closed myself in the little room at the end of the train with a sign above the door that said SERVICE.

"Service" turned out to mean "commode." Phew. It smelled fouler here than the privy in August. The floor was slippery and yellowish water was sloshing around in the stopped-up sink. The toilet bowl opened directly through the bottom of the train. Peering into it, I could see the tracks speeding by below. What a thing! I latched the door but pushed it open a little bit. Through the crack I could see the policemen moving down the aisle again. They passed where I'd been sitting and kept going out of view.

I stayed still. A minute passed, then another. I'd just stay here until the train got to Atlantic Beach, then I'd slip off in the crowd. But a moment later there was a tug at the door, then a hard, angry-sounding knock. "Excuse me," a woman said. "Excuse me. My little boy needs the commode."

I froze. If I didn't say anything, maybe she'd think the commode was broken, and she'd move down the train to find another one. This was a long train; there had to be more than one commode?

But then she rattled at the door again. "I saw you go in there."

I stayed quiet. Please go away. Please go away.

"Do I need to get the conductor?" she called.

"Just a minute," I said in my best fancy-lady voice.

"Mommy, I need to go," said a child.

Damnit. I opened the door a crack, casting my eyes down the aisle. It seemed clear, so I stepped out. I pushed past the woman and her hopping-up-and-down boy and walked back to my seat. I opened up the newspaper. Maybe the police had stopped at the back of the train and sat down?

But not a moment later I heard them again. They were behind me, not far back from the sound of it, talking to somebody in their slow deep voices.

I wondered if the train window opened. I wondered what would happen to a body, jumping at such a speed.

But lucky me, just then the train gave a bone-shivering hiss and started to slow down. Buildings rose up around us, and then a platform appeared. A wooden sign swinging on chains from the edge of the platform roof said NEW BERN.

I stood up, still holding my newspaper, and moved towards the front of the train. We were still moving, but slowly now, and the conductor opened the door and began tossing bags to a worker standing on the platform. I walked towards him slowly. *Just be normal. Ain't nothing to see.*

"Miss," said a man's voice behind me.

My heart began flopping in my throat like a dead fish. I kept walking.

"Miss," said the voice again. "Excuse me."

The train was still moving. Goddamn it, how long did it take to stop this thing?

I heard one low voice speaking to another. Were they about to grab me, to wrestle me to the floor like Matty Barnwell had done that time a first-floor girl had a fit in the cafeteria, her head and hands slamming against the floor over and over?

I wasn't gonna wait to find out. I pushed past the conductor, stood at the edge of the train step, and jumped.

I landed on my feet, and for a moment I thought everything was fine. But then my ankle rolled and I pitched forward onto the ground. My chin hit first, and I tasted blood, hot and salty. Goddamn it. I scrambled up again and started to run.

I ran across the platform and across the street on the other side. Now there was a house in front of me, a woman on the porch hollering. I ran right through her yard, a chained dog nipping at my heels. On the other side was a bare field of sun-scorched grass. I tore across it, praying I wouldn't break a leg in a vole hole. Behind me the dog barked again. The police. They must be chasing! I couldn't stop to turn around. I ran and ran, hot air burning my nose, blood from my busted lip dripping down my chin and flying off behind me.

I was running down a road now, with big low buildings on either side, but no people that I could see. To my right was a stand of scrubby pines, too shallow to hide in. Beyond was a gleam of water. The ocean?

Then I saw it. A white building near as big as the Casteen School. A church, I reckoned. Wasn't it true you could always hide in a church and no police were even allowed inside? I tore through the trees like a possum running from the devil himself. There! A gray metal door. I grabbed the handle, twisted, and pulled as hard as I could. It was locked. Damn. Damn. Damn.

I ran around the other side and there, in front of me, at the corner of the building, was a great big round grain bin, twice as tall as me. It looked just like Frank Sproul's, except his was metal and this one was wood. Next to it was a row of regular wood barrels like you'd store moonshine in. Guess this wasn't a church after all, but some kind of a barn?

A rustling sound came from the other side of the building. The police. I would not let them get me. I would not. I jumped onto the lid of one of the moonshine barrels and from there pushed the wooden lid of the grain bin until it opened a crack. Just enough for me to pull myself up and slip inside.

Splash.

Oh hell. This was not a grain bin. This bin was full of water. Salty, stinging water. I was in it, under it, my nose and eyes and mouth full of dark wet, choking gasping, pushing my head to the surface, sucking air, then slipping. My feet kicking out, nothing but emptiness below. But not empty, because the water was full of something. Many somethings. Small, hard, floating bars, rough against my skin. I flailed out, and my arm grabbed hold of something—a nail? Slipped off, slipped under again. Again, I flailed, and this time caught the lip of the bin. Grabbed on so tight I could feel the blood squeeze out of my fingertips. I hung there, half in and half out of the water, trying not to cough. Were the police still there?

It felt like an hour went by, but maybe it was only five minutes, I really don't know. I held my breath and listened. Nothing but the soft sloshing sound of the water around me.

Finally, when I could feel my arms going numb, I worked side to side, inching up until I could hook a leg over the edge of the bin. I pulled until the rest of my body lifted out of the water and tipped right out. I fell. I fell to the ground and landed on my side in the sharp, tiny rocks. For a moment, I lay there, just breathing, the sunlight feeling like a miracle after the darkness of the bin. After a moment, I half crawled behind the row of barrels, then flopped back to the ground.

My ears felt full of bubbles and my skin was stinging from

the salty water and the scrape of the tiny rocks. The bottom lip I'd smashed jumping off the train beat in time to my heart. The air around me smelled strange and sharp, like something they used to clean the cafeteria at Casteen.

Oh damn. Where was my sack with the food and the money? I felt in my pocket; the keys were still there. But the sack, the sack was . . . sitting on the seat of the first-class train car. *Miss. Miss. Excuse me.* The man on the train who'd been calling at me was probably just trying to give me my sack. It might not have been a policeman talking at all. Which meant . . . which meant I might have just jumped off a moving train for no dang reason. And now I was somewhere called New Bern, lord knows how far from Wilmington, with a busted face and no money, and Matty Barnwell back at Casteen telling everyone how I'd stole his keys and run.

Think! I yelled to myself, inside my head. *Think! Think!*

The girls at the Chalet School always had someone to rescue them when they got into trouble. A handsome doctor would pull them out of the lake, or a passing soldier would see them get swept away by a snowstorm and race after them on his horse.

When was somebody coming to save me?

Just when I had that thought, I heard footsteps crunching on the rocks. I lay stiff and still. It wasn't the police, I didn't think. It was just one person, and they were walking slowly, like they were heading towards somewhere they didn't especially want to get to.

Could this be my handsome doctor? My brave soldier?

I just needed a story to tell him.

Crunch. Crunch. The footsteps got closer.

I fell off a traveling circus train. I'm a half orphan from New York City. I was sleepwalking. I just need your help. You're so strong, you're so brave, you're my hero.

Suddenly a face was leaning over the barrel and looking at me. It was a narrow face, with very dark eyes below dark eyebrows all V-shaped with worry. But the face didn't belong to a man. It belonged to a woman.

Everybody knows what a man wants.

But what on earth did this woman want? How was I supposed to know what story to tell her?

"Are you all right?" she said, leaning over me.

For once, I didn't have a single thing to say.

Chapter 33

MILLIE

1939

"Why did you think I wouldn't have helped you if you'd told me the truth!" I demanded, then, thinking of everything Cecilia had told me, steadied my voice. "I mean, do you really think I'm as bad as they are?"

"Of course I don't, not now," Cecilia said. "But I didn't know then. You could have been anybody. Look at that sweet old lady, Mrs. Pattishall. I told her the truth, she called Dr. McDevil, and now I've been cut open and gutted like a hog."

"So what now?" I was practically vibrating, emotions popping like firecrackers under my skin. I sat down on a kitchen chair, then stood up again immediately and began pacing in a tight little circle in front of the sink. "What do you want now?"

"You know what I want." Cecilia's pale eyes bored into me.

"Jean."

"Jean. Will you help me?"

I was trying to formulate an answer—I was trying to wrap my mind around the question, really—when there were footsteps on the front steps and the door began to open. Immediately Cecilia's posture changed. Her relaxed, confidential look vanished and her big doll eyes came back, lashes batting.

My mother stood in front of me in her green crepe dress, her face dark. She didn't say a word, just shook her head back and forth like a heavy bell.

Jesse came up behind her and whistled. "I always knew you were bats, but, boy oh boy, Millie, that was something else. The ladies'll be talking about that one till they're old and gray. One of the pearls from Sophie's necklace bounced right into the cake, y'know—Old Man Lefkowitz nearly choked on it."

"*Shvaig*, Jesse!" commanded Fanny in the sharpest tone I've ever heard her use, and Jesse, for once in his life, fell silent. He followed Fanny out of the room, a smirk still on his face.

From the corner of my eye I could see a small spasm of suppressed laughter ripple Cecilia's chest. Had she been doing this all along—swallowing her laughter as we all walked around like fools, looking for language books, buying dresses, arranging translators? Except for Jesse. He hadn't believed her, had he? That was the worst, that my idiot brother had been right after all.

But, no, that wasn't the worst thing.

I'd killed a man.

All at once I heard the thwack of the mallet again, saw the shock on his face in the moment before the blood began to spurt. I rushed to the sink and retched.

I felt a hand on my back. Cecilia had glided up close. "Remember," she whispered. "He deserved it. You did a good thing."

I swung around and faced her. "Don't say that," I hissed. I brushed by her and rushed upstairs. I needed to think.

In my bedroom with the lamp on, I stared at my face in the oval dressing mirror, breathing hard yet feeling like I wasn't getting any air. I looked frightful—pale and wild-eyed, the sort of lunatic who'd start a fight at a wedding. Did I look crazy enough to murder a man?

Murder. That wasn't the word, was it? I'd only hit him in self-defense—he was coming at us.

But *was* he really coming at us? He was reaching out for Cecilia. But did he have a weapon? Did he present a threat? What had he been planning to do?

All I'd known was that he had evil intentions towards Cecilia, and that my job was to protect her, the poor lost Swedish girl.

Would I have protected her if I'd known she was just a poor farm girl from Lenoir County, the kind of girl I wouldn't have given a second look at if she'd come to unload cucumbers at the warehouse on a Monday morning, her dress ragged? The kind of girl who—I didn't want to admit this, but it was true—I would have thought myself above. I'd have pitied her, of course. I'd have happily given her a sandwich. But would I have immediately dedicated myself to saving her, if I hadn't thought she was someone special? The thought made me feel nauseated with shame.

But the shame was knocked sideways by an even worse feeling—the image of the tall man, Matty Barnwell, crumpling to the ground once again struck me like a bullet between the eyes. I buried my face in my hands. What was I going to do? Someone—a fisherman, a sailor, a child on a beach holiday, God forbid—would find the barrel bobbing in the ocean, pry it open, and find a brine-stinking body. The police would be called. They'd find me, the woman who'd punched someone in the middle of the hora at her cousin's wedding. If I was lucky the loony bin was where they'd put me again, I supposed. Otherwise it'd be prison.

But as I turned that thought over and over in my mind, I found it didn't frighten me as much as it should have.

On the contrary: it made me feel, in the oddest way, *free*. If

I was to be known as a criminally insane murderer, then there'd be no more pretending. No more sitting in parlors making polite chitchat with unmarried Jewish butchers. No more discussing wedding dresses. No more holding my tears inside. No more pretending as if the world hadn't stopped spinning when Auggie died. I could weep. I could scream. I could tear my hair.

The relief flooded through me like cool water. I took off my dress and let it crumple to the floor. Hanging up clothing seemed absurd at a time like this. I pulled on a nightdress and lay down on my bed. The police might be here in the morning; they'd haul me out in my stocking feet, all the neighbors staring. The thought made me giggle to myself. Oh, well. I'd done what I could. I'd done what I could and it had all ended like this. I wasn't surprised. I'd never done things right. I couldn't help Auggie. I was a humiliation to my family. I found a woman behind the pickle barrels and brought her home and now I was a *murderer*. Well. What's done is done.

I closed my eyes and fell asleep almost instantly. More proof, I suppose, that I really am insane.

I WOKE BEFORE dawn and went to Auggie's room. Cecilia was already awake; I supposed that was the Casteen School bell ringing in her head. She was sitting at Auggie's desk, looking at his photo album. When I walked in, she closed it slowly and slid it under another book. I sat down on the bed.

"All right," I said.

Cecilia looked at me. Her face was remarkably untroubled. The bruises were almost entirely gone. "All right?"

I gathered up my breath. I was confused and angry and hurt and shocked, but I could only see one path forward. "I'll help you," I said. "Let's go get your sister."

Chapter 34

CECILIA

1939

When Millie said she'd help me, I just about threw my arms around her, but I could tell she was still skittish after what happened with Matty Barnwell. Can't blame her. Even if she knows the truth about him, it's still hard to understand something deep down in your bones if it didn't happen to you. So I just smiled and said thank you and let her go find Zeke, her skinny friend from the train station, to see about borrowing his car.

That boy's a funny one. He's jumpy as a hound dog, but he ain't half bad looking. Got eyes as blue as cornflowers and a sweet way of smiling. All the men I've known have been somewhere between stupid and evil, so it's kinda nice to see one that ain't neither of those things.

I went down to the kitchen and saw Millie's ma had left breakfast on the table. Griddle cakes and butter, a bowl of soft cheese with strawberry jam, a silver pot full of coffee with a little pitcher of fresh cream. I gave a little shiver of happiness, just seeing it. I don't know much about Jews—the only Jew I ever met before Millie and her family was a peddler called Abraham who'd come through Tobacco Run a few times a year on a mule, selling tin pots and hairbrushes and little bottles of Florida

Water. He'd always give us a horehound stick, whether or not Mama bought anything—she almost never did. So as far as I'm concerned, Jews are like everybody else, only with better food.

I made myself a plate of griddle cakes and smeared on a layer of butter so thick I could see my tooth marks in it. Then I helped myself to a bowl of cheese and jam, and a cup of coffee with cream and sugar, just like the girls at Chalet School had. I was fixing a second plate of griddle cakes when the door opened, and I turned, expecting Millie and Zeke.

Except it wasn't. It was her thickheaded brother, Jesse, who looked like Bluto from the *Popeye* funnies. The one who tried to take the picture of me. He was lucky I only broke the camera, not his jaw.

He saw me and stopped, looking around for his sister, I reckon. When he didn't see her, a smile came over his big Bluto face.

"Enjoying your breakfast?"

I gave him one of my blank, blinky looks.

"I hope so," he went on, leaning against the doorframe. "I worked hard for that food. I work hard for everything you're enjoying for free, you know. The food, the electricity, that goofy dress. I'm guessing you don't know much about hard work, huh?"

It was a matter of strength to keep my face still and smooth just then. Hard work? He sits in some office in a big building full of cucumbers! You want to moan about hard work, you can haul buckets of water through the 'backer rows in the blazing August sun, mosquitoes eating you alive. You want to complain about hard work, you wash cabbages in the middle of winter till your fingertips turn blue. Hard work, my fanny!

Jesse got a plate and slid the rest of the griddle cakes onto it, then slopped on half the bowl of jam. He sat down across the table from me. "My family relies on my hard work, you know? My mother wore herself nearly to death until I was old enough to step up. Millie can read three books in a day, but does she know how to run a cutting machine? No."

He started to chew with his mouth open. His sweet wife really ought to train him out of that, but I reckon she's got enough on her hands.

"Auggie was the same," Jesse said, slurping his coffee. "The two of them were peas in a pod. Always reading. The brain bunch. You know, they say being smart is so great, but that's a load of baloney. Look at Zeke—he won some state math contest when we were kids, got a medal and his picture in the paper and everything. Now he's sitting up in the rail shop all day, holes in his socks like a hobo. Never gonna get married. And Millie?" He made a spluttering sound with his lips, like a horse, and tiny dots of jam splattered the table. "Everyone was so proud when she went off to college. Was gonna be some big-shot lady newspaper writer. But now look. If it weren't for me, she'd be rotting in the loony bin in Raleigh. But I don't get any appreciation!"

I couldn't help narrowing my eyes just a tiny bit. He looked back at me with a small smile curling the edge of his lips. He ain't book smart like Millie and Zeke, but he can read a person better than either of them. He's never believed my story, not for a minute. But since Millie and the rest think he's stupid, they don't pay him any mind. They think he's just being a bully.

"I reckon someone's gonna see my ad in the paper soon, come to fetch you," he said. "Your daddy? Or your husband? Whoever you're running away from."

If only I'd had a daddy worth running away from, I thought, imagining my pa snoring away on the bed in the kitchen, his muddy boots still on his feet. I took another bite of warm sweet griddle cake and thought of my mama, all alone now in the house in the middle of the 'backer with just the little ones, nothing to eat but mush and boiled peanuts. Maybe she should have run away from her husband before she started having all those babies.

Poor Mama. Married on a Tuesday morning in winter, wearing the same dress she wore to church my whole life. She was sixteen. A neighbor had her and my pa's families over afterwards for cake and coffee. My ma always talked about that cake with a smile, like it was the best thing she ever ate.

No. Not for me. I'm not one to take the unfairness and meanness of this world with a smile, all grateful-like, the way the pastor says you oughta. I always knew I was gonna get more out of life, and I am. Casteen won't stop me, hard as it tried.

Thinking of my mama, I leaned over, looking Jesse right in the eye, and forked one of his griddle cakes straight off his plate. He froze for a moment, then started to sputter. But I'd already swallowed it down.

JESSE WAS GONE when Millie came back a half hour later with Zeke a step behind her. From his shocked white face I could tell she'd already told him about me. I only wondered if she'd left in the part about the dead body in the pickle barrel.

"Let's go upstairs," she whispered, looking around the parlor fearfully, though nobody else was there.

In the bedroom, I sat on the desk chair and Millie sat on her bed, giving me a sharp-eyed stare. Zeke leaned up against the wall, staring at Millie like she was a fortune teller about to tell him his fate.

"Here's Zeke," Millie said quickly. "Explain what you want."

"Hey there, Zeke," I said.

He turned even paler, hearing my voice for the first time. He looked at Millie, then back at me. "You *are* really American."

"Born right in the dirt of Lenoir County," I said, grinning.

"Gosh," he said. "Gosh. So what do you want me to do?" He looked around as if looking for a rescuer. "I'm supposed to be at work now; my boss thinks I'm just getting a sandwich."

"I want you to come with us to the Casteen Training School to help get my sister out," I said. "It's outside Kinston town. How far do you reckon that is?"

"Forty miles," Zeke said right away, then swallowed hard.

"When?" asked Millie.

"No time like today. Later, though, so we get there after dark, of course."

"Why after dark?" asked Millie.

"The teachers will be asleep, so you'll just have to talk to the house warden. Her name's Miss Grieve, and she's real soft, won't give you any trouble."

"Wait, who is the 'you' talking to the night warden?" Zeke asked. He looked at me, wary, arms folded across his chest.

"You and Millie," I said sweetly.

He began to ask another question, but Millie interrupted. "So nobody will be there but the house warden?"

"The doctor and Auntie Sybil live on the grounds, but they have their own houses. The only ones in the building overnight are Miss Grieve and the nurse and Matty Barnwell. And with Matty Barnwell gone . . ."

"Who's Matty Barnwell?" asked Zeke.

"Just a guard at the training school," said Millie quickly.

I guess she didn't tell him about the pickle barrel, then. Probably best; boy already looked like he was fixing to keel over.

"All right, we'll go tonight," Millie added. "We don't want

Jean to stay there any longer than she has to." She started rooting through one of the desk drawers, pulling out pieces of paper. "There's got to be a road atlas in here," she muttered.

"Tonight?" Zeke said. "But how will you—we—get there?"

I gave him a look. "Your daddy's car, Zeke. Isn't that why you're here?"

Zeke looked at Millie. "It's not going to get messed up, is it? My father likes that car better than me."

"Depends on whether they try to shoot the tires out," I said. I couldn't help myself.

Zeke's mouth hung open. I started to laugh. I should be nicer—they're helping me. But, oh, it felt so good to laugh. There wasn't much to laugh at in Casteen, and I haven't been able to say a word since I landed in New Bern. Laughing gave me a happy, shimmery feeling, like the way I felt when I was back at Mrs. Randall's school, with a cheese sandwich and a brand-new Chalet School book.

"I'm just joking—you can close your mouth," I said after a minute. "Don't worry, nothing's gonna happen to the car."

"But how are we going to get inside to get Jean?" Millie asked.

I smiled at her—my real smile, the one Miss Pritchard said was "brazen." "Easy," I said. "Y'all are gonna tell them a story."

Chapter 35

MILLIE

1939

Cecilia's pale eyes were twinkling as she leaned back in my desk chair and stretched her arms. Then she smiled and clapped her hands together. "Here's how the plan goes," she said brightly. "Millie and Zeke, you're gonna pretend to be my parents. Zeke, your name is Roy. You walk dragging your right leg on account of bad liquor. Millie, your name is Sarah. You're gonna mostly look down at your feet. Mess up your hair a little." She reached over and pulled at the clip holding my bun in place. I bristled at her touch, but she didn't seem to take any heed, just gave me a hard up-and-down look. "My mama never had a dress so nice. What else you got?"

"What do you mean?" This sudden turnaround—Cecilia being in charge, me being led around like a child—was confusing and irritating.

"If she was taking a trip out of Tobacco Run, my mama would wear her church dress, the one she got married in. It's a real pale pink cotton with buttons, worn to heck, mended about a thousand times. You got anything like that?" She stood and opened my closet door, rifling through my dresses like they were items on the rack at the Marie Antoinette.

"Of course not," I said, then, feeling ashamed at my snobbery, added, "I suppose I could wear one of my old housedresses."

Cecilia nodded. "And take off that necklace."

"No," I said, reaching up to cradle my locket.

Cecilia rolled her eyes. "Well, tuck it inside the dress, then. And no lipstick."

I snorted. As if I'd wear lipstick to jailbreak a girl from a training school. Anyhow, lipstick and necklaces were the least of our problems, I thought, looking at Cecilia's pale hair. "Who's going to believe that I'm your mother?" I demanded. "We look nothing alike. And Zeke and I are barely older than you. How could we be your parents?"

"Don't worry—the house warden doesn't know what my parents look like," Cecilia said smoothly. "The only one at Casteen who ever saw them was Auntie Sybil, and she'll be tucked up in her little house down yonder for the night. And it's not so strange that y'all are young; I knew a girl in Tobacco Run who was a grandma before she turned twenty-five."

A grandmother at twenty-five? I tried to work out the horrible math of that, then decided not to think about it.

"Anyways, just keep your hair in front of your face a little. Zeke, pull that cap down so it shades your eyes. And act country, all right?"

"No," said Zeke, looking even paler and shaking his head. "No way. There has to be a better plan. If this school is holding your sister captive, shouldn't we go to the authorities?"

I put my hands on my hips, my skin prickling with anger. "Zeke, you know exactly what happened last time I tried to get the police to help me."

His brow furrowed. "Well, no, Millie. I really don't."

"What do you mean?" I said impatiently. "Everybody knows."

He shook his head. "I know you got into trouble somehow

when Auggie died, wound up in the hospital in Raleigh. But I don't know anything else, not really—I asked you, but you didn't want to talk about it. That's fine. You don't owe me an explanation. But I don't know what happened with you and the police, no."

I thought for a moment, hands still on my hips. It was true. Zeke *had* asked me, in his own offhand way. *If you ever want to talk about what happened, I'm a pretty good listener*, he'd said. But I hadn't wanted to talk. I'd wanted to sit alone in the sharp glass cage of my anger and sadness.

"Oh." I sighed. "I suppose it just feels like everyone in Little Jerusalem knows every single detail of what happened, and they all talk about it and judge me for it."

"I understand," he said. "I felt the same after I came back from college. It's a small town. But I think . . . I think people are mostly just caught up in their own business."

Cecilia made a loud clucking sound. "This is a very nice conversation, I'm glad y'all are having a little heart-to-heart and all that. But can we move it along?"

I held up my hand. Cecilia had gotten me into this fine mess. The least she could do was wait a second before it got even messier.

"I'll tell you the whole story later," I said, looking at Zeke. "But the short version is this: I tried to get help for Auggie—and, no, I was not in my right mind, but the police didn't even listen to what I was saying, not for a second. They just hog-tied me and shipped me off to Dix Hill."

Zeke looked down. "I'm sorry, Millie. That sounds awful." His blue eyes were fixed on mine. I felt a funny heat in my stomach, part embarrassment, part pleasure, like he'd seen something in my private soul and understood.

"It *was* awful," I said, feeling my voice break. "So tell me, what do you think would happen if Cecilia—a girl they've already said is feebleminded and degenerate and worse—tried to tell the police what was happening at Casteen?"

Zeke swallowed. "You're right. But—but, if I come, do I have to talk? You know I'm a terrible liar."

Cecilia laughed. "Best you don't talk, I reckon. We'll let Millie do it. Just don't use your fancy college words, all right, Millie? Remember, you don't barely even know how to read. Zeke, you got some liquor you could have a swig of? Get some real smell on you, like my pa."

"My mother keeps some Shabbat wine in the cabinet. It smells like grape juice and I don't like it, but—"

Cecilia shook her head. "Never mind. At least you're already dressed like a field hand."

I giggled, then stopped myself. Zeke was dressed like he always was—old pants worn gray at the knees, shirt untucked, like he'd just rolled down a hill.

"What will I say?" I asked.

"Tell the warden you're here for your daughter Jean," Cecilia said. "Tell her Cecilia made it home, all sunburnt and feet bloody from walking through the fields all the way to Tobacco Run. Tell her Cecilia told you everything, and now you're taking Jean away."

"Will she fight it?"

"I reckon not," Cecilia said. "If she does, just say you know about the whippings and the infirmary. Tell her you'll be calling the sheriff, and you'll make sure he knows that she's the leader of the bunch. She'll crack easy. Like I said, she's soft."

I had a sudden thought. "But what about Jean? She'll know we're not her parents, of course. Won't she be frightened?"

"I thought about that. You'll have to give her kind of a secret message. Tell her Cecilia says to remember the party at the Lintons' house."

"What does that mean?"

"It's something from the books we like, the ones about the Chalet School. She'll know what I mean."

"Are you sure?"

Cecilia nodded confidently. Then she looked out the window, her posture wilting a little. "Poor Jean. Locked up there at Casteen when she hasn't done nothing wrong. Life ain't fair."

No, I thought silently. Life isn't fair. That's one thing Cecilia and I can agree on.

"Let's meet out front after supper," Cecilia said, regaining her upright pose. "Zeke, you bring the car. We'll get there just after lights-out."

"But where will we say we're going?" Zeke asked.

Cecilia laughed. "Ain't y'all grown-ups? What's the worst thing that could happen—your mama and daddy get mad? They ain't gonna give you a thrashing, are they?"

Zeke and I exchanged looks. Cecilia was right. Sometimes I did forget I was a grown woman. I *could* do what I wanted. A tiny window opened inside my chest.

Zeke nodded, still nervous. "All right. I'll meet you at seven—I can pick you up outside the arch, so no one will see us. But give me a story to tell my parents, please. You know I can't do it myself."

I had to smile. Zeke was incapable of lying. Auggie always did that for him, making elaborate excuses to the mayor when they crashed one of their model airplanes into a window at city hall, coaxing their parents into giving them more money to buy supplies for their experiments ("I read that the chemistry program at Duke really wants students with experience. Gee, I sure hope I'm getting enough practice"). What would Auggie say?

"Tell them we're driving to the bluffs of the Neuse to see the meteor shower," I said.

"What meteor shower?" Zeke asked, clearly alarmed to think he'd missed knowing such a date.

"Zeke." I gave him a look.

"Oh. Right. Okay."

Cecilia smiled.

It was sort of a cat-who-ate-the-canary smile, I thought. Dangerous. I felt a shiver of fear, but underneath was a hot glowing coal of something I hadn't felt in a long, long time: excitement. This was an adventure, the kind of thing I'd imagined for myself back at college, when Professor Snett had us read the work of the muckrakers—Nellie Bly and Ida Tarbell and Ida B. Wells, who was both a lady and a Negro. I'd lain in my dormitory bed at night, fantasizing about the stories I'd uncover, the politicians who'd resign in disgrace after my articles. How had I let this part of myself fall away?

We stood to adjourn our little meeting when I heard a creak in the hallway. The middle board outside my doorway always creaks. Auggie knew that. When we were little, he'd tiptoe around the creaky board and scare the living daylights out of me when I opened the door. Once he was wearing a wolf mask he'd fashioned out of newspaper and paste. I screamed loud enough to wake the neighbors.

But Jesse didn't know about the creaky board.

He was standing in the hallway, just outside the open door. Oh God. How long had he been there?

"Just came up to tell you lunch is ready, and afterwards Mama wants you to go to Benji's for some flounder," he said, a funny look on his face.

"All right," I said, trying to keep my voice level.

Cecilia stood behind me with her hands folded in front of her, transformed back into the silent Swedish girl.

Jesse gave her a long look. She stared right back, her face a perfect blank. He was the first one to look away.

Chapter 36

MILLIE

1939

"Stay in the shadow," I hissed at Cecilia. "No, not under the arch!"

We were standing at the edge of Cedar Grove Cemetery, where the Confederate dead are buried by the dozen under Spanish moss–dripping oaks. It was early evening, the sky pinkening at the edges, the shadows black as pits. No one was around at this time of day, which was why we were waiting here for Zeke to pick us up.

"Why not stand under the arch, if you're so worried about someone seeing us?" Cecilia asked.

"Just don't, all right?" I said. "I'm helping you, aren't I?"

I didn't want to explain to Cecilia that the coquina stone arch at the cemetery entrance was the subject of a silly children's legend: If a drop of water from the arch falls on your head, you'll be the next to die. The Weeping Arch, they call it. As children we darted underneath, back and forth, back and forth, daring each other to go again.

Fortunately, before Cecilia could respond, Zeke drove up.

"Nice motor," said Cecilia, whistling.

"*Shhhh*," I said, though of course no one in the cemetery could hear her.

Solomon Abramowitz, Zeke's father, had a maroon LaSalle with whitewall tires. He refused to buy a Ford on account of what Henry Ford wrote about Jews. Uncle Abe always laughed at Mr. Abramowitz for that. "If I didn't buy from Jew haters, my home would be empty," Abe said.

The car was handsome, and I usually enjoyed riding in it, but now its color and newness made me nervous. It stood out in this part of North Carolina, where most people drove farm trucks or old black Model Ts. We'd surely have to hide it outside the Casteen Training School, lest someone see it and realize we weren't poor farm folk at all.

I climbed in the front seat next to Zeke, while Cecilia slipped into the back, stretching her arms out luxuriously against the maroon fabric seat.

"Are you still sure about this?" Zeke asked in a low voice, leaning in so close our heads nearly touched. "We don't have to do anything you're not sure about."

"No, I'm not sure," I said, looking into his eyes. "But every time I've been sure about something before, I've been wrong. So let's go."

"All right, then," said Zeke, giving me a small smile. "Let's go."

We drove through Riverside, the factories and warehouses empty, the Neuse smooth and flat beyond. We reached the edge of town, marked by a scattered handful of tin-roof houses set in a scrubby field along the river.

Cecilia leaned over the seatback, watching Zeke's hand work the gearshift like driving was still a marvel to her. After a few minutes, she spotted the road atlas sitting between me and Zeke.

"Never seen one of these in real life," she said, grabbing it.

I turned and watched her unfold the map. She squinted at it. "Wilmington ain't nowhere near Atlantic Beach!" she muttered.

The summer sun didn't want to set that evening, instead growing larger and rosier as we drove west, bathing the fields in gold. Zeke shielded his eyes with one hand to see. My mind turned to Jesse and that creaking floorboard. Would he snitch? Would he tell our mother what he'd heard? Would he—God forbid—go to the police? I knew my brother was a jackass, but was he a rat? How far would he go to prove he'd been right about Cecilia all along? I set my worries aside. If I was going to prison for murdering Matty Barnwell, Jesse would be the least of my problems. Again I got that strange weightless feeling.

After a while, Cecilia looked up from the map. "You told me you wanted to be a newspaper story writer, right?"

"Once," I said stiffly, my stomach twisting with embarrassment as my mind raced over all the confessions I'd made to Cecilia when I thought she didn't understand.

"When this is all over, you'll write a story about it," she said. "Get it published in the paper. Then everyone will know about Dr. McDevitt and Auntie Sybil and the rest. They won't dare try to send me and Jean back after that. And nobody else'll ever send their girls there again, thinking they'll get eggs and fresh milk. The state will have to close them down!" She laughed, a merry cackling sound.

For a moment, I allowed myself to imagine it. My name beneath a story. An *exposé*. I just hoped they'd let me write it from prison. The idea made me stifle a weird, hiccuppy giggle. I should have made Zeke bring his mother's Shabbat wine after all, I thought madly; we could have made this strange drive into a proper party.

"So," said Cecilia, turning to Zeke. "Why did you have to leave college? You hit a teacher or something?"

Zeke looked horrified. "Of course not."

I laughed, imagining Zeke hitting someone. "No, he just

missed being around trains too much, and the assistant timekeeper job was open, so—"

I stopped speaking when I noticed Zeke tightening his jaw. He opened his mouth, then closed it again.

Cecilia, in the back seat, noticed too. She got a little smirk on her face. "Is there something you wanna tell Millie, Zeke?"

Zeke began to look red. He gripped the steering wheel harder but didn't say anything.

"What is it, Zeke?" I asked, confused.

He took a sharp inhale and said, "I didn't leave school to take the job, all right! I got expelled."

Cecilia hooted. "I knew you were a naughty boy in secret, ha!"

I gave her a dirty look. "*Expelled*? For what?"

Zeke was crimson now, his Adam's apple joggling as he swallowed. "I broke a wind tunnel."

Cecilia hooted even more loudly. "They kicked you out of college for breaking wind! Must have been some fart, boy!"

"A wind *tunnel*! For aeronautics experiments. I wanted to test out an airfoil design I'd come up with, and, well, I managed to snap one of the blades off the fan."

"They kicked you out for that?" I said. "Couldn't you have just had it fixed?"

"It was expensive. Very expensive. And also, well, I wasn't actually supposed to be in the aeronautics laboratory at all. It was only for professors and senior students. I had to go at night and sort of . . . broke in. I mean, I didn't break down the door; I just climbed up the fire escape and went in the window."

Cecilia piped up. "And you told everyone you left college cuz you wanted to! Reckon you're a better liar than you said, ha! You'll do just fine tonight."

"I didn't *lie*, exactly," Zeke said, wounded. "I just didn't, well, tell the whole story. But nobody asked! Everyone just assumed I'd come back for the station job, because I'm Zeke, the train maniac, right? So I let them think it."

I wanted to laugh, but I bit my lip, seeing Zeke's distress. Breaking into a lab in the middle of the night! It made perfect sense now that I thought about it. Zeke had always been someone who followed his passions wherever they led, too absorbed to consider the trouble it might bring. Like the homemade hot air balloon that had got him a caution from the sheriff. Or the time he'd argued with our high school science teacher about Darwinism and gotten himself a week of detention—he wasn't trying be a troublemaker, he just couldn't let Mr. Brooks get away with saying something he knew wasn't true. I patted his arm. "Your mother must have had a stroke of apoplexy."

"She stayed in bed for a week," he said grimly, and we both laughed.

All of a sudden Cecilia gave a little hiccup. There, on the pink edge of the horizon, was a building.

The Casteen Training School looked very little like the Gothic mansion I'd imagined, no Castle Udolpho or Northanger Abbey. It was just a rather ordinary tall brick building with double doors like a regular schoolhouse. It was surrounded by fields and several barns and outbuildings, which gave it a pleasant, country feel. Fresh bales of hay were stacked in pyramids by the edge of the field, glowing red in the last smudge of summer sun as the sky above went dark.

"That's it?" I asked.

"That's it," Cecilia said, setting her mouth in a grim line. "If there's a God in the sky, this better be the last time I lay eyes on the Casteen Training School."

Chapter 37

MILLIE

1939

Zeke parked behind the brick pillar marking the entrance to the school's driveway. The blue was quickly draining from the sky, and inside the car it was almost too dark to see. "What will you do while we're inside?" I asked Cecilia.

"Stand guard. If anyone comes, I'll honk the car horn."

I looked at Zeke. In the fading light he was green as a frog, but his mouth was set in a determined line.

"You can do this," I whispered to him. "Just let me do the talking."

He nodded.

Together, we got out of the car and began to walk down the paved driveway towards the main building. In the gathering shadows the building did look a little more like a Gothic castle. Some of the windows on the left side of the building were lit, while the ones on the right were all dark.

"What'll happen to Cecilia if we get caught?" Zeke whispered. "You think she'll get sent to jail?"

"I don't see how running away is a crime," I whispered back. *Of course, killing someone with a mallet and hiding their body in a pickle barrel* is *a crime*, I thought. I imagined my mother's face when she opened the front door to see the police standing on the other side. *We're here for your daughter.* Again I got the feeling that I wanted to laugh and scream at the same time.

"Anyway, we won't get caught," I added. "We'll get Jean, and we'll get out, and that's that."

Zeke gave a half smile. "If anyone can do it, it's you."

I reached over and took Zeke's big puppy paw of a hand in mine. He gave it a squeeze and I suddenly felt, contrary to my pounding heart and the sweat already dripping down the back of my dress, that it would all be fine. We could do this. Together. We climbed the steps to the front door. It had two old-fashioned iron knockers. I took one and let it fall against the wood. I could feel the thud in the pit of my stomach. For a moment, there was silence. Then footsteps. Then the door opened.

A woman in a white nurse's uniform stood at the threshold. Her face was plump and pleasant, her expression entirely unsuspicious. "Hello. Can I help you?"

"We're here for our daughter. Jean."

"Jean?" said the woman.

I froze, realizing I didn't know her full name. Cecilia had never told us her surname. I had the desperate urge to run back to the car. *Solve your own problem*, I'd tell Cecilia. Then I thought of Auggie. I squared my shoulders.

I stepped across the threshold and stood several inches too close to the woman in white. "Cecilia came home to Tobacco Run," I hissed in what I hoped was a passable country accent. "She told us all about what y'all are doing here. We're taking Jean home from this devil place. Where is she?"

The woman's mouth hung open in a little O of surprise. "I see," she said finally. "Follow me."

I gave a short sharp nod. The woman led us into the corridor and up a set of stairs. When we got to the third floor, she asked us to wait.

Zeke and I stood together, uneasy. The walls of the hallway were lined with photographs. Though it was dim, I could see they were of the school staff—women in nurses' whites, women with schoolteachers' buns, all standing on the steps of the main building. Each picture had the year printed at the top: 1912, 1913, 1914. In the center of each photograph was an enormous man with a white coat and a long beard. He stood at least a half a head taller than anyone else in the photo. His smile was a dark straight line.

I shivered.

The woman in white came back. "This way, please."

We followed her down the hall, where the light was on in the last room. Too late, I realized it wasn't the dim light of a dormitory. It was the bright light of an office.

"Hello," said a deep voice.

I jumped back.

A man was sitting behind a vast gleaming wooden desk. His face was large and round and almost childlike with its plump cheeks, which made his hard pink twist of a smile seem even more frightening. The man from the pictures. Doctor McDevitt. Doctor McDevil.

"How fortuitous that I was here working late," he said. "Normally I'm at home with Mrs. McDevitt by now. I'm glad to meet you—Mr. and Mrs. Aiken, I presume?"

Aiken. Cecilia Aiken. Jean Aiken.

"That's right," I said, then immediately wished I'd said "yessir," the way a poor Lenoir County farmer's wife might have.

"Cecilia made it home safely? We've been so worried."

So worried, my foot!

"Cecilia done told us everything," I said, Cecilia's voice in my head. "We're here to take Jean home."

"Jean," the doctor said, stepping closer. The lights in the office were very bright. "May we talk a minute first?"

I nodded. "Jest for a minute, we got to be getting back to our other young'uns."

The doctor nodded back, his big inflated face all sincere looking. He did look just like the Santa in the Coca-Cola ads. "Sit, please," he said, holding out one puffy hand to indicate the chairs on the other side of the desk.

Zeke practically collapsed into the chair, sweating. I sat next to him.

The doctor sat on the other side of the desk and folded his hands in front of himself.

My mind flashed to that day at Duke with Doctor Weasel Face, folding his hands similarly before he told us the cancer had spread. I felt my heart beating hard in my neck.

Clearing his throat, the doctor began to talk in his deep, soothing voice, the exact voice you'd imagine the Coca-Cola Santa having. "We've so enjoyed having Cecilia at our school," he said. "She seemed to be making such great strides. With the firm discipline, wholesome work, and religious instruction she received here, she'd truly blossomed. She was excelling in her trade class—the sewing instructor said she made the straightest hems of the bunch. She could have graduated from Casteen and gotten useful, honest work as a seamstress or in a textile mill. That's why it was so terribly, terribly disappointing to see she'd reverted to old behaviors by running off."

"Wholesome work? Firm discipline? Y'all made them sew sheets for your store, you made them harvest in the cold, you starved them half to death! How is that wholesome work? How is that firm discipline?"

"Mrs. Aiken," the doctor said, shaking his big head. "That's at best a . . . mischaracterization of our techniques here. Exposing overexcited girls to cool air and exercise calms the brain and nervous system and helps them control themselves. It's the opposite of cruel, really."

I narrowed my eyes at him. How sinister it was that a man so evil would look so jolly, with his snowy Santa Claus beard and his pink smile. "You said this was a school," I said. "You lied. Now, give us our Jean and we'll go."

"Mrs. Aiken," he went on, not moving from his seat, "when Cecilia first arrived at Casteen, we did a series of scientific tests to determine how best to educate her. Cecilia's test, unfortunately, showed something rather complicated. In addition to her abnormal sexual impulse, she suffers from a disorder known as 'pseudologia fantastica'—though I prefer the label 'mythomania.' Are you familiar with either term?"

He looked out at us, and behind his level gaze I thought I could see a smirk of enjoyment. He knew perfectly well Cecilia's parents wouldn't know what he was talking about. *I* didn't even know what he was talking about, and I'd gone to college!

"No, sir," I said, in a small voice, though inside I was seething.

"They both refer to a chronic condition in which an individual tells continuous falsehoods—lies, if you will. We're not certain of the origin of the disorder, though the German physician who first described it believed it was hereditary—that is, it was passed down from parent to child." He gave us another long look. "I prefer the more modern interpretation, which posits that the mythomaniac lies not out of wickedness but from a desire for stimulation, for excitement. Someone with a brain like Cecilia's simply needs more spark than the ordinary world offers. Is Cecilia fond of fiction—storybooks?"

I nodded. I had to. He already knew the answer.

The doctor shook his head slowly. "That's very common among mythomaniacs. We're not blaming you—of course not, you wouldn't have known the best treatment for mythomania is to keep the patient calm and away from brain-exciting materials. That's the sort of knowledge we have here at Casteen. You understand, don't you?"

I saw now with perfect clarity how parents like Cecilia's could send their children away to Casteen. It wasn't just the eggs and fresh milk. It was the shame. I could feel it all over my body, even though I wasn't really Cecilia's mother. I was stupid; the doctor was smart. He knew everything; I knew nothing. He could help my child; I could only damage her. Of course Cecilia's mother had done what she did.

"You're saying Cecilia is a liar?"

The doctor clucked. "'Liar' is an ugly word, with such negative moral connotations. Cecilia is not in control of her capacities the way a liar is. She's suffering from an illness. The only question is—are you willing to do what it takes to help her?"

"You mean bring her back?"

He smiled with his big rubbery lips. "You *do* understand, *Mrs. Aiken.*"

"But you cut her open," I said, feeling myself sitting up straighter. "You made it so she couldn't have children. What right did you have? She didn't say you could. We didn't say you could."

"Mrs. Aiken. I'm so sorry, but you did. It's right here in the papers." He pulled a sheaf of paper out of an envelope. "See, this line here, it says you give us at Casteen permission to care for Cecilia in loco parentis—in the place of her parents. You signed away your rights."

I wanted to rush at him and slap his face, tear at his hair. "You know gosh darn well I don't know Latin."

The doctor leaned back in his chair, and his awful pink smile grew wider. "You don't know Latin," he said. "Yet you know that 'in loco parentis' *is* Latin. Interesting."

Shit.

"Don't treat me like I'm stupid," I said, stepping closer to him to show him I wasn't scared. "I may not have book learning, but I ain't stupid. I want my daughter right now!"

"You said Cecilia had come home already."

"My other daughter. Jean."

He looked at the nurse and smirked. Then he looked back at me. "We don't have any Jean here, *Mrs. Aiken.*"

"Liar!"

He put his hand to his chest, pretending to be insulted. "Mrs. Aiken, I haven't lied to you about anything. But you aren't being honest with me, are you?"

"What do you mean?" I said in my most indignant tone. "Give me Jean, now!"

He smiled again—a smile of real delight—and I could see he'd been toying with me, like a cat toys with a mouse. He'd known I wasn't Cecilia's mother. He'd just been waiting for me to trip, so he could sink his claws in.

"The Aiken family is from the backwoods of Lenoir County—some blighted little field called Tobacco Run, I believe," he said. "So please, explain this to me—if Cecilia came home like you claim, *Mrs. Aiken*, then why did a description of her appear in a missing-person ad in the Kinston *Free Press*?"

Shit again. Of course. Matty Barnwell came because someone here at Casteen saw the ad Jesse took out.

That blasted my story apart completely.

Suddenly, a deep voice spoke in a thick country accent. "Goddamn, you bastard, give us our daughter or I'll wallop you good!"

Zeke had pulled himself up to his full height and was angling his body menacingly towards the doctor, raising a balled fist above his head.

I don't know which was the bigger shock of my life—Cecilia turning out to be a Lenoir County farm girl, or Zeke speaking in a fake accent and threatening to punch a doctor.

The doctor held up his hands. "There's no need to act rashly."

"Give us our daughter," Zeke growled again.

"Like I told you, *Mr. and Mrs. Aiken*, Cecilia is the only Aiken girl we've ever had here. There is no such girl as Jean. I'm afraid you've been bamboozled."

I felt a flood of vinegary panic in the back of my throat, and my heart began to beat even faster. *There is no such girl as Jean.* My mind flipped quickly through all Cecilia had told me. Jean. who screamed when they cut her hair. Jean, who loved hearing the Chalet School stories. Jean looking out the window as Cecilia escaped into the snow. Cecilia had lied about plenty of things, but she'd told me the truth in the end, hadn't she? If there was no Jean, then none of this made sense. If there was no Jean, then why would Cecilia have wanted to come back here? Surely the doctor was lying. I only hoped Jean hadn't been hurt or—thinking about little Ruthie in the unmarked grave—worse. My dress was damp with sweat, a buzzing sound in my ears. No, I told myself. No, he's lying.

I'd almost convinced myself when, through the open doorway, I saw Cecilia running full speed down the hall. As she passed, she mouthed something to me, but I couldn't make it out. She was alone. There was no girl with her.

Oh God.

She *was* lying.

There is no Jean.

What had I done?

Chapter 38

CECILIA

1939

Those Casteen bastards will for sure tell Millie that I'm a liar and worse.

I am a liar. But who taught me to lie? They did.

They said we'd get fresh milk and eggs, and they fed us mush.

They said I was born feebleminded, but I'm just as smart as anyone I've met.

The worst lie of all was that they'd take care of Ruthie in the infirmary. Instead, they left her alone with that long-fingered monster.

The liars ain't just at Casteen. They're everywhere. In Tobacco Run, Fred Sproul said if my pa worked hard, we'd make a good living out of his 'backer field. Yet not one year went by where we had enough food. Not once did we earn enough to put glass in the windows. His boy, Jimmy, said he loved me, and if I let him put his hand up my dress he might even marry me. You see a ring on my finger?

At church, the preacher said the poor were closest to Jesus's heart. Well, weren't *we* the poor? And what did Jesus ever do for us? Didn't give us no loaves or fishes, that's for sure.

If Mama heard me, she'd wash my mouth out with soap, but it's just the damn truth. Pastors can lie too.

The lie about Jean wasn't just a lie, though. It was a story. It was a story I told myself while I was at Casteen, to help me bear it. A little sister who I could protect, like Madge Bettany protects Jo in the Chalet School, the way I always protected the young'uns back home. I could just see her: red hair and freckles, sweet and good. I'd talk to her in my head at night—*Don't worry, Jean*, I'd say, *I won't let them get you*. I knew I was just talking to myself. But it made me feel less alone.

I waited in the car till Millie and Zeke went inside. Then I slid out the car window so as not to make a noise, and crept along the front path and up the side of the building. When I came to the kitchen door, I stopped.

I pulled the key ring out of my pocket. The key ring I'd taken from Matty Barnwell. The one I'd kept close to myself, night and day, ever since. I hadn't known why I kept it until this morning, when I woke up knowing in my heart what I needed to do. Was this the way it felt for Miss Elinor Brent-Dyer, the English lady who wrote the Chalet School books? Did she wake up in the morning with new Chalet School books in her head, just waiting to be put down on paper?

I pulled out the big silver key marked KITCHEN and unlocked the door. Now I was standing in the dark pantry. The flour and cornmeal sacks lined up against the wall looked like children playing at being ghosts. I crept through the kitchen and into the cafeteria. The floor was sticky and the air smelled of sour cabbage. I shuddered at the smell, thinking of those dinners I'd eaten, sitting stick straight like Miss Pritchard said to, scraping my bowl clean and still aching with hunger an hour later. But then I smiled. I wouldn't have to sit at the long table eating half-cold mush ever again.

There were two staircases at Casteen: the main one that

starts by the front door, the one visitors see, and then there was the bare, narrow back stairs, the ones we took to classes and to the cafeteria. Quick as I could, I made for the back stairs, ducking as I passed each door, in case there was a warden in there who might spy me through the wired glass pane. I pushed open the staircase's door. It was dark inside, with just the one yellow lamp at the bottom of the stairs to light the whole staircase. I began to run, leaping two or three stairs at a time.

I was passing the second-floor landing when I heard a noise. The creak of a door opening somewhere above me. I stopped, still as a statue. From above, I heard slow footsteps, growing louder. There was nowhere to hide. So I did what I had to. I crossed my arms over my chest to hide the big flappy blue bow on my dress and tilted my chin downward. Then I started walking up the stairs again, but slow this time, the way you'd climb stairs if you had no reason to hurry, nothing to hide. The footsteps got louder, and as the stairs turned again I could see a shadow in the moonlight falling against the wall. A narrow, pointy shadow.

Nurse Chilcott. That skinny witch who cut off my hair. Goddamn it, what was she doing here?

"Is that you again, Miss Pritchard?" she called from the landing above. "Have you not gone home yet?"

I froze for a moment. Then I gathered myself and called back, in Miss Pritchard's high silly voice: "Yes, Nurse Chilcott. I'm afraid I've left my *Ladies' Guide to Household Management* upstairs. I simply had to return for it."

"I see, Miss Pritchard," said Nurse Chilcott.

I didn't look up. But the footsteps stopped. Goddamn goddamn. I kept walking. From above, I heard Nurse Chilcott call out. My stomach squeezed like I'd ate too many crab apples.

"Do you mind checking on the girls in three C?" she said. "They were unsettled this evening; I've given several of them a dose of veronal, but I'm going home now."

"Of course, Nurse Chilcott," I said, my voice coming out even higher than I'd meant it to.

The footsteps started again, this time getting quieter and quieter. My stomach loosened. Any more of this and I'd need the privy.

A minute later I was at the third floor. I pushed the door open real slow, in case there were any more wardens on the other side. But the hall was empty and very, very dark. With the keys in my hand, I made for the 3B door. My hands were sweaty and cold pressed up against the heavy dented metal. Which key was it? I could barely see the marks in the darkness. A small one, right? I tried one, then another, and another, and another, my hands getting wetter and slipperier. As soon as I dropped one key, it would disappear into the rest of the bunch with a little tinkling sound, like it was laughing at me. I couldn't tell which ones I'd tried and which ones I hadn't. My heart was beating faster and faster. Another key. No. Another. No. No. No.

And then one fit. Slotted right in with a solid heavy thunk like it was nothing.

The door opened. I stood for a moment in the silence, looking at all the sleeping girls. How many nights had I spent here, sleeping in the bed on the far wall? How many girls had come before me? What had they done to deserve this? Being brazen, losing their virtue, stealing candy, being touched by their fathers and brothers and cousins. Daring to be born girls and poor.

Old Mollie lay on her back by the far wall, mouth open. What was she dreaming of? Did she even have dreams anymore? What about the soldiers that paid her to lie with them? Were *they* locked in reform schools and fed mush? Ha!

The twins lay facing each other, taking turns snoring. Maybe they did steal the candlesticks. But why had their father given them to the rich man in Goldsboro in the first place and kept their brothers at home on the farm? Why were they so worthless to him?

Jacy was by the door, curled in a ball under the sheet. Jacy, who missed the wind and water of her island something fierce. Jacy, who missed her baby boy who smelled like the sea. He was born sleeping, she said. She'd known she was expecting, but she also hadn't known. You can lock things up in a special part of your mind, if you try hard enough. Like Bertie Lou, the one whose brothers strung her Negro sweetheart from the tree. *He's coming for me*, she told us again and again, even though she'd seen his body swinging.

How dare they? I thought. Auntie Sybil and Dr. McDevil and the teachers and the wardens. How dare they keep us here like this? How dare they keep us here, in darkness and shame? What made them think they were better than us?

I kneeled down and poked Jacy in the side. She popped right up, almost like she wasn't asleep at all. You live long enough in a place like Casteen and you learn to sleep light. "Cecilia! What the heck? Where have you been?"

"Hush, Jacy. You gotta get out of here. Wake up everybody on the third floor, then go wake up the downstairs girls. Y'all have to help them get outside." I pulled the dormitory key off the key ring. "Here, take it."

"What? Why?" Jacy's light eyes flashed in the darkness.

"Just go!" I hissed at her. "Quick!"

Jacy frowned, but got out of bed and went over to shake Mollie awake. I ran back out the door and down the hall. I poked my head into the stairwell to make sure nobody was there, then jumped down the steps three at a time and raced across the hallway that connected the west and the east wings. When I got to the east wing I stopped running. Took a deep breath and made myself quiet as a cat. I walked with tiny tiptoe steps past the classrooms, then stopped in front of the door.

The infirmary. Just looking at the big red cross made me swell with anger. I didn't have to try out a bunch of keys to open this door. I knew exactly which one it was. I'd seen its shiny gold gleam in Matty Barnwell's hand enough times.

The door opened real smoothly, like the room had been waiting for me. It was dark, but I could see well enough now that my eyes were used to it. There, below the window, was the bed Ruthie had lain on, shrieking. The bed where Matty Barnwell had pinned me down while Dr. McDevil held the kerosene-smelling rag over my face.

Along the wall above Matty's cot was the cabinet. I pushed a stool to the wall and stood on it. I reached up and unlocked the cabinet with the tiniest silver key on the key ring. Inside, I reached for the biggest bottle on the shelf. I pulled it down and cradled it like a baby. It felt cold and heavy and good in my arms. I carried it across the room, to the bed under the window.

Then someone said my name.

A man.

I didn't need to turn to know who it was.

I knew that voice.

In my head, my mother sang: *Rawhead and Bloody Bones . . .*

He was dead, rotting in a barrel halfway to China. But he was also here. Standing at the back of the infirmary, his head almost touching the ceiling, like being dead had made him grow even taller.

"Hey there, Cecilia," said Matty Barnwell.

Chapter 39

CECILIA

1939

"You're dead," I said. My voice sounded flat and strange in my ears.

"Then I reckon I'm a ghost," he said. He smiled, but the smile quit halfway through and he raised his hand to his face to rub his jaw. In the moonlight I could see the dark blotch on the side of his long bean-shaped head. Running down the middle of the bruise was a line of rough black stitches, like the ones I had on my belly when I woke up from the appendix.

"Don't come near me."

"Or what?" He narrowed his mean glittery little eyes at me. "Or you'll hit me with a hammer? You don't have no hammer now, do you? And you don't have your friend, neither." He took a step forward. "Y'all girls are all the same. Tramps and thieves and whores and liars and feebleminded bitches, but putting on airs like you deserve something better. You think you're better than me? You think you're smarter than me?"

"No," I said. "No, you're dead."

Matty Barnwell got a prideful little smirk on his face.

"Y'all didn't put the lid on tight enough," he said. "If you'd have used the hammer to wedge it on good, I'd have been done for. 'Stead, I woke up and popped it right open, hopped out. I might have drowned, 'cept it was low tide, that river's not even deep as my shoulders. I just walked right to land."

Goddamn too-tall Matty Barnwell.

"You were lucky to be here, you know?" he said, taking another step towards me. "Now they're gonna send you to prison or the asylum for the white insane for the rest of your life. Then you'll wish you were back here at Casteen with me."

"I'm sorry, Matty," I said in my smallest voice.

He took another step.

I shifted the bottle to my left hand and slowly raised it over my head. In the moonlight you could just read the words: ANESTHETIC ETHER: HIGHLY FLAMMABLE.

I thought of Mollie. I thought of Jacy. I thought of Ruthie. I thought of myself. I thought of all the words Matty Barnwell used. Tramps and thieves and whores and liars and feebleminded bitches. Somebody's been calling me something since the day I was born. My daddy said I was fresh and needed a smack in the mouth. The Sprouls said I was field trash. Auntie Sybil said I was wayward. Dr. McDevil said I was a degenerate. A curse on all of them.

The scar on my belly throbbed. *Imagine you trying to care for a child!* McDevil had said. *It would be a catastrophe.*

I hadn't known what that word meant, I just knew it wasn't nothing good. I know what it means now. I looked it up in the dictionary in Millie's brother's room. *Catastrophe: an event that causes great trouble or destruction.*

I was going to cause Dr. McDevil a catastrophe.

That catastrophe was in my hand right now. I raised it over my head. I reared back on one foot. Then, with all my force, I launched it into the air.

The bottle flew through the infirmary. It flew through the dark air and it came down and smashed on the frame of Ruthie's bed. My bed. Its insides rained down on the white sheets. I took a deep breath and held it, so the gas wouldn't get me. Then I pulled the little metal square from my pocket. FELIX's FAMOUS PICKLES: THE FINEST IN NORTH CAROLINA, it said. A "lighter," they'd called it.

"What the hell are you doing?" Matty Barnwell said.

I flicked the little wheel on the lighter the way I'd seen Jesse do. A little flame leapt up from a hole in the top of the square like magic. For a moment I watched the flame glow. Then I threw it.

There was a second when I thought the flame had gone out. But all at once the bed exploded in fire with a great whoosh.

Matty Barnwell screamed.

I ran.

His rawbones arm shot out towards me, but it was too late. I was already out the door. As I ran down the hall, I could see the flame leaping as high as the infirmary ceiling.

Has anything ever looked so pretty?

Chapter 40

MILLIE

1939

The doctor, facing the opposite direction, hadn't seen Cecilia run by. But hearing the commotion, he frowned and stood up. "What's going on?"

"We gotta go," I whispered to Zeke. "Something's wrong."

We followed the doctor out of the office and into the hallway. Cecilia stood with her back to the dead end of the hall. The look on her face made me stop walking.

Her eyes were narrowed with determination, and something else. Anger. No, rage.

I turned to see what she was looking at. There, coming up the stairs opposite her, was a tall, gaunt shadow, coming from the tall, gaunt figure of Matty Barnwell.

Matty Barnwell, whose head had made a wet thwacking sound when I hit him with the mallet. Matty Barnwell, whose limbs had folded up like a rag doll's when we'd sunk him in the brine. He was walking with a deliberate step, his legs like a spider's.

I thought again of the golem, the man made of clay who couldn't be killed because he was never alive.

When he turned, I saw the side of his face was a hideous purple pulp knit by black stitches like train tracks.

"You," he said, turning to me, unfolding a horrible smile. "You tried to kill me."

Anger leapt up in me, smothering the terror for a moment. "You tried to kidnap Cecilia," I shouted. "I was defending her."

Dr. McDevitt and the nurse, who had reappeared, exchanged a look.

"Why don't we all sit down in my office, and we can discuss how to proceed?" said the doctor.

Cecilia had regained her composure. "Your office ain't gonna be around for much longer," she said, smiling.

The doctor looked at the nurse, then back at Cecilia. "Cecilia," he said very slowly. "What have you done?"

"Don't worry," Cecilia said. "I got the other girls out."

"Cecilia." The doctor took a small step towards her.

"The whole world's gonna learn what you are, what you do," Cecilia said. "Taking girls from their homes and treating them like farm animals. Worse! You work them, you starve them, you steal their wombs, you leave them alone with Matty Barnwell. You ain't a doctor. You're a monster."

"Oh, Cecilia." The doctor shook his head. "I would love nothing more than for the whole world to learn what we do here. I write papers for medical journals, letters to newspapers, trying to explain, to spread the word. Training wayward girls in a firm manner to make good citizens out of them, and—if they cannot be trained—making sure they don't breed. Keeping incorrigibles and the morally defective from sullying bloodlines is crucial for our nation's health. It's not punishment, it's progress. I suppose I can't expect you to understand, but other, more educated minds will."

"That's absurd," said Zeke, stepping away from the wall. "You think you can breed humans like fruit flies in a laboratory? Do you know the first thing about science?" He sounded perfectly calm, like he was asking a question in a high school biology class.

"I assure you, young man, this is a very sound science indeed."

Zeke laughed. Remarkably, he didn't look frightened at all. "Absurd," he said again. "That's a child's understanding of genetic science. I'm more of an engineer myself, but even I know human breeding doesn't work like that."

But the doctor had turned back towards Cecilia. He took another step towards her.

Quick as a squirrel, Cecilia leapt up on the radiator at the end of the hallway, and from there climbed onto a high windowsill. She turned halfway, keeping her eyes carefully on the small crowd.

"I might not be 'educated,'" she said. "Y'all made sure of that. But I know what a monster is. And I ain't gonna let you do this to any more girls. Not here."

She pulled open the hinged window. A blast of hot summer air filled the hallway. Blackness outside.

"No!" I screamed.

But it was too late.

Cecilia squeezed through the small window and disappeared into the empty night air.

Time froze and twisted. The hall went silent. No. No. No. For a moment my body felt paralyzed. Then, my terror blotted by a sudden burst of energy, I ran to the radiator, Zeke at my heels, stepped up, and poked my head out the small window. I looked down.

Nothing but darkness. Sickening, dizzying darkness.

No.

I felt in that moment what I'd felt three years ago atop the Lucky Strike tower. Like every other human on earth had disappeared and I was alone. Totally alone. I heard myself wail. I banged my forehead softly against the sill.

She was gone.

I wanted to dissolve into the wall, to disappear.

Then a noise came from somewhere far below. A *pssst* sound. I leaned out a little farther, my stomach lurching. Now my eyes had adjusted a bit to the darkness and I could see the pale patch of drive below, with a dark square shape on it. A smaller shape was next to it.

"*Pssst*," went the smaller shape in Cecilia's voice. "Just jump. There's hay!"

I leaned out even farther, though every bit of my body resisted. My fingers gripped the sill so tightly I could feel the blood cut off.

"C'mon," Cecilia hissed again. "You can do it. You're tougher than those bastards."

Then her shadowy shape began to run.

I turned back towards the hall. The doctor and Matty Barnwell were now advancing towards me, moving slowly like dog catchers about to net a mad dog. Zeke stood between me and them, holding his hands up as if ready to throw a punch. I saw something behind him, a large dark greasy smudge. It was growing.

Smoke.

As soon as I saw it I smelled it, and as soon as I smelled it I heard it. An angry crackling, like a thousand feet stomping on fall leaves. A tongue of orange flame appeared around the corner, moving quickly.

I looked back at the window. The small figure that was Cecilia was moving quickly away from the building, her pale hair flashing in the moonlight.

The ground was so very far away. My vision went wobbly

and I could feel my knees sagging. But when I turned back to look at Zeke, the flames seemed to have multiplied in size. The crackling filled my head, and the dark greasy smoke made me choke.

"Just follow me, Zeke," I whispered. "It'll be fine, I promise."

Swallowing hard, Zeke moved forward to stand next to me at the window.

"Give me a boost," I whispered. "Wait ten seconds after I've gone, then follow me."

"What?" Zeke's face was creased with concern. But he wove his fingers together into a basket like we did when we were kids, and let me step on his hands.

Now I was lying on the windowsill, half my body outside, my hands gripping the outer edge of the sill. Oh God. Oh God. I can't. I can't. I can't. The ground was somewhere below, shrouded in blackness, an impossible distance.

Then an image came to my mind, clear as a picture. It was Auggie, in that derby car he never got a chance to ride. He was flying down the wooden ramp he and Zeke built, going so fast he rose into the air. He turned to me and smiled.

You'll be fine, he said.

Out I went.

Out.

Down.

Chapter 41

MILLIE

1939

I fell.

I fell for what felt like a hundred years.

But then I landed. I landed in something soft but scratchy. I clawed the scratchy substance away from my face and sneezed. It was hay. Cecilia must have pushed the bales from the edge of the field to the driveway beneath the window. I coughed the hay dust from my lungs and rolled away just quickly enough to avoid being hit by Zeke, who landed in the same spot.

"Come on," I called to him. "To the car."

He scrambled up and we hurried across the yard. As we did, I saw girls in nightclothes streaming out the side door of the building. Flames were leaping from the upper windows now, bathing the girls' upturned faces in orange light. I wondered which one was Jacy, which one was Mollie. But I didn't have long to wonder, because just then the front door burst open and I saw Matty Barnwell's skinny frame silhouetted by the yellow hallway light. Behind him loomed the wider figure of Dr. McDevitt. "Hurry," I cried.

Zeke and I ran down the gravel drive, past the cabbage fields and the barn and the little cottage where Auntie Sybil lived. I ran full speed, head forward, arms akimbo. I hadn't run like that since I tore across Durham, running from my mother and the rabbi, running from the truth. But tonight, the running made me feel powerful as a wild animal, my legs carrying me in huge deerlike bounds.

Finally, reaching the gate, we stopped, lungs burning, and nearly collapsed. I leaned over, hands on my thighs, wondering if I might vomit. "Are they following?" I gasped.

Zeke coughed up dust and spit on the ground. "I don't think so," he said. "It looks like they've got bigger things to worry about."

I turned to see the entire top half of the building in flames, fire leaping towards the sky in an ecstatic dance. I could hear voices in the distance—girls' voices—hooting and yipping and singing. They sounded happy. More than happy, delighted. They were watching their prison burn.

Suddenly, Zeke cried out: "Hey!"

I whirled around to see the LaSalle lurch onto the road. It juddered back and forth, then screeched to a halt. We took a step towards it, but it shot off and careened down the road.

"What the heck?" Zeke said. "Is she driving off with my father's car?"

That was exactly what she was doing. Cecilia was driving away in Zeke's father's car. It was clearly her first time behind the wheel; I could hear the gears grinding even as the car disappeared into the darkness.

"The headlights aren't even on," Zeke said.

I opened my mouth to speak, but what came pouring out was laughter. Uncontrollable waves of laughter. I laughed so hard I could barely breathe. I laughed so hard my stomach cramped. When I finally rose, my sides throbbed with exertion, and I wiped sweat and hay dust off my forehead with the back of my hand.

Zeke stared at me, mouth half-open.

I felt light, giddy. Was this how people felt when they survived a disaster, were plucked from the water after a shipwreck or hauled from beneath the snow after an avalanche? Like all of a sudden you could see what mattered and what didn't matter in blinking neon. I wasn't a murderer. I wouldn't go to prison. And I wasn't useless. I'd helped Cecilia. It wasn't the way I'd imagined it, but it was help nonetheless. In an instant, the future rearranged itself before me. Where I'd long seen an endless gray grid of days, each one the same as the next, I now saw images of myself flash by. Laughing. Eating ice cream. Typing on an emerald-green Royal typewriter. Being free.

ZEKE AND I walked along the two-lane road, the black tar still radiating the summer day's heat. When a car's headlights would appear, we'd hide in the pines until it passed, in case it was a sheriff.

Zeke was mostly quiet, thinking. "About the sister . . . I don't understand?" he said.

"There was no sister."

Zeke frowned. "No sister at all? Why would she lie about that?"

"I think she learned to survive by telling people what they needed to hear. She knew I wouldn't have driven her back to Casteen so she could burn it down. But if I was driving her there to help her save her sister, well."

"Right." Zeke was quiet for a moment. "You would have done anything to help her save her sister."

"Right," I said. "I would have done anything."

Zeke didn't speak. But he reached out and took my hand.

"I'm sorry about your father's car," I said. "I had no idea she'd do that."

"That's all right," Zeke said. "I'll just move to the Arctic Circle, and I won't give my father my forwarding address."

"Ha ha."

"I'm serious." He laughed.

"I suppose I should feel bad I let her trick me," I said. "Jesse will probably gloat that she was a fraud all along. But I don't feel bad. I feel . . . free."

Zeke nodded. "You know, my mother always refused to give me any food to take along when Auggie gave out sandwiches to the hobos. She said some of them weren't even poor, they were just lazy and riding the rails for a laugh. She read so in the papers, she said. And, sure, I suppose that's possible. But I always figured it was better to feed a faker than starve someone truly hungry because you were so worried about being tricked."

"I never thought of it like that," I said. "But that's exactly right." What *was* so great about being untrickable? It only meant you had a hard shell around you.

We walked for a little while longer in silence. It felt good to walk at night, without the sun prickling my scalp and burning my neck.

"Zeke," I asked, "do you ever feel bad about . . . about the way things have turned out?"

"Like what?"

"Like, do you ever wish you'd gone back to college, or had a different job, or were married, or lived somewhere else? Do you ever wish you had . . . something different? What would your life look like, if you could wish it?"

Zeke was quiet for a minute. "Well," he said, "I would work with airplanes. That's the future, you know. I mean, trains will always be important, but airplanes, wow—they're going to change everything, and soon."

I started to cut him off—I didn't really want to hear about airplane design right now—then thought better of it.

"I don't care about college," he went on. "Most of it was a waste of time—but I do wish I had a bigger workshop. The engineering laboratories at State were something else. And New Bern? I guess, well, the town is nothing special, but why would I want to live somewhere else?"

"You don't dream about visiting other places? About seeing New York? Or Paris?"

"I mean, sure, that would be swell. But, well, but . . ." He coughed and cleared his throat, then cleared it again. "But, well, you're not in those places. So, yeah, they'd be nice to visit, but only with you."

Sometimes you know something without knowing it. The knowledge is in your body, perhaps, but has never made its way to your brain. Now it was hitting me all at once. Zeke had always been there. And he'd always loved me. I saw him sitting in the parlor with me at sixteen, smiling bashfully as our hands accidentally touched over the plate of oatmeal cookies. I saw him at eighteen, coming by the house before we left for college, writing down his dormitory address "just in case you feel like writing." I saw him at twenty-one, when I was back from the hospital and barely speaking, bumping into me and Fanny on our long riverside walks so often it could hardly have been a coincidence. "Oh," was all I could say. But that was enough, because instead of talking, I stopped, stood up on my tiptoes, and kissed Zeke right on the mouth.

IT MUST HAVE been midnight before we got to Kinston town, its downtown empty and eerie in the darkness. "When's the earliest train?" I asked.

"There's a freighter at ten after three," he answered immediately. "No passenger cars, but I know the engineer—we can ride in a boxcar if there's room."

We sat together on the ground outside the freight station, waiting. The moon rose above the pines, large and white as a scoop of Maola vanilla ice cream. Zeke and I leaned against each other's shoulders. It felt so natural.

"So who was that tall guy with the stitches?" he asked, turning towards me. "Didn't look like a doctor."

"No," I said slowly. From somewhere in the hot night came the long trembling call of an owl. I took a deep breath. "His name is Matty Barnwell. I thought I'd killed him, but seems like I was wrong."

Zeke's eyes examined my face, as if he was unsure whether I was joking. "You're going to have to explain that one."

So I did. I explained the horrible night after the wedding. The long fingers reaching towards me and Cecilia. The swing of the mallet. The horrible smacking sound. The splash as the pickle barrel tumbled into the Neuse.

When I finished, the big round station clock said three. My bottom felt numb from sitting on the hard ground for so long. Zeke's mouth hung half-open. I felt a little flash of fear: Was this too much? Would he recoil?

But finally Zeke simply squeezed my arm and said, "I guess it's good that Jesse taught you a decent batting technique."

I smiled. It was true. Jesse had insisted on teaching me and Auggie and the cousins to play baseball one summer when we were small. How desperate he must have been for someone to play with that he dragged his bookworm little siblings and prissy girl cousins to the sandlot.

"In all seriousness, if you had actually killed him, he would have deserved it," Zeke said. "Cecilia was right on that count. Fellows have gotten the electric chair for far less."

"I suppose," I said. "Still, I'm glad I don't have to live with that."

I must have fallen asleep, leaning against Zeke's shoulder in the warm night, because the next thing I heard was the screech of the freight train. Zeke pulled me upright, and we ran to the end of the platform to find an open car. Zeke gave me a boost the way he'd done at the window, and I flopped face forward onto the dusty floor of the boxcar. I scrambled upright and reached a hand to Zeke, who heaved himself up after.

I sat, blinking in the darkness, my hands scrabbling for something to hold on to as the train gave a long groan and began clacking forward. I grinned to myself. Hopping a freight train on a dark North Carolina night! This was the sort of thing you could write about.

As I settled into the rhythm of the rails, I became aware of another noise. Something soft and alive.

Breathing.

"Evening," said a voice from somewhere in the shadows. "Or morning. I ain't too sure."

Chapter 42

MILLIE

1939

I startled and drew my knees towards myself, ready to spring.

"It's all right," said Zeke, patting my shoulder. "It's just some other freight hoppers."

I squinted and made out the shapes of four people sitting on sacks on the other side of the car. One of them leaned forward out of the shadow and I saw that he was just a boy, with a narrow, wary face and overalls held together with rope where the strap had torn.

Hobos.

"Hello," said Zeke. "I'm Zeke, and this is Millie. We'll only be sharing your ride as far as New Bern, just an hour or so down the track."

"Y'all are welcome to it," said the boy. "Rails are free to anyone who can hop on. Last free thing in America, I reckon. I'm Jer, by the way. Jeremiah Carthew to my ma."

"Nice to meet you, Jer," said Zeke pleasantly. "Where's home to you?"

"Harper County, Oklahoma," Jer said. "But I ain't seen it since I was twelve."

The boy didn't look too much older than that now, sixteen at the most, though hunger had carved the puppy fat from his cheeks. I thought of Auggie at the same age, just before he got sick, eating cookies under the blankets in his own bedroom, a copy of Jules Verne balanced on his knees.

"That there's Billy and Bobby Kenan, from the turpentine camps down in Florida," Jer said, gesturing towards two young Negro men sitting knee to knee. They looked a few years older than Jer, both of them wearing white shirts and pants held up with suspenders. "And that's Patsy, though he won't say where he's really from—big ol' mystery, that one."

"I *told* y'all I'm from Lizard Lick," grumbled a stocky shape from the back of the car. "It ain't but twenty miles from Raleigh."

"That sound like a real place to y'all?" asked Jer, grinning and slapping his knee. "Anyhow"—he looked back at us—"y'all have anything to eat? I ain't had nothing but a handful of boiled peanuts since yesterday morning."

"Sorry, no," Zeke said.

"Sorry," I said, wishing I had my satchel full of sandwiches.

"That's all right," the boy said. "Can't hurt to ask."

"Where are you all headed?" asked Zeke.

"Coastward," Jer said. "See, we were working the melon harvest out near Goldsboro, met a fellow who said the fish on that coast get so thick in the water come September, you can scoop them up with your hands and sell 'em by the pound."

Zeke nodded, but his brow was furrowed. When the mullet ran down at the beaches south of New Bern, people would come from up and down the coast to net them. They pitched camp and lived out of tents for weeks. It was hard work, and clannish—families camped on the same spots they'd had for generations. I couldn't imagine a boy from Oklahoma would know much about fishing. Nor would he likely have the money for a net or anything else.

Then I had an idea. The moment it popped into my head it was out of my mouth. "We can get you some food," I said to Jer and the others, "if you get off with us at New Bern."

I could feel Zeke looking at me curiously. I gave him a look back, one that said *I know what I'm doing*, and he nodded.

Jer raised his eyebrows warily. "Y'all church people?" he asked. "Nothing against church people, but last time I went to a church for food they made me listen to the preacher talk about sin for about two hours before they let me eat."

"No," I assured him. "We're not church people."

"Sounds good to me, then," said Jer. A second later, as if remembering the manners taught to him by his mother, he added, "Thank you very much. But how about them? I reckon they're just as hungry as me." He pointed his chin towards the brothers and the boy from Lizard Lick.

"We've got plenty for anyone who wants to come," I said.

Two hours later, Zeke and I and the four boys were traipsing up the front path to my house in the thin pink dawn light. We entered, and I motioned for the boys to sit at the dining table while I went into the kitchen. I opened the icebox and saw there was half a lemon pie, a crock of farmer's cheese, and a bowl of stewed prunes covered with an upside-down plate. On the counter was a basket of eggs and two loaves of my mother's homemade bread. This would do.

I cracked the eggs one by one into the bowl with the green stripe, and added a pinch of salt. I couldn't remember the last time I'd cooked something. The words *Millie's useless in the kitchen, just like she's useless at everything else* rang in my ears, but I stopped—who had actually said that? No one. The words sprang from my own head, but they weren't the truth.

I heard a creaking on the stairs and a moment later my

mother's voice said sharply, "Zeke? What's going on? Who are these people? Where's Millie?"

"In the kitchen," I heard Zeke say.

How a woman as short as my mother moved across the room so fast I cannot tell you, but not a second later she was standing in the kitchen doorway with a thunderous expression on her face. "Millie! What's happening? Why didn't you come home last night? And who are these dirty boys at the table?"

I decided to tell her the most simple truth possible. "Zeke and I stayed out late to help Elisaveta get back home."

"You found her family?" My mother's face was creased in confusion.

"Sort of," I said.

"And these boys?"

From over my mother's shoulder I could see the young hobos staring at the floor, like puppies expecting a hard slap with a rolled-up newspaper.

"They're here for breakfast. I was going to scramble some eggs and slice the bread for toast. But if you think there's not enough, I'll send them off." I stood tensely, waiting for a reaction.

My mother was silent for a moment. Her eyes scanned the boys up and down. Finally, she snorted. "Not enough? I was expecting that bottomless pit Elisaveta to be here today. I've enough for the tsar's army." She threw open the cabinets and began taking out more food—a cantaloupe melon, a raisin cake, a tin of chocolate cookies.

Sometimes people surprise you, I was learning. And that's not always a bad thing.

The boys sat stiffly, as if it had been years since they'd eaten at a table. But as soon as my mother and I began bringing in the food, their hunger overtook their manners. A fluffy yellow mountain of scrambled eggs disappeared in minutes, along with both loaves of bread smeared in butter and jam. They scooped up farmer's cheese with stewed prunes until their spoons scraped the bottom of their bowls and I refilled them.

My mother stood in the doorway with her hands on her hips, with the same satisfied expression she'd had watching Cecilia eat. "*Ess, ess,*" she murmured to herself.

When all the food was gone, the boys sat nervously, unsure of what to do.

"Just carry the plates to the sink, if you don't mind," I said. "And feel free to come back next week. You or anyone you meet. Sunday. We'll serve breakfast at eight. And we'll have no talk of sin, I promise."

My mother looked at me but said nothing.

The boys left with Zeke, who was going to take them down to the cannery and make an introduction. Apparently they were hiring again, after nearly a decade. I wished them well.

I went to begin washing dishes, though I was so tired my vision was fuzzy at the corners. My mother sat down heavily at the kitchen table, shaking her head back and forth, her gray-brown curls jiggling, her face unreadable.

I waited for her to say something, but she didn't.

"I'm sorry about the wedding," I said, breaking the silence. "I know you're angry. I'll apologize to Violet and Aunt Zora and Uncle Abe. And to Sophie."

"I'm not thinking about the wedding, Millie."

"Oh."

She was silent.

"Well, what then?"

"I'm thinking of how much I love you and how little I understand you."

"I see." I turned off the taps but didn't move, just stood still amid the empty bowls and dirty pans, the morning sun bathing the kitchen in pale buttery-yellow light.

"When you were born, I was so happy," she went on. "A girl. I was so lonely then, your father working every hour God made. I had Jesse, but even at three Jesse hardly needed me. I used to try to read him fairy tales at bedtime and one night he turned to me and said, 'These stories aren't even true—let's just go to sleep.'" She laughed darkly. "Then you arrived, and I thought, 'Thank you, God, a girl for me.' I thought, here's a girl I can teach to cook and embroider, who'll listen to my fairy tales. And when she's grown up, we'll be best friends, just like me and Misha."

I turned around and leaned with my back against the sink. Misha had been my mother's best friend growing up. She'd died not long before my mother moved to New Bern. My mother kept a picture of her in a small silver frame on her bedside table.

"But then you were just a tiny girl when your father died, and I had to work so much," she said. "I suppose I should have tried harder to make time, to tell you stories, to teach you things, to build understanding. Because"—her voice broke—"now you're all grown and I don't even know how to talk to you! I don't know what you're thinking. I don't know what you want!"

"Oh, Mother," I said. "I'm sorry I've disappointed you."

"That's not it, Millie," she said, turning her large face towards me. "I don't understand you. But I'm not disappointed in you. I'm proud of you."

I turned back to the sink as if to start washing again. I wasn't sure I could control the expression on my face anymore.

"You don't just accept what God gives you," my mother went on. "You want more. You don't give up. It worries me for you. But I admire it too. That girl—Elisaveta—was lucky it was you who found her. Who else but you would have fought for a stranger like that?"

"Auggie," I whispered.

"Auggie," my mother replied.

I turned. My mother's eyes were shining with tears.

"I miss him," I said.

"I know," she said. "I miss him every day. I dream about him every night."

"You do?"

"Oh, yes. I know you think I was hard-hearted when Auggie got sick, but you have to understand—I knew he was going to die from the moment we met that doctor at Duke, the terrible one with the pointy face. You and Auggie, you had your hopes, and I didn't want to crush those. But I've seen people die from this same disease. Misha, she had cancer too, you know? They never used that word. All Misha knew was that she had a womanly complaint. But she got thinner and thinner, and then she was gone." Her voice broke. "So when Auggie was ill, I knew what it meant. I had to keep myself together. First for Auggie, then for you."

For me. Of course.

You can't fall to pieces when you have a daughter in Dix Hill, having fallen to pieces herself.

"I'm so sorry," I whispered. "I kept you from mourning your own son."

"No, that's not how I feel, and please don't be sorry," she said. "Perhaps I should have told you what I truly believed when Auggie first got sick, but your hope seemed so good for him—for both of you. I didn't realize how difficult it would be to fall from those high hopes."

I stood for a moment, a question trembling on my tongue.

"When . . . when you dream of Auggie," I began. "What is he doing in the dream?"

My mother smiled, and for a moment her face looked ten years younger. "Sometimes I dream I'm in the kitchen, cooking, and I look out the window and see him," she said. "He's small again, playing in the yard. And I think to myself, *I thought you were lost, but you're right here.* And sometimes I dream he's almost grown, the way he looked just before he got sick. He's sitting in that thing—that meshuga contraption he and Zeke were building—and he's at the top of a hill, which is strange, since there are no hills around here, and he waves to me." She looked up, and there were tears in her eyes, but they were bright tears, happy tears. "I always wake up feeling so peaceful from that one, just for a moment."

I sat down next to her and laid my hand on top of hers. "That sounds really nice," I said.

We were both quiet for a moment, then she wiped her eyes on her apron and stood up. She pushed her sleeves back, as if to finish washing the dishes. But before she went to the sink, she said, "Maybe next Sunday I'll make the challah French toast. Do you think those boys would like that?"

"I think they'd love it," I said.

I stood up as well, my whole body feeling dazed and sore from the long strange night. But just as I was walking up the stairs, there was a rude, insistent knocking on the front door.

"It's not locked, Jesse," I called out.

But wait. Why would Jesse be knocking on the door this early in the morning? Surely he was still asleep?

The door opened. It wasn't Jesse. It was the police.

Chapter 43

MILLIE

1939

Three policemen stood in the parlor. One I recognized as Josiah Riggsby, who was in my year at school. He looked uncomfortable. They all did.

"We're sorry to bother you so early, ma'am," said one of the officers to my mother, taking off his hat.

"We get up early," my mother said, one hand on her hip like a general. "What do you want?"

"Well, ma'am, we got a call from officers out in Kinston. They're investigating a fire at a school for girls. Nobody got hurt, thank the Lord, but the building is pretty well destroyed." The officer, a heavy man with salt-and-pepper curls and a piggy, pushed-in nose, shifted his weight.

I held my breath and went rigid as a board. My knees began to wobble, and I squeezed them together. If I fell to the floor now, there'd be no chance for me.

"Oh?" said my mother. "What does this have to do with us?"

"Well, ma'am, the officers in Kinston found a cigarette lighter in the ash. Said 'Felix's Pickles' on it. I understand y'all are the owners of that operation?"

My mother shook her head dismissively. "Yes? Many people

have our cigarette lighters—we give them away to grocers as advertisements. What of it?"

Josiah Riggsby turned towards the window, the tips of his ears red.

"See," said the older officer, "it's that the doctor that runs the school for the wayward girls, he says he knows who started the fire—some poor mad girl who'd run away from there some weeks ago. They're already on her trail. But the doctor says she didn't act alone. He says she was with another young woman and a young man, and he described someone looking quite a bit like Miss Green here."

"Officers," said my mother, "I don't mean any offense to my daughter, but she's as common looking as a girl can be. Brown hair and brown eyes? How many girls between here and Kinston look just the same? This is absurd."

"I understand, ma'am," said the officer. "It's just that when we got the call about the cigarette lighter and the suspects, Officer Riggsby here remembered his wife saying she'd seen Miss Green with a strange woman here in New Bern. Which makes us wonder if you, Miss Green, somehow got tangled with the mad girl from that school." Here his expression softened and he looked at me. "Miss, if you did get tangled with this mess, just tell us now and you'll surely not be in nearly as much trouble. The staff at the school says she's a scheming person, real devious. It wouldn't hardly be your fault if she drew you into something unwholesome."

"Officers, come on now."

I was so startled to hear Jesse speak from behind me, I nearly lost my balance. He'd come into the room so quietly, very unlike himself.

Jesse stepped forward, smiling, wearing the chest-forward

posture he uses to meet with businessmen. "I'm the head of the household; it's me you'll want to be speaking with. Though I already know the two of you"—he gestured towards the older two officers—"from our mutual association. Good to see you fellows."

Masons, ugh.

Jesse slapped the two Masons on the back and held out his hand for Josiah Riggsby to shake. "I'm certain this is a mistake on the part of Kinston. First of all, we send off dozens of those lighters with every new order. If I'm doing my job right, every groceryman in the state has a box of them on the counter by now." He grinned and winked.

I struggled to keep my face neutral.

"As for the 'strange' woman," Jesse went on, "that was my wife's cousin who was visiting from Baltimore. German, just off the boat—doesn't speak a lick of English, poor girl."

I tried not to let my face show my utter shock. Not only was Jesse lying for me, he was lying so quickly and smoothly.

"Do you mind if we talk to your wife, just so we can tell Kinston we've confirmed it?" said the older officer.

"I'm sorry," Jesse said, shaking his head, "she's not well." He dropped his voice lower. "She's been upchucking, if you get my drift. If you'd like to come back in the afternoon, she may be feeling a bit steadier."

"Oh, no, it's fine, we'll tell Kinston we've confirmed," said the officer. "And, uh, congratulations."

"Thanks." Jesse grinned so broadly and genuinely I realized that, on this count, he was telling the truth. Fanny *was* expecting. Despite the circumstance, my heart leapt.

"Sorry to bother you," said the officer. Josiah Riggsby, beet red now, gave a curt nod.

"Not a problem at all, just doing your job," said Jesse in the same hearty, doing-business-with-bigwigs voice. "See you fellows Thursday." He smiled at the officers before closing the door. Then he turned back to me and my mother, who had sat down heavily in the parlor chair. "Dummies," he scoffed. "McKinley, the one with the gray hair, couldn't find his way out of a paper bag."

"Jesse." I gasped, looking out the window to make sure they were truly gone. "You lied to the police for me."

"Course I did. You think I'm gonna let those weasels haul my sister away? And anyway"—his voice dropped lower—"if you burned down some school, good for you—education's overrated."

"I didn't!" I cried.

"I don't need to know," Jesse said, holding his hands up.

For a moment, I thought of spilling the beans about everything that had happened the night before. But Jesse was right—he and my mother didn't need to know any more than they already did. I strode across the room and did something I hadn't done since I was a child—I threw my arms around Jesse and hugged him.

"All right, all right," Jesse said, stiffening. "Gotta go bring Fanny her tea."

My mother spoke up, her voice trembling slightly, like she was trying to keep down a strong emotion. "Is Fanny really . . . Could it be true . . . a baby?"

"Looks like," Jesse said, grinning. "She's been upchucking every morning for the past few days, so . . ."

"How wonderful!" my mother exclaimed, then quickly added, "*Kein ayin hara*," and pretended to spit, to keep away the evil eye.

"Wow, Jesse," I said sincerely. "That's wonderful news."

"Thanks, Sis," he said, then disappeared into the kitchen to make the tea. Jesse making tea! I was seeing something new each minute this morning, wasn't I?

My mother, still sitting in the armchair, let out an enormous breath. "What a morning," she said. "What a summer. You think you get to my age, your life becomes peaceful, you get to sit on your porch with your knitting, ha!"

"I'm afraid you're not that old yet, Mother," I said. "Though I guess you *are* going to be a grandmother."

"A grandmother," she repeated in wonder. "I never thought it would happen." She looked up at me, a guilty expression on her face. "I didn't mean it like that! I'm sure you'll get married and be a mother one day. If that's what you want, that is."

"I don't know what I want yet," I said truthfully. "Not when it comes to marriage and children, that is."

"I understand," she said. "My children have been such a joy, it's been hard to imagine anyone wanting something different. But you've never been a girl to take the common path, Millie. So about Richmond, if you don't want to go, I'll call Mrs. Tepper and—"

"It's fine," I said. "I said I'd go, I'll go. I know you wanted to visit Mrs. Tepper anyway. I'm not making any promises, though. I think—I think I may not need a matchmaker after all. But I will need a new dress, of course."

My mother raised her eyebrows. "Charge it to my account."

Chapter 44

MILLIE

"Sorry, we don't open till eleven," called Sophie Cohen as the bells on the doors of the Marie Antoinette jingled. Then she looked up and saw it was me. "Oh," she said.

I moved past the racks of autumn dresses and marten fur stoles to stand by the counter. Sophie was doing some sort of inventory, writing in a book of lined paper with a red pencil. "Hi, Sophie," I said.

"Hi," she said, her face blank. She looked back down at her paper and kept writing.

"Is it all right if I sit?" I asked, motioning to the little wire chair next to the mirror where ladies tried on hats.

"Suit yourself."

I sat down. "I wanted to say I'm sorry," I said. "The way I acted at the wedding was completely awful. I'll pay to have the pearls fixed."

Sophie looked up. Her blue eyes studied my face. "It was inappropriate, yes," she said. "No one has ever tried to hit me before. But until the wedding, I hadn't understood why you were so angry at me."

"Didn't you?"

"No, Millie, I didn't. I hadn't known that you didn't read my letters."

"Like I said, I wasn't in a state of mind to read about yacht parties," I said, hearing the bitterness creeping into my voice.

"My letters weren't about yacht parties, Millie," Sophie said, putting down her pencil. "Maybe the first one was, but that was written before I knew that Auggie had died or that you were in the hospital. All I knew then was that Auggie was ill; I was trying to be cheerful."

"All right, Sophie," I said, taking a deep breath. "I'm sorry. Tell me what the other letters said."

Sophie dropped her head towards her chest. When she raised it again, her voice was thick with tears. "Now I don't want to tell you," she whispered. "When I wrote those letters about what happened to me, we were still friends. But now you hate me. If I tell you now, you'll just hate me more."

"Sophie"—I sighed—"I don't hate you. I've just been angry. Angry and jealous. My life fell to pieces three years ago, and yours has been just marching along so perfectly. You've got a store, a husband, a place in the world. And here I am, useless as a third leg."

"You're not useless, Millie," Sophie said. "And my life hasn't been marching along perfectly. Do you think I wanted to move back to New Bern? Do you think I wanted to marry Sam?"

"Didn't you?"

"No!" she cried, a flush of red appearing on her pale cheeks. Then, as if pained by a sudden guilt, she looked down and said, "Sam's been very good to me. I'm grateful for that. Or I should be. But, no, I wanted to live in New York and be a dress designer, just like we always planned."

"So why didn't you?"

"Because I was ruined, Millie!" A sob wrenched her body.

"Ruined?" The word sounded so old-fashioned, like something from a Victorian lady's novel. Or, I thought, my mind flashing to Cecilia and the girls of the third floor, like something from a place like Casteen.

"Yes, ruined." Sophie pulled a handkerchief from a drawer and wiped her eyes. She must have been wearing mascara to darken her eyelashes, because her cheeks were now streaked with black. "By a man. Of course."

"Tell me," I said. "I promise, I don't hate you. And I couldn't possibly judge you. Remember, I'm the loon who started a fight at my cousin's wedding."

Sophie smiled faintly. "You're not a loon, Millie. And don't say you won't judge me until you've heard the rest."

I nodded.

Sophie sniffed and straightened. "I met a man in New York. A fur dealer. His name was Bernard. He wasn't handsome, exactly, and he was much older than me. But he had . . . something. Charm? More than charm, really—when I was with him, I felt like the only person in the world. I felt so beautiful, so smart, so understood. My job at Bonwit Teller only paid eighteen dollars a week, and I was living with two other girls in a flat with a bathroom in the hallway and eating egg sandwiches half off at the Automat. It was fine—that's how everyone gets their start in New York—but I was used to having my own bedroom, my own bathroom. I guess I was spoiled.

"Then Bernard comes into Bonwit Teller one day and spends an hour at my counter, just chatting to me. The next day he sends a dozen red roses! I'm so stupid, to be impressed by something like roses. But, oh, they were so pretty, and Bernard was charming like you wouldn't believe. The next thing I know, he's taking me to dinner at Delmonico's and Luchow's, and he knows everyone there. He took me on his sailboat, he took me for a weekend at his country house; he promised he'd take me to Paris. And then he said I should quit my job and he'd set me up in my very own rooms at the Sherry-Netherland, which is the most beautiful hotel."

She closed her eyes for a moment, as if recalling the pleasure of the hotel's beauty.

"And oh, Millie, I'm so ashamed of myself—I should have known better. It's the oldest story in the world, isn't it? Naïve young girl swindled by a charming liar. Because that's what he was—a liar. I hadn't been in the hotel for a month when management came and said the bill was unpaid. I called Bernard and he said, 'Oh, it's a misunderstanding, I'll take care of it.' But then a week later management sends the bellman to remove my belongings and put me out on the street. Literally on the street!

"I tried to find Bernard—I went by the house where he said he lived, this gorgeous brick mansion on the Upper East Side that he'd pointed out when we'd go walking at night. And it turns out it wasn't even a home! It was the Portuguese consulate! I'd seen the flag outside, of course, but Bernard had told me it was his family crest! I would have known better, but remember I had scarlet fever the week we studied flags at school?" Sophie looked up, tearstained.

I looked back at her and burst into giggles. "Oh, Sophie," I said.

Her lip trembled, and I could tell she was deciding whether or not to be angry that I was laughing. Then she too began to laugh. "You should have seen the confused Portuguese secretaries when I burst in, demanding to see Bernard. They thought I was an absolute madwoman." Immediately her face turned pink. "I'm sorry, Millie, I shouldn't have said that."

"It's fine, Sophie. I'm beginning to be proud of being a madwoman."

"I don't think you're a madwoman," Sophie said, reaching out to put her hand over mine. "You had a horrible thing happen and you didn't pretend everything was fine. I'm in awe of that. A much smaller bad thing happened to me, and I've driven myself to misery acting like my life is still perfect."

"What do you mean?" It seemed from my perspective that Sophie had landed on her feet as prettily as a Persian cat.

"Sam," Sophie said unhappily.

"What about him?"

Sophie buried her face in her manicured hands. "He's just . . . oh, Millie. He's so . . . so *boring*."

I maintained a carefully neutral face. "Does he have other . . . qualities?"

Sophie sighed. "He's kind. He's hardworking. He loves his mother. He loves me too, I suppose, though he doesn't understand me. Maybe understanding from a man is too much to expect, though."

I thought for a moment. You can't criticize the husband of your friend, even if they've criticized him first, everyone knows that. "Do you feel like you could grow to be happy being his wife?"

Sophie began to cry again. "I don't know. No. I don't know. But it's not even a question I can ask; it's too late. I was ruined, and now I'm married to Sam, and that's that."

"Ruined? Who says?" Anger stirred inside me. Here was Sophie, beautiful and clever and whole. Why should a woman—again, I thought of Cecilia and the girls of the third floor—be declared "ruined" while men like Bernard and Jimmy Spruill hitch up their pants and walk away, smirking? What kind of world is that?

"Mother, for one. I would never have told her, of course—I would have never told anyone but you—but my cousin Florence from Greensboro came to visit when I was at a low ebb and wrangled everything out of me. Then she went and blabbed to all of Jewish Greensboro, who blabbed to all of Jewish Durham, who blabbed to all of Jewish New Bern and Wilmington and probably the rest of North Carolina too, and, oh, now I'm ruined.

"Mother was so angry. She called me a whore! You wouldn't have thought she'd even known that word. She and my father said they'd send me to live with my aunt in Atlanta who's religious—you know, married to one of those men with the hats and side curls, with a dozen children. She said they'd find a religious man to marry me off to, someone who'd keep me in line. Millie, can you imagine! I don't want a dozen children! But then Sam came over one evening and offered to marry me, just like that. I guess he's been sweet on me since school, and it didn't matter to him that I'm a whore."

"Sophie! Stop." I spoke more loudly than I'd intended, and I could feel my face had grown red.

"I ruined my career in New York, quitting Bonwit Teller like that—what designer would hire me now?—and I ruined my marriage prospects, letting myself become a kept woman. You know, after he disappeared, I realized I didn't even know Bernard's last name!"

"What a lout," I said. "Would you like me to have him murdered?"

Sophie looked at me, her blue eyes wide in surprise, before realizing I was joking and dissolving into giggles again.

"Here we are, the 'Cleverest' and the 'Teacher's Pet' in the yearbook, the prides of Jewish New Bern, a lunatic and a ruined woman," I said.

Sophie snorted in a most unladylike way.

"But in all seriousness," I went on, "if this whole thing had never happened, what would you want to be doing with your life now?"

Sophie didn't even need to think. "I'd be working in an atelier, learning to design dresses, not selling them."

"You don't like selling them?" That surprised me a bit. Sophie seemed so confident and poised as the chatelaine of her boutique. She did, as my mother said, have such nice taste.

"Why do you think I named this place the Marie Antoinette? From the outside the queen's life seemed perfect, but she was so bored, so miserable, like a bird in a fancy cage."

"I see. But you're not actually in a cage."

"No," said Sophie. "It just feels like it. If only I had your bravery."

"Bravery?" I laughed, but with a feeling like a fish bone was caught in my throat. "I've done nothing with my life since Auggie died. I'm wandering around New Bern like a ghost, like it was me who died. It's one thing to feel grief, it's another to let it be the entirety of your life. I haven't written a word in three years."

"So why don't you write something now?" Sophie asked.

"I'll do it when you start designing dresses," I joked.

"Deal," said Sophie, looking right at me with perfect seriousness. She reached out her hand to shake.

Oh. I felt a swirl of fear, of shame.

Then I remembered standing on the edge of the windowsill at Casteen, staring down into the blackness, choosing to jump.

I could choose to jump again. I could trust that if I broke, I would heal.

I reached out and shook Sophie's hand.

Epilogue

MILLIE

New Bern
August 1940

I have never seen the parlor in quite such a state. The new luggage set my mother bought me—a trunk, three cases, and a hatbox, all in yellow leather—is stacked against the wall. The top suitcase is open; there are so many books inside it won't latch. Still more books are stacked in crooked piles on the floor. The chesterfield is strewn with brassieres and socks and underwear.

"Oh, my," says Lizzy as she comes in the front door. The twins, who are walking now, zip in behind her, burbling in glee. They can tell something exciting is happening. "Your mother must be having a conniption at the mess."

"Hardly," says my mother, huffing down the stairs with another armful of clothes—these ones are Auggie's. "It's good to have a big clean-out. It'll be tidy again in no time." Knowing my mother, it'll be tidy again before supper.

Lizzy turns back to me. "I was hoping you could watch the twins for a bit while I go to the grocery," she says. "Mother's at work, Violet's in a mood, and Bea has her hands full—Eugene is teething. But I see you have your hands full too. When's your train again?"

"Not till Tuesday," I say. "And of course I'll watch them—come here, bubbies!" The boys careen, shrieking, into my arms.

I used to find the twins exhausting, but now they're such *people*—Aaron with his bright little eyes darting everywhere, Adam with his slow shy smile. And it feels different to spend time with them now that time is so short. I'll be back, of course, for holidays and weddings and brises and birthdays. But it won't be the same.

On Tuesday, the Palmetto Limited will take me and Sophie to Baltimore, where we'll start our new jobs. Sophie will be working for Claire Vandermeer, the designer, who's made gowns for all sorts of movie stars and even the president's wife. It's a junior job, starting at the bottom. But I remind her that she could still be sitting behind the counter at the Marie Antoinette.

What I don't say: She could still be married to Sam Cohen.

Their divorce has given the yentas of Little Jerusalem something to gossip about for the next century. Sophie's father took her to Mexico at Christmas to get the divorce papers, which was a scandal in and of itself, not to mention a shock to anyone who knows pious, grouchy Mr. Zucker. Sophie's mother was so angry, it's a wonder she didn't file for divorce herself. She's still not speaking to Sophie, which is just fine with Sophie.

Sweet boring Sam landed on his feet. He's already engaged to a pretty girl from Durham.

"Thank you. I'll be back in an hour," says Lizzy, blowing kisses to the twins.

As soon as she leaves, my mother takes the boys to the table for slices of cake, and I turn my attention to sorting Auggie's clothes. Some of the shirts and sweaters have holes in them and will be used for rags or unraveled for yarn. The rest will go into the hall closet, to be given away on Sundays.

A few minutes later, Fanny arrives with her cousin Rivka. Fanny is holding baby Susan, who's sleeping. Skinny, big-eyed Rivka is carrying a basket of figs and another of butter beans. Now that Fanny and Jesse have their own house, Fanny has a bigger garden, which has been bursting all summer.

"Hello, bubbies," Fanny says, kissing the twins on their heads. To my mother, she says, "I thought we could do the figs in a cake at breakfast, and the beans in a chicken stew at supper?"

"Oh, yes," says my mother. "The boys loved your chicken stew last time."

"Anything tastes good when you have nothing," Fanny says modestly.

"That's true, but come on, Fanny, you're a wonderful cook," I say.

Fanny smiles. "One of the boys did say my peach pie was better than his own mother's."

The first breakfast we cooked for the boys from the train that morning last summer has turned into many more breakfasts, then suppers as well. Our mailbox now bears a proud chalk *X*, so hungry, desperate boys know it's a place they will be welcomed and fed. There are more of them now, since word's gotten out that the New Bern cannery's hiring. My mother will soon begin letting my and Auggie's old rooms for a dollar a night.

"You don't need the money, Ma," Jesse sometimes says. He still likes to be the big man, taking care of everyone. He's got plenty of other people to take care of now, though, what with baby Susan and Fanny's family from Germany living with them.

"Maybe I don't need the money," my mother says to him, "but I do like the company."

"Look," Fanny says to Rivka, tapping the framed New Bern *Sun Journal* article on the wall next to the pictures of Auggie and my father. "Newspaper."

"News-paper," Rivka repeats.

"Your English is getting so much better, Rivka," I tell her.

I should be embarrassed that my mother insisted on framing my article. But mostly I'm just proud. Will it ever stop being a thrill, seeing my name right there in black ink? I guess I'll find out, once I get to Baltimore and start my new job at the *Jewish Times.*

An impressive exposé, the editor called it, at my interview. Then his face turned dark. *And yet we say what's happening in Germany could never happen here.*

The article—the exposé—took months to report. I had to track down the social worker named Sybil Leigh, who was living—hiding, if you ask me—in a boardinghouse in Raleigh. When I told her I was a reporter, she slammed the door right on my foot. Miss Pritchard, the Behavior teacher, was even harder to find, as she'd married and was now a Mrs. Norbert Janes of Goldsboro. She was no more friendly than Sybil Leigh. It wasn't until I found Miss Grieve, the Casteen night warden, that I got anywhere at all. She sat me down in her tiny Kinston kitchen with a cup of tea and began to cry. Miss Grieve led me to Bertie Lou Rice, who was working in a cotton mill just down the road.

"I'll tell you exactly what happened," Bertie Lou said bitterly. "But I don't reckon anyone will care."

Miss Grieve also gave me the address of Jacy Bragg of Ocracoke Island. It took me two days to get there, and I arrived green with seasickness.

Jacy had a round face and a crown of braids atop her head. She smiled as she stared off her aunt's porch at the wild gray Atlantic.

"Burning down that place was God's own work," she said.

The article caused quite a scandal among the board of directors at Casteen, which included some of the most prominent business and government men in North Carolina. Dr. McDevitt was fired, and the old, half-burned Casteen building razed. But they're rebuilding the facilities—the state has given the board a large grant to construct something "modern"—and soon they'll hire a new director. There'll always be a place to lock up girls the world considers crazy or bad or broken.

The police looked for Cecilia for a while after the fire, but after the article came out, they said the case was closed for lack of leads.

"I reckon we'll never know what happened to her," the police officer told me.

I just nodded.

They may never know. But I do.

I tell my mother I'm going to bring down some more of Auggie's clothes, but once I'm upstairs I slip into my own bedroom and open my desk drawer. There's one last thing in here I need to pack. The letter lies folded underneath Captain Kennedy's copy of the *Atlas of European Languages*. I should probably give that back, though I doubt I will. I open the letter and, for the hundredth time, smooth it out and begin to read.

Dear Millie,

I guess you can see from the postmark I'm in California. Los Angeles—it means "the Angels" in Spanish, which is pretty funny to us girls at the Silver Spoon.

Out here, nobody has their real name or their real story. Jean Harlow is really a girl from Kansas City called Harlean. Paulette Goddard's got a fancy French name, but she's just a girl from Kansas City too—Marion Levy. Carole Lombard's really a plain "Jane" from Indiana.

I learned all this from Loretta, who works with me at the Silver Spoon diner. Loretta was born a Ruth Svenson in

Duluth, Minnesota, but she renamed herself after Loretta Young, who is really a "Gretchen" from Utah—so you understand how it goes now, out here in California.

Loretta and I wear the cutest little black uniforms with sharp white collars and little peaked caps. If it's cool, we wear trousers with a smart crease. I've only worn trousers once before, but these are better. We carry trays of fried chicken and ham steaks and malted milk to customers, and if we giggle and flatter the men, we might get a good tip.

On her afternoons off, Loretta goes to auditions. That's when you dance in an empty ballroom in front of three men sitting on chairs, and they decide whether they want you for a chorus. Being a chorus girl is the first step to being a movie star, Loretta says, or getting a rich husband. Billie Dove (born a "Bertha") started as a chorus girl and now she's a movie star and was once engaged to Howard Hughes—it could happen to anyone, Loretta says.

Sometimes I go with her to the auditions, though I don't have what Loretta calls a "good shape." Sitting in the waiting room is a good place to watch and listen. When I hear names that seem important—like Howard Hughes—I write them down in a notebook. That way, when I chat with someone I can seem like I belong, like I'm not a farm girl from Tobacco Run. I've also practiced talking the way the movie stars talk. I'll go to the double feature whenever I can, no matter what's playing, and just sit in the back practicing. I haven't said "y'all" since I got here. My hair has grown down to my chin, and I curl it in rags at night. You'd hardly recognize me if you sat down in my section at the Silver Spoon.

The Silver Spoon's a real nice spot. We get Salisbury steak for our shift meal with as much mashed potatoes as we want. Sometimes, when my boss isn't looking I'll have a little spoonful of the hot fudge we put on the ice cream. But nothing's quite as good as those breakfasts your mother fed me.

That time with your family was real happy for me. I do hope you're not sore about everything. You know by now Jean wasn't real. But you see why I said she was, don't you? I know you do.

Anyway, I won't say I'm sorry, because I'm not. I did what I needed to do. And I reckon it was good for you too in the end. If Madge Bettany hadn't been left alone with no money by her brother, she wouldn't have needed to start the Chalet School. Then there wouldn't have been any story.

We all need a story.

Sincerely,
Cecilia Aiken

PS: Zeke is in love with you. If you don't know it by now, you're not as smart as I thought.

I laugh every time I read that. Zeke laughs too. He's the only one I've shown the letter to.

Zeke says he needed the push too, and that he's also grateful to Cecilia, even though he'll be paying his father back for the stolen car until he's old and gray; he told Mr. Abramowitz he left the brake off and the car rolled into the Neuse. At least he has a better salary now. He's not working at the railroad any longer. In fact, he's not in New Bern at all. He's in Washington, DC—just a short trip from Baltimore—working for the US Army Air Corps. He sent them one of his plane designs, and they hired him right away, despite his having been expelled from NC State. He can't say much about what he does—it's all very secret—but he does say he believes we'll go to war with Germany sooner than later.

Will we ever get married? My mother would like to know, though I don't have an answer for her.

I fold the letter back in the drawer. Then I go to Auggie's room and scoop up an armful of clothes. I stand for a moment, looking around. It's already unrecognizable. The bed has been replaced with two narrower ones, his science books donated to the school, his teddy bear given to little Susan.

It's as if he was never here.

But that's okay. A room is just a room. Auggie *was* here. He's still here. I see him in the mischievous eyes of Aaron when he grabs for something he knows he's not supposed to have. I see him in the dirty faces of the young boys gathered around the breakfast table. I see him in my mother, sitting down to listen as the boys tell her about their lives.

I see him in myself: at the top of my own ramp, about to shoot off into the unknown future, terrified but so, so alive.

Author's Note

Though my characters are imaginary, their setting and context are drawn from real history. The following were invaluable research resources (as well as hugely interesting reads for anyone wanting to learn more): Eli N. Evans's *The Provincials: A Personal History of Jews in the South*; Roy G. Taylor's *Sharecroppers: The Way We Really Were*; Karin L. Zipf's *Bad Girls at Samarcand: Sexuality and Sterilization in a Southern Juvenile Reformatory*; Steven Noll's *Feeble-Minded in Our Midst*; Kevin Begos, Danielle Deaver, John Railey, and Scott Sexton's *Against Their Will: North Carolina's Sterilization Program and the Campaign for Reparations*; and the Memories of New Bern Oral History Project from the Memories of New Bern Committee.

Acknowledgments

Enormous thanks to Kate Dresser at Putnam, Allison Hunter at Trellis Literary Management, and all the other team members who put their hard work and brilliance into the book, including Tarini Sipahimalani and Natalie Edwards. Thank you to Hazel Gaynor for invaluable mentorship on the nitty-gritty of author life. Thanks to Bobbi Matchar and Deborah Shlian for providing great early reader feedback, and the rest of my family and friends who are always happy to be sounding boards for book news. Thank you to my husband, Jamin Asay, for running everything while I disappear into writer mode, then being ready to read the draft as soon as I emerge. Thank you to my children, who have fallen asleep to the sound of typing for much of their lives.

ABOUT THE AUTHOR

©JAMIN ASAY

Emily Matchar is the author of *In the Shadow of the Greenbrier* and *The Lost Girl of Craven County.* She's written for many publications, including *The New York Times*, *The Washington Post*, *Outside*, *Smithsonian*, and *The Atlantic*. She has a bachelor's degree in English from Harvard University, and has taught writing at the University of North Carolina and the University of Hong Kong. Originally from North Carolina, she lives with her husband and two sons.

Visit Emily Matchar Online

emilymatchar.com

@EmilyMatcharWriter